WAKING MAYA

A Novel

Warren Goldie

WONDERLIN PRESS

Visionary Fiction / New Age Fiction

This book was printed in the United States of America

Cover Design: George Foster

Copyright © 2004, 2008, 2014, 2017 by Warren Goldie

ISBN: 978-1493625239

WAKING MAYA

You have attracted certain events into your life, based upon your thoughts and beliefs. This principle is called the Law of Attraction.

If you've searched for evidence of it, you've found it. If you deny it, it will remain forever invisible to you.

If you observe the greater world, you may suspect that large-scale events—the sweeping cultural changes of recent years, the rise of new technologies, the rapid growth in social awareness—may not be random occurrences.

If so, you would be correct. They are manifestations. Not of a single person or group, but of all humankind.

Our race is searching. It has been since the beginning. It does this using one of the most exquisitely powerful tools in the universe: the human mind.

How do we create events? What are the processes? Why must they remain a secret?

We will examine these matters now.

— *From the journal of Ben Ambrose*

1

One Into the Earth, One Out of It

Maya Burke stopped digging and leaned on the shovel, her gaze drawn to the bundle on the grass a few feet away. What had been Livingston an hour ago was now an unmoving mass pressing at the seams of a burlap sack. It was awful. And she had not slid him all the way in, for the tip of a white paw was peeking out, as if the old cat were trying to grab hold of some grass and pull himself free. She winced. Why had she rushed this?

She didn't want to think about that. She didn't want to think at all. She quickened her pace, digging intently under the hot sun, pausing now and again to wipe the tears and sweat from her cheeks, which only spread the brown smudge further across her face. At one point she raised the shovel up over her head and plunged it down as hard as she could into the pit, like a harpoon. When she touched the vibrating handle she could have sworn she sensed the pulse of the earth beating within the wood. Quickly she tossed off the idea as absurd.

She dug furiously, pouring everything she had into it, which was mostly the energy of anxiety; a putrid, festering anxiety that needed to be expelled. An anxiety born not only from losing her sweet brittle-boned companion, but that derived from a profound aimlessness and unsettledness that had been infecting every aspect of her life. She'd gone off the rails and she knew it.

Maya had graduated from Towson University in May, and now, well into September, still she was languishing at her mother's house. Most of her friends had left Plainfield, like seeds scattered across the country. They were working, furnishing apartments, traveling in Europe and South America. And what was she doing? Stewing in indecision. She'd made no real plan in her senior year and was reaping what she'd did not sow. Her grand idea was to wait for inspiration—a magical event or an idea that would light her up and get her in gear. In truth, it was no plan at all.

But at least she had this: the catharsis of physical exertion. She dug and she tossed, and the hole grew deeper. There was a satisfaction in being laser-focused. Well, mostly. Every so often her gaze would wander over toward the driveway in search of her mother's Lexus. If Muriel pulled in now—well, it wouldn't be pretty. She would experience no thought nor consideration for Livingston, or for Maya's grief, no *pause*—only reaction. How *could* you? Do you know how much I pay the gardener? Unbelievable!

But none of that would happen because Muriel was working again as a real estate agent, showing houses most nights, right up until happy hour and beyond. Maya, who had sputtered uneventfully through her twenty-second birthday in August, had been attempting not to care what her mother thought about her for years, if not most of her life. But for reasons she didn't fully understand, she had never quite managed to get there.

Maya stomped her boot down on the shovel's blade, felt it cut into the earth.

Clink.

What was this? She tapped around with the tip, probing, then plunged the blade in again.

Clink.

Intrigued, she dropped the shovel and fell to her knees, curious to see what was down there, and glimpsed a sparkle at the bottom of the hole. Eagerly she brushed away the loose soil and saw a metal surface begin to appear—the top of a box. She wedged her fingertips down under it and yanked it up, as loose soil spilled down into the space it had occupied.

She found a clean patch of lawn on which to sit and placed the box ceremoniously before her. Clapping the dirt from her hands, she lifted the clasp and popped open the lid, and glimpsed the treasure inside: a leather-bound notebook. She stared at it, mesmerized. Without wasting another moment, she opened it.

"Oh, my God," she whispered aloud, staring wide-eyed at the first page. "This is impossible. This cannot be."

Yet there it was—the answer to a riddle Maya had tried to solve for as long as she could remember. On the page was a single handwritten sentence, seven words that reached forward from the distant past to change her life forever.

To Maya, with love from your father

He'd written his name down at the bottom. Ben Ambrose. She spoke it. *Ben Ambrose.* It was a revelation. Until this moment she'd never known her father's name. Eagerly, she turned the brittle pages, skimming a few paragraphs of the text, realizing that she held his story in her hands. What happened, why he left.

Memories came, unbidden: the years spent searching, the wanting, the sickening feeling of something always missing. All the times as a little girl when she would search the house in the early morning hours, dressed in her flowered pajama shirt and matching shorts, rummaging through the piles of junk in the basement in the hope of finding some evidence of him—a page with his signature on it, an ID card, a wallet, a baseball glove, anything. And then, succeeding. It was a photograph pressed into the pages of an old map book. A precocious seven-year-old with gaps around her front teeth, Maya had proudly presented it to her mother. Muriel stared at it for a quick moment, then deftly slid the prize into her purse without a word. And that was it. Maya never saw the photo again. Somehow, the blurry image lived on in her memory: Muriel and, yes, *Ben*, sitting on a park bench, the tall buildings of a city rising up behind them.

And now … this! She lay back on the grass grinning, hugging the slender volume to her chest. She would savor it. She would consume it. She would read each line a hundred times. She would read *between* the lines.

But not yet. First, there was the task at hand. Carefully she placed the journal back in its box and fetched the sack with Livingston in it, slingshotted back to reality by the recognition of the weight—eleven pounds that had always stirred and purred—and again Maya had to wipe away tears. He had been struck down crossing Allenswood Road and had heroically limped to the front porch where Maya found him. She'd laid him carefully on a towel on the car's front seat and sped to the clinic, but he was gone before she even made it to the front door.

She set him down at the bottom of the hole and glanced at the box on the grass a few feet away. *One into the earth, one out of it. Was life like that?* she wondered. *An even exchange through a revolving door?*

Staring into the grave, leaning on the shovel, Maya could find no words. "Thank you, love," was the best she could manage, which didn't even sound like her. She'd never called anyone "love" in her life. But that's what escaped her lips.

As the soil pattered against the sack, Maya's thoughts kept coming back to the question of *how?* How had she come upon this magical spot with its incredible bounty, within the entirety of a one-acre lawn? Why dig here?

Half an hour earlier, when she had emerged from the back door, she had difficulty settling on a grave site, and so she decided to ask for guidance—from the beyond, the Universe, the out-there. Closing her eyes, Maya grew quiet and made her query. *Where?*

Listening within, seeking for the narrow space between her thoughts where an answer might be found, she had walked the grounds slowly, deliberately, tracing a path along yesterday's still-crisp lawnmower tracks. When she had reached the end of the yard where the fence met the woods, something happened that sent a shudder through her: a tug at the sleeve of her T-shirt. Unnerved, she had frozen in place. Then, another tug.

When she'd recovered from the shock, she knew she had received her answer. An urge came to gaze upon a specific patch of lawn. *There, over by the old oak tree, do you see it?* A minute later she was digging...

Maya took a seat on the rusted iron swing-set that stood like an apparatus from a bygone age under the oak tree, and stared at the journal in her lap. Looking at the first page, she was struck by the handwriting, a tortured jumble of cursive and printed letters, barely legible—and nearly identical to her own writing. She smiled.

Had Ben Ambrose had as difficult a history around penmanship as Maya? The trials she'd endured in grade school had often gotten the best of her. She was a child who could not write a single sentence from start to finish without all sorts of interference coming in, as if her brain and hand weren't properly synced up. Sometimes she pressed the pen so deeply into the page that she managed to punch right through it. Someone had once said her grade school papers resembled relief maps. Her fourth-grade teacher, the prune-faced, disagreeable Mrs. Booth, had suggested she take up engraving. Engraving! Maya had been doing her best, and was just as bothered as everyone else. It was not until years later, when she'd gotten her fingers on a keyboard that the clouds parted and she found she could express herself in writing.

Now, for the first time, she viewed her labored penmanship not as a liability but as an inevitability. An inheritance, even— from her father. She slid her fingertips lightly across the page, savoring the little peaks and valleys, and she began to read.

Maya, I miss you already. And you are right in front of me. Whatever has happened or will happen, this much is true: I love you.

There is no way to explain why I must leave. It is necessary. My reasons, which are—or, I should say *were*—compelling, cannot match the

disappointment you must feel in not knowing
me. I hope this can change.

It is early evening as I write to you in my
study. My window looks out onto the farm—

Maya stopped reading right there and closed the journal.
Her hands were trembling. She grabbed tightly on one of the
swing's support poles, seeking comfort in the solidity of the iron.
His words—to me.

What he'd written indeed was true. This place had once
been a farm. Maya had no trouble recalling that time. The
summer afternoons spent ranging the fields in search of Indian
arrowheads. The evenings playing Capture the Flag with the
neighborhood kids in the tall grasses. Or just staring lovingly out
her bedroom window at the rolling hills as dusk melted into
night. Then everything changed. When Grandpa Burke died and
Muriel took possession of the property, Muriel sold most of the
land to the developers. So what if the farm had been in the Burke
family for more than a hundred years? It was prime real estate
situated in the woodlands of northern Baltimore County.
Making a buck was what Muriel was after.

In time the neighboring farms were sold, too, and Plainfield
became a well-coiffed suburb, its rural character sliding into the
forgotten past. Muriel had the Burke farmhouse leveled and a
tract mansion built in its place. It was "upscale." It was "nice."
The sole artifact that remained from Maya's early childhood was
a single lonely section of wooden fence that lingered at the far
end of the yard like a headstone beneath the low-hanging
branches reaching over from the woods. It was strange, Maya
had often thought, that it still stood. She imagined her father
looking at it.

Steeling herself, she opened the journal again and breezed
through a few passages detailing his guilt about leaving, then she
came upon something interesting.

So let me get on with it. I am a researcher at
the university and elsewhere, and this is where
it begins. In my work, I have stumbled (and that

is the right word) onto phenomena having to do with the way that change comes about. By *change* I mean in all ways—small and large, micro and macro, personal and societal.

In the course of my work I became aware of dynamics previously unknown. As I dove further and further in, examining the data from every possible angle, seeing the results confirmed in test after test, I came to believe that what I had discovered was truly extraordinary. I tell you this with some gravity after long consideration because you must be warned. Everyone must be warned.

What is clear is this: A sweeping global change is in the offing, of such magnitude that every human system—every nation, government and people—will shift markedly. Societies will be permanently altered. Nothing will remain the same. We are poised at the dawn of a transformation unseen in centuries. Monumental forces churn, even now as I write to you. But it is not what you might think, Maya. The change will be *internal*. It will come from the inside of man, not from without.

This must sound fantastic to you! I know. But please, hear me out. Much work has been done and many others know what is to come.

I tell you all this because discord usually accompanies change. The old does not yield willingly to the new. You, dear daughter, must prepare. But take heart. The storm will not last. As it strikes, look beyond its violence for the nourishment of the rain to come, for that is its greater purpose—

Maya closed the journal, feeling even shakier than before. Thinking. Rocking. Comprehending, or trying to. This was much to take in. Fantastic is what it was.

It was crazy, even.

No great global change had occurred in the years since he had written those words. No "storm" had struck. One could say the world was dizzyingly in flux and incredibly unpredictable, but it was pretty much the same world from day to day.

Maya frowned, disappointed. What kind of a man was he? Why would he write such things? Was this how he wanted to introduce himself to his daughter? She mused unhappily for a time, swinging vigorously and kicking nervously at the swing's support pole.

Then an idea came to her. She sat bolt upright. *Maybe*, she thought. *Just maybe* there was validity to his prognostications, for hadn't the most incredible one, the assertion that bordered on the impossible, actually happened? She'd found the journal! His choice to bury it had presupposed her digging it up. Why plant it there unless he knew she'd find it?

But how could that be?

She opened it again, hoping to find the answers in its unread pages, but the honk of a car horn startled her, and the book almost fell from her hands. Josh's Mustang was idling in the driveway. He waved to her.

She sat for a moment, thinking. Then staring at Josh, whose timing couldn't be worse. She wanted so badly to remain on the swing, to continue to take in this miracle, this catalog not only of her father's life but of hers, too, which he'd written to her and no one else. The pull was intense. But she couldn't just send Josh off, especially not today, after the way he had insisted they see each other.

She gave a little frustrated huff, then shook it off and waved at him, forcing a smile and calling out for him to wait. She placed the journal back in its box, held it tightly, and dashed for the house.

She slid the box under her bed, stirring up the dust balls that danced like spiders over the hardwood floor. She washed her face, and stood at the mirror, running a comb through her long auburn hair, pleased to be looking at an attractive young woman with well-tanned skin that had nicely held its color through the long summer.

She couldn't help but notice the changes in her face and body over the last few years. The gawkiness that had plagued her in her mid-teens had transformed into five-foot-eight-inch stateliness. All was good and she was happy with what she was seeing.

She grabbed her jean jacket from the back of the chair and started for the door but then stopped, bent down low and glanced beneath the bed. "*Later, Dad,*" she whispered, noting the strange feel of that word on her lips.

2

Falling

J osh Rosenberg leaned his tall, lanky frame against the driver's side door of his black Mustang GT and absentmindedly tapped his boot to the beat of one of the rock songs that played perpetually in his head. When Maya appeared beside him, he had completely forgotten where he was and gave her a look of surprise. "Oh … hey," he said.

"Hey yourself," Maya said, giving his arm a squeeze. They got in the car.

As Josh backed out of the driveway, he flipped back his long black hair, which tumbled right back down over his eyes. He did it again, twice, as Maya watched, stifling a chuckle. Josh was the only guy she knew who could manage to be cool *and* a caricature of cool at the same time.

Though they had passed each other for three years in the halls of Plainfield High School—with Maya dashing off to honors classes while Josh goofed off in the back rows of the rooms for kids in pursuit of a different future—they had not spoken back then. They met for the first time four months ago, the last week in May, right before Maya walked the stage at her college graduation. Josh's band was playing at a house party in Stoneleigh Heights. Maya was uncharacteristically at ease in the crowd that night, dancing to near exhaustion, blissfully lost in the throng and the heat of the dimly lit room. With Becky driving Maya had allowed herself a few glasses of wine. She was surprised when she locked eyes with Josh whaling on his guitar a few feet away and he flashed her a big smile. When his band took a break, Maya made her way outside and he followed after her and they talked. At one point Josh stared up at the night sky and said some poetic thing about the stars, and Maya, the avowed science and history geek, went right ahead and reeled off the names of those same stars for him. She looked down at her shoes, embarrassed and he gently lifted up her chin and kissed her.

The months since then had been good, mostly. Josh was spontaneous and fun. He had lifted her out of her lowest moods without any idea that he was doing it. But something had changed a few weeks back because their time together, which had been fluid and easy, was now labored and strained.

Stealing a sideways glance at him sitting beside her on the worn cloth seat of the clunker he loved so much, Maya wondered what exactly they had. Was it a *relationship*? She wasn't even sure she understood the concept, because every time she thought she was in one, it didn't seem to be the case. There was a breaking point—usually at about three months, for some reason—when things could go awry, when the drama would kick in. Some terrible fear she couldn't quite identify would assert itself, her stable world would flip upside down and she'd have a hard time thinking clearly or even trusting her judgment. The agreeable, eager face of her guy would start to look angry and hostile, as if she'd done something wrong. And maybe she had. The bond would fray, she'd be unsure how to fix it, black would become white, and up, down, and she'd end up in a bathroom stall crying into a wad of toilet paper. Something was obviously wrong with her. The Maya who started relationships wasn't the one who finished them. Pain wound itself into love, and love seemed neither stable nor reliable, and certainly not comfortable. And *that* couldn't be what all those happy couples out there were experiencing. And lately this—whatever it was with Josh—had been starting to feel exactly that way.

* * *

The Orion Cafe was packed with the regulars, students from the art institute across the street. Talented kids who knew what they loved and wanted to do. *How nice that would be*, Maya thought as she settled in at a sidewalk table and watched Josh walk inside for mocha lattes. He returned a few minutes later and set the tall glasses down, dropped into the chair opposite Maya and pulled a squished pack of Marlboros out of his front pocket.

Maya stared at the kids crowding the other tables while fidgeting rapturously with her hemp bracelet, adjusting and readjusting it, pushing it up and pulling it down her wrist like someone in need of a Xanax. Why was she even here? Surely she should be at home reading her father's journal. Going out had clearly been lunatic. It was a serious breach of logic and rightness, whatever Josh wanted. What if her mother burned down the house, or worse, found the journal and read it herself?

Maya released her bracelet and looked over at Josh. "You'll never guess what just happened," she said.

"I'm sure you're right," he said, clicking his Zippo, lighting the cigarette hanging from his mouth.

"I just met my dad," Maya said, watching for his reaction.

Josh stared at her, nonplussed. That was the thing about Josh. It was really hard to surprise him.

"I thought he died," he said.

"Where did you hear that?" Maya said, bristling.

"Where do you think?"

"Me?"

He nodded.

She thought about it. Yes, she may have said something like that at one time. Her feelings about her father had changed often over the years, not that she had any actual data to base them on.

"Well, whatever," she went on. "But listen, seriously—this journal? He wrote it to *me*."

"What's it say?"

"I don't know," Maya said. "I've hardly read it. *You* showed up." *Too harsh*, she thought. She'd meant it lightly, as a joke, but it didn't come out that way. She took note of that.

Josh tapped an ash off the cigarette. The gray cinder spun and fluttered toward the sidewalk and danced off in the breeze.

"Maybe you shouldn't read it," he said.

"Yeah," Maya said. "Maybe I'll just toss it out with the trash. Can't be anything important."

"No," he said. "I'm serious."

Was he? *Serious* wasn't a concept with which Josh was all that familiar. He preferred to play the part of the contrarian, always going against the grain, doing the thing you'd least expect. Josh would pet a dog's fur *backward*. And here he was at it again, trying to get a rise out of her. Maya glared at him.

Then he smiled—and changed. It took only an instant. The *other* Josh emerged. The warm, caring guy shoved away the too-cool hipster who played with his hair and smirked a lot. His smile reminded Maya what it was about him that thrilled her.

This Josh was the one whose vintage Telecaster guitar could transform a room full of strangers into a single pulsating being. He was connected to a power that was deep and untamed, that you could *feel*. He knew how to channel the primal energy force. Maya had always been drawn to people like that. What a gift to have. But the fact that he was so blasé about his talents could make him hard to take at times.

"Livingston died," she blurted out.

"Who?"

"My cat, Josh. I just buried him. That's how I found the journal. In the very spot I put him."

Josh took a pull off his cigarette, sailed a plume of smoke out toward the street.

"I'm devastated about the little guy, of course," Maya went on. "That goes without saying. But there's something else, it's crazy, I can't even describe it. It's like this ... *existential* pressure. Like I have to figure out my purpose in life. I'm having a purpose attack. Jesus. It's like this high command in my head has ordered me to get moving, or else. Or else *what*? Frankly I'm sick of it. What is my purpose in life? You know what? I don't care! How about that?"

"Maybe your purpose is to live and be happy," Josh said.

"Easy for you to say," Maya shot back. "You're the next Kurt Cobain. What do I do? I know how to take a history test. I run a fast mile. So what?"

"Do you want to know what your problem is?" Josh said.

Maya stared at him, feeling suddenly confused. His directness gave her pause. This was not exactly a Josh Rosenberg conversation, yet here he was, engaged.

"Go on," she said cautiously.

"You're always looking for the meaning of life, Maya, wondering where you'll find it. You're so into that. Well, I can tell you where it *isn't*: inside your head. The place you're always so gung-ho to look. Because you know what you'll find in there? The past. What's done and gone. Journals that take you backward when what you want to do is go forward—"

"Josh, it was written by my father. Seriously, you can't be telling me not to read it."

"I'm not saying that. You're not hearing me."

He grazed his fingers over the nautical star tattoo on his wrist, as he searched for the right words.

He said, "You don't discover what to do with your life, Maya. It's not something you *find*. It doesn't exist anywhere. So looking for it is a waste of time."

She stared at him.

"You make it up as you go," he said.

"Excuse me?"

"Yeah," Josh said. "No signposts, no guides. Just what you decide, here and now. The rest is a bunch of garbage. What I don't understand is how you can't see that."

This was the schism between them. Maya saw life as a grand journey informed by some higher ideal or principle, whatever that might be—God, science, philosophy, building aircraft carriers—that whispered in one's ear, urging you to look deeper. It couldn't be ignored or minimized. No, you didn't "make it up." You listened for it.

"Don't you think there's more to life than *this*?" Maya said, holding out her arms to indicate the surroundings. "Why do we have these big brains? How was it I found that journal? Was that dumb luck? I dug that hole exactly where he buried it all those years ago."

"You got lucky," he said.

"That is so ... small," Maya said.

Josh turned away. And that was it. Conversation over. No surprise there. This was ground they had covered many times. Too many times.

"I know," Maya said. "Blah, blah, blah. You don't care about any of this. Go ahead and make a face. I don't care."

He stared at her with an expression of—pity? Could that be? As if she were an idiot, unable to understand his simple idea. He dropped the spent cigarette on the sidewalk and stamped it out under his boot heel.

"You're overreacting," he said.

"I know what you think," Maya said. "I don't know how to live life. I'm just some stupid old fool."

"I didn't say that."

"Like you have to," she said.

Again he turned away. She waited for him to turn back but he just kept staring at the parked cars out on the street.

She saw his pained expression and understood. *Of course.* This was why he had wanted to go out, what he needed to talk about. She hadn't let him say it, grousing on and on about her miserable, screwed up life. *Perfect.*

"Josh?"

She waited for him to respond but he just sat there looking at anything but her. A few feet away a car started up and pulled out onto the street and drove off. An ambulance screamed down the next block, leaving a wake of noise ricocheting between the buildings.

Maya held her breath. She *knew.* She knew what was about to happen.

Oh no.

"I'm not saying we should break up," Josh said.

Maya drew a quick breath and held it. Her skin felt hot and prickly. *Not again.* She could feel herself starting to wilt, deflate, transform from the spirited Maya into her mother's girl: the mouse, the doormat.

"I just need some time," Josh said.

"Huh?" Maya said, hardly hearing him.

"I want to work on some songs," he said.

Songs? What exactly did that mean? He always worked on songs. That wasn't it. It was her. Obviously.

Thoughts whirred in her head. As hard as she tried, she couldn't grasp a single one.

"What are you saying Josh?" she said finally.

"I'm sorry," he said. "I've been thinking about it awhile."

"You acted like everything was OK."

"It's not," he said. "Come on, we both know it. I'm just the one who brought it up. We need to take a break. Air it out."

She almost laughed, hearing that. But she was too miserable to do that. *Air it out.* Now that was precious. As if a relationship were a bedroom with windows that needed to be flung open.

"You're right," Maya said. He was. Of course he was. She knew that. Still, it burned. She looked at him, her eyes freighted with despair and hopelessness. A shudder passed through her, and she felt the tears coming on. *Not now.*

She stood up. "Then that's that," she said with a certainty she did not feel. She flashed him a pained smile and started to walk down the sidewalk. She must not let him to see her cry. That would destroy whatever shred of dignity remained.

"Hey, Maya, wait up," Josh called out, running to catch up with her. "Let me give you a ride."

"Don't bother," she shouted back at him. She would call someone to pick her up. She ran. She could feel him following behind her. She sped up, crossing to the other side of the street, pressing on even faster, then sprinting as fast as she could go, her long legs pumping beneath her, her hair blowing and jumping around wildly, as Josh's pleading words grew fainter in the distance. Through tears that blurred her vision, she gazed up at those same stars she had named for him when they had first met, remote specks in a forbidding firmament, impossibly distant, throwing their dying light pointlessly into the vacuum of space.

*   *   *

Maya's friend Betsy gave her a ride home. When Maya arrived at the house she bolted for her room and shut the door, and thudded onto her bed face first into the pillows. More than anything she wanted to cuddle with Livingston, to feel his soft fur on her cheek and hear the little motor purring, to know that he was content to be with her. But life was too cruel for that. He was gone. On this day worst of all. She sensed the finality of death—permanent, infinite separation. And now Josh was gone, too. A sob barked from her throat. More tears flowed, pattering onto the pillow. How hard it was to breathe, to simply live.

And then she remembered. Of course! How could she have forgotten? Hurriedly she reached under the bed for the metal box with the treasure inside, sat it on her lap and lifted up the lid. Just touching the cool leather cover of the journal brought rays of sunshine through the clouds. This book, she thought. This book. It would be a talisman for her, a support to lean upon that would carry her through challenges and difficulties. Like a father would. All that remained was to learn its secrets.

3

Watching the Sleepwalkers

Maya lay back in bed and opened the journal, but she heard sounds coming from the living room and she quickly shut it. She switched off the lamp and lay still in the dark. Waiting.

Footsteps echoed in the hallway outside her door. She heard a man's deep voice mingling with her mother's flirtatious squeals, whispers turned to giggles, there was a loud burst of laughter followed by a "Shhh!" and all sounds faded away as her mother's bedroom door clicked shut down the hall.

A moment later Maya heard a tapping at her own.

"Maya?"

Go away.

"Honey?"

"What do you want? I'm tired."

"Can I open the door, please?"

"Sure," Maya relented.

The door opened, but only a crack. Muriel's tall, slender figure filled the vertical slot of light coming from the hallway, her face hidden in shadow. A breeze wafted in, carrying on it a hint of tequila, and Maya felt her hands clench.

"How are you?" Muriel asked. It was a random question, and a puzzling one coming from her mother. Maya couldn't make out the details of Muriel's face, but she imagined a blank, unfocused look in her eyes.

"I'm fine," Maya said.

"That's good," Muriel said brightly. "That's really, *really* good." Her head was tilted to the side like it was being pulled down by a heavy weight. "What was I saying—Maya?"

"Still here."

"There was something I wanted to tell you," Muriel said, straining to recall what that might be. But she couldn't quite get hold of it.

"Mom?" Maya said worriedly.

"Oh yeah!" Muriel said. "It's this: I try. I do. Honest. You can't fault me for that. For trying?"

Maya felt herself start to panic. Was this an apology? For what? She clicked back mentally through the hours and days. She'd barely even seen her mother lately. The housing market had been picking up and Muriel was out working long hours, closing more than a few sales. Or she was at the gym. The Pilates teachers could have made a living off of her alone.

"It's all good, Mom," Maya said.

"You mean that? Honest?"

"I do."

Muriel nodded her head, apparently relieved, and Maya wondered, *Why am I still here?* It was a good question. A good question without a good answer.

"By the way," Muriel said, "Henry is over. You know Henry, right? I introduced you."

"He's great," Maya said, though she had no recollection of the man.

Muriel remained in the doorway, staring at Maya. Again Maya clenched. *Here it comes.*

But it didn't. Incredibly, her mother's voice was gentle: "Whatever you may think, I love you. I—love—you. Just so you know. That's all I wanted to say. OK? Goodnight."

"Goodnight, me, too," Maya said, holding back a sigh of relief.

Muriel shut the door and was gone. Maya felt suddenly exhausted. It was amazing how fast that happened. She tried counting off breaths in an effort to put whatever that was out of mind. There was much to do tonight.

She switched on the lamp and reached for the journal, but she didn't want her reading of it polluted by the reek of tequila, still tinging the air. She opened the window all the way and leaned out, breathing deeply of the night air. It was ambrosia to her. The full moon shone brightly overhead, drenching the yard and the woods in a soft silvery light. The treetops looked like giant crowns of broccoli, rustling to get her attention. *Look here! Here! No, here!*

Maya smiled, secure in the peacefulness of one a.m. She imagined herself growing wings and leaping out of the window to fly up into the night sky, like a bird—an eagle, pumping its powerful wings, ascending the air currents, gliding majestically in ever widening circles over the cities and towns, peering down at the strange and restless beings below, sleepwalkers who must remain earthbound, in so many ways.

She felt the day's burden start to fall away. Muriel, Josh, Livingston, and her own confusion and stuckness. It was possible everything would be OK. *Things do work out.* And so she returned from her flight, pulled in her wings and glided back down to the house and into the second-floor bedroom and into her body.

But when she pulled away from the window, her T-shirt caught on a nail in the frame, ripping the fabric. She bristled, but then quickly shrugged it off. It was a small thing, on a night that might hold big things. She did like the threadbare shirt, though, which she'd bought years ago at an open market downtown. She had been drawn to its large yin-yang symbol displayed on the front, now faded with age.

She mused on the ancient mark for a moment—the black and white teardrops caught in a circular embrace. It seemed as if they were pursuing each other. Would one catch the other? What then? And what about the seeds inside? Would they grow larger and take over their hosts? Where would that lead? The questions brought up more questions. The symbol was a doorway into mystery. And mystery was cool.

Maya liked that symbol so much she'd drawn one on the back of one of her Converse All Star sneakers, stretched to abstraction, designed to go undetected by all but the most perceptive of observers. If she ever met a guy who saw that yin-yang, *well*... But what were the chances of that, especially in Plainfield, the dullest of all places? She'd hardly met a soul here who connected with Eastern symbols.

She pressed her ear against the door. All was quiet. Muriel was in for the night with this Henry guy, whoever he was. Maya sat up in her bed, lay the journal in her lap and opened it and began to read.

My research is in a field called psychosocial meta-dynamics, which explores the idea that the *beliefs* of groups of people, en masse, affect and even create large-scale cultural and global events. Why do some gain enough momentum to change the world, while others fade away? What are the actual metaphysics of change?

I didn't stay long at the university. I signed on with the U.S. government. There I—

Here several lines had been struck out with a heavy black marker.

—cannot be more specific about this. Suffice to say that recently I left a project of great importance.

My purpose here is to give you a little something in the hours before I go. A primer of the old man's work, if you will. But practical. For you. I cannot be there but I will give you a little bit of what I am, or was.

There is a bank in Calhoun called First Street Federal. There you will find a safe deposit box registered in your name. Take the key from the back of this book and—

Electrified by these words, Maya flipped to the back cover and indeed, a small slit had been cut in the flap. She reached in and pulled out a flat key.

—go there and remove the contents of the box.

Two significant phenomena occurred at that moment. The first was a sensation like a mild electrical current moving through Maya's body. It was familiar, for she'd felt it many times before. It was like a buzzing in her arms and legs that lasted a few moments, and then was gone.

The second phenomena was new and unknown: the feeling of a presence in the room with her. Excitement quickly turned to panic. *Get out.* Carefully, so as not to disturb the very air around her, Maya tiptoed across the carpeted floor, opened the bedroom door, stepped into the hallway, and sprinted full out for the living room, ending her dash a stocking-footed slide across the hardwood floor. She went around switching on all the lights until the room was as bright as an operating room. She turned on the TV, too, but muted it for fear of rousing her mother and her guest.

Maya found the perfect anesthesia on channel sixty-eight: The Weather Channel. The colorful maps and big, bold temperature figures had always been oddly comforting. And she needed that comfort because the power, *her* power, was in play. The electrical buzzing was a sure sign.

Since she'd been a small child, Maya had demonstrated an ability in precognition. Its onset was impossible to foresee; months could go by without a single episode occurring. Then, out of the blue, a detailed scene would materialize as images in her mind. It could happen anytime—while standing at the bathroom mirror, or driving to a friend's house, or wandering the aisles at Everybody's Whole Foods—and would last a few seconds before fading away into the mind's normal thoughts and chatter. The images were always unnervingly clear, of people she didn't know, places she'd never been. And with them came that charge of electricity. Who were these people who had found their way into her head? Maya didn't know, until sometime later when she would witness the scene manifested in the real world exactly as it had appeared to her. Once, in her mind, she'd "seen" a bearded man arguing with his pregnant wife at the eatery in the mall, then saw it at the actual location. Another time she'd recognized a car accident on Liberty Road. And there was the time her friends took her to a party at a house she'd never been to but that she actually *did* know.

This is like that, Maya thought. *But it's different, too.* She hadn't actually visualized anything, just felt the electrical sensation. And no images had come. She wasn't sure what to make of that.

She nestled into the deep, cushiony sofa and pulled a blanket around her, and stared at the high and low pressure systems coming and going on the TV. Perhaps it was the strangeness of reading the highly personal writing from the hand of an unknown father, which spoke directly to her, that had spooked her and stirred all this up.

The town of Calhoun was a twenty-minute drive on Route 32, past some of the oldest homes in the county, imposing two-hundred-year-old stone structures situated along the river like fortresses built to stand for a thousand years. The countryside was lush and thickly wooded, and Maya enjoyed the drive down the winding road, as she always had.

She was singing along with an Indigo Girls song that had come on the radio. A few years ago she'd had an intense month-long Indigos phase when she was drawn to the raw passion and searching lyrics in their folk songs. She had listened to them non-stop, at times replaying the same song over and over until she knew every word, every chord change, every evoked emotion by heart. In doing this, there was no mistaking the lightness she felt, as if she'd been liberated of something foul and unwanted.

As she rounded a soft curve singing the line "and learn to yield," she passed by a YIELD sign on the road's shoulder. She switched off the radio, her curiosity piqued. *Yield* had occurred twice at the exact same moment. Was that just chance? Or was it meaningful in some way, like a synchronicity? Since she'd become aware of the concept of these so-called meaningful coincidences, she actively sought them out. There were surprisingly many.

Maya believed that meaning could be found most anywhere and most all the time—in every thought, every action and every event. Everyone was a part of a larger story. Nothing was random. If the batteries in her music player died on a particular song, then hearing that song at that time may have been inauspicious. Perhaps she would have picked up a book instead that revealed a needed insight, or made a call that proved useful. If she turned her car onto a wrong street, the reason could be avoiding an accident, or slowing someone down who needed to go fast. And most certainly, if she saw a road sign displaying the very word she was singing at that moment, it was significant. How?

A Big Picture existed in everyone's life, Maya believed, and it was up to each person to discover what it was. If you succeeded, then you reaped the reward of that knowledge— greater awareness and greater fulfillment. If you didn't find it, or didn't even try, then your life was going to make about as much sense as the back of an embroidery, a mishmash of threads going every which way with no rhyme or reason. *Seeing* the big picture, or parts of it, amounted to viewing the perfectly stitched scene on the other side. A synchronicity was a clue that came to you from the perspective of The Whole, critical information which had found its way to you for a good reason.

So, what did the *yield* synchronicity mean? Maya didn't know—yet.

She rubbed her eyes and stared at the center-line dashes passing rapidly beneath the car. She had slept fitfully on the couch last night, awakened many times by her thoughts, imagining what she might find at the bank. Surprisingly, Josh had been completely absent from her thoughts. She could hardly even summon a care about him. *Ben Ambrose, whoever you are, thank you*, she thought with satisfaction.

She swerved her red Honda Civic into an angled parking spot beneath the tower clock on Main Street just as the ten o'clock gongs clanged, echoing throughout the walking mall.

When she pulled open the door of First Street Federal Bank, she paused, burdened by worry: Would it be safe to access the box? When she revealed its number, would the clerk press a secret alarm button that would bring the police rushing in? Maya shrugged off the paranoia and stepped inside. There was no turning back now.

She walked over to where a clerk was filing papers at a desk and waited, but he didn't look up.

She sighed.

"I know you're there, young lady," the man said curtly. "I'll just be a moment."

"Sorry," Maya said.

He was in his late-fifties, pink-faced and balding, with a few random hairs swept over a shiny forehead. He peered up at Maya and forced himself to smile, and in a voice that mocked by its very nature, asked what he could do for her.

"I'd like to get into a safe deposit box, please," Maya said.

"Name?"

"Maya Burke."

"Just a moment."

He reached for a small metal file box crammed with four-by-six index cards, dog-eared from years of use, and searched through them. He pulled one out and set it on the desk.

"ID?"

Maya handed over her driver's license, which he placed beside the card. Glancing at it, he registered a look of surprise.

"Huh," he said. "This is rather unusual."

Maya felt herself tighten up. She watched the man closely, certain he was going to reach under the desk for the secret button. But he kept both hands in view.

"This box hasn't been used in twenty years," he said.

"Is that OK?" Maya said nervously.

"Never saw this before," he said.

"What's that?"

"The box has been prepaid for thirty," he said. "As in *years*."

Maya stared at him, astonished. Is that how long Ben Ambrose expected her to take to find the journal? How could that be?

"Well, so it goes," the man said, taking on a business-like look. "Sign here, Ms. Burke." He slid the card across the desk.

And there it was—Ben Ambrose's signature, swerved gracelessly in the line above where she herself wrote her name. Seeing it sent a chill through her.

"This way," the clerk said, rising.

He led her into a walk-in vault where safety deposit boxes lined the walls from floor to ceiling, and bent down to the bottom row. He slid a key into box 1230 and waited, staring up at her.

"Oh, right," Maya said sheepishly, handing him the key she'd pulled from journal's back cover. He slid it into the companion keyhole and turned both keys simultaneously. He pulled out a small strongbox and handed it to her.

"Viewing rooms are over there," he said, pointing to three doors in a narrow hallway.

Maya stepped into the first room, shut the door and sat at the small wooden table. Breathing. Readying herself. Staring at the box. Hoping. Here was another message from the past in front of her. An image arose in her mind: she was standing at the outskirts of a glorious, magical city. All she had to do was to take a step forward and enter it.

She pulled up the lid.

The box was empty.

She gasped. She shut her eyes and reopened them as if to repair a temporary malfunction. The metal box indeed was bare. *This can't be.* Her first step into the magical city had landed her in a pothole, and she was falling fast.

No. Wait.

There was something at the far end, under the two-inch section that formed the back of the latch. The color of the gray envelope closely matched the gunmetal hue of the drawer. She snatched it up and tore it open.

Staring at its contents, Maya fell back against the wooden chair as if blown by a strong wind. A smile spread across her face. In a lightning-quick reaction of emotional alchemy, despair had transformed into joy. The envelope held a stack of bills— fifty neatly folded hundreds, which she spread out on the table in front of her. *Five thousand dollars.* She'd never seen so much cash in all her life. But that wasn't all. The real gift was a scrap of paper on which Ben Ambrose had written, "Dr. Edgar Porter, 3706 N. Hillside, Chicago. A colleague, Maya. See Dr. Porter first."

She read over these words several times. One of them filled her with hope. "See Dr. Porter *first*." She raised her fists in triumph. Her father was sending her on a mission.

4

The In-Between Time

A t breakfast the next morning, Maya desperately wanted to ask Muriel about Ben Ambrose. The urge was stronger than it had been in years. The flame of her father, which had almost gone out, now burned as brightly as ever. Intense dreams had plagued Maya through the night and she found herself arguing nonstop in her mind about whether or not to speak out and break the longstanding taboo around the subject. But caution, as usual, won out. Provoking Muriel could mean long days of suffering, and Maya didn't want to risk that, especially now, when she would need all of her energy and focus for the days ahead.

Maya watched her mother from a chair at the kitchen table, as Muriel stared out the sliding glass doors in the direction of the patch of backyard grass that had sent a seismic jolt into Maya's life. She was wearing a terry-cloth robe and matching slippers, and sipping at a fruit smoothie. She brushed aside a strand of her messy morning hair, its dark roots visible beneath wild the blond tangles. Faint circles ringed her eyes, which would clear up as they always did after her morning shower.

Muriel drew men's stares easily, Maya had noticed over the years. Her sexy allure eclipsed Maya's wholesome good looks, even with the twenty-year age difference. Maya didn't much care. Muriel had earned those glances, and wanted them. But she would often go too far, restricting her food intake and sweating through intense workouts she refused to miss, even for important events such as Maya's high school graduation, which Muriel had made with just minutes to spare.

"You're not too attached to that TV in the living room, are you?" Muriel said, still staring outside.

"Why? Are you getting rid of it?" Maya said.

"Thinking about it," Muriel said, turning around. "I may get one of those gigantic ones everybody's got these days." She sipped at the smoothie, leaving a froth mustache on her upper lip. "Henry is into sports. The man practically breathes and eats it, and if he doesn't get his fill, I believe he'll up and expire, or at least go dim. I thought he might like a bigger set to watch it on."

"That TV is forty-three inches," Maya pointed out.

"Well, it's not big enough," Muriel said, giving Maya a stare. "Men like their sports and they like 'em big. How they can get so worked up over a bunch of guys chasing a ball is something I'll never understand, though let's keep that between us."

"The guys I know aren't into sports," Maya said.

Muriel arched an eyebrow, then burst into laughter. "I'm talking about *men*, honey, not boys." Then, in a softer tone, she said, "But, hell, there's time. You need to meet some new people, get out once in a while. You've got your head buried so deep in those books of yours, you wouldn't know a real man if he was pressing up against you. How's anything ever going to happen if you don't *do* something once in a while?"

Maya tossed the last bite of the corn muffin she'd been nibbling at into the plastic bakery box on the table and flipped the lid shut. Normally the fireworks would be starting right about now. But not today. Muriel was right. Maya was one of life's great spectators.

"This might come as a shock, Mom, but I'm going to follow your advice. For once."

"Oh?" said Muriel. "Pray tell?"

"Camping," Maya said.

"What?"

"I'm going camping."

"That's your big idea?"

"What's wrong with that?"

"Whatever you say, kiddo. Who with?"

"Josh."

"Oh, come on, you can do better than that freakazoid."

Maya wanted to tell her she was so right. But she couldn't, not yet.

"You're beautiful," Muriel said. "But you act like you don't even know it. *Use* it. That boy—he owns more earrings than me except I've got the good sense to wear one pair at a time."

"He's creative," Maya said, wincing at defending a guy who had just dumped her, yet dutifully doing what had to be done.

"He doesn't even have a job," Muriel said.

"He works at a music store," Maya said. "And he's a serious musician. He's really good."

"Whatever you say," Muriel said. "Who knows, maybe he'll hit it big and you two can move out to Hollywood and live in style."

Maya examined her mother closely. The beautiful profile. The statuesque figure. The quick confidence. But there was something else, and it was new: a troubled expression on her face. It had persisted for weeks now. And there was a sadness in her voice. It would sneak in, in the middle of her diatribes, at the edge of her quips.

"You must like this Henry guy," Maya offered.

"Why do you say that?"

"I mean, you're buying him a TV, right?"

"That's for us," Muriel snapped. "Henry is one fine man but he's a teetotaler. I haven't figured him out yet, but I will, don't you doubt it."

"But you like him," Maya said.

"Sure. I like him just fine."

"That's good."

Muriel gave her daughter a wary glance. The burden in her eyes was unmistakable. "Yeah, good," she said.

"I want to pack," Maya said, standing up. "We're leaving tomorrow."

"Sure, you go right ahead and do that. I hope you have a good time."

Maya started for the basement, but the camping gear would remain untouched. In fact, she would have to remember to hide it. For now, there was Googling to do.

On the drive to the airport, Maya got caught in freeway gridlock, which she hadn't expected so early in the afternoon. But she managed to make it into the terminal with time to spare, and now found herself onboard the Chicago-bound flight, staring out a scuffed up window and paging desultorily through the *City Paper* in her lap. Mostly she was trying not to steal glances over the empty seat at the handsome man sitting by the aisle. He looked like he'd stepped off the pages of *GQ* magazine. Maya had never been so close to a guy like that, and though he hadn't as much as glanced her way, she was flustered. He had perfectly cut sandy-brown hair, a square jaw, and bronzed, chiseled features. His movements belied an off-the-charts confidence that was beyond any of the guys Maya had encountered in Plainfield, which she could see just by the way he paged through the magazine he was reading.

His destination was Los Angeles. Maya *knew* it. She knew it because the thought had come with that familiar, unmistakable feeling of certainty that presented itself when her precognitive abilities were engaged.

Outside, two mechanics were probing at a complex of gears in a hatch on the wing. Maya squeezed the armrest tightly, straining to see what they were doing. Was something wrong with the wing?

Quickly the fear spread in her. What if the wing failed in flight? What if birds dive-bombed into an engine? Hadn't she read that a flock of geese had once brought a jet down? Or was that lightning? Or worse—what if a meteor smashed into the cockpit and immolated the pilots? What if—

Maya's own mind took flight. She wondered how she'd react to any of that, for wasn't staring into the face of death the true test of one's mettle, illuminating the unvarnished beliefs that lived beneath the surface? She recalled a Buddhist sect that focused on nothing but preparing for one's final moment on this earth. What would *she* do? Would she accept it, try to fight it, or might she actually *embrace* it?

She groaned. These were not thoughts she wanted to be having a half hour before liftoff. Flying had always been difficult. Maya could hardly bear being cooped up with all these strangers, hurtling across the sky in a machine that amounted to a tin can with rocket engines on it. She wondered how these people could immerse themselves in their novels and computer screens with those comfortable, satisfied looks on their faces.

She twirled her hair with icy cold fingers. *Think.* A strategy did come to mind which had succeeded in derailing this kind anticipatory fear in the past. It was simple. Preemptively strike at it with paradoxical intention: imagine the worst, play it out in the mind—and thus maintain control by not being surprised. It was a medicine could seem worse than the illness.

So, sitting safely in the stationary aircraft, Maya imagined the coming disaster: the stomach-wrenching descent, the crushing G-force pressure that would stretch out the skin of her face and disfigure her, the bone-shattering impact that would smash body, melt organs—and then—

What?

Maya had often tried to view the end in positive terms, as a step in a spiritual evolution, a transition, a passage into a different state of consciousness. Perhaps fabulous experiences were in store that defied even the most creative imagination. Maybe Earth was the *bottom* rung on the soul's journey, a hell, and things got better once the mortal journey was completed.

One thing did seem certain. Death was change. Why was that such a problem? Why did people get so worked up about something as natural as a tulip closing for the night? It would open again, in some way, in some form, somewhere.

Wouldn't it?

It was easy to be all cool and theoretical about something Maya essentially knew nothing about. Livingston had been her first real loss, and she hadn't even fully experienced it yet. Her theories were just mind-stuff. Chatter. She knew that. Like everyone else, she had no idea what would happen when she felt the grim reaper's bony-fingered tap on her shoulder.

Out on the tarmac, uniformed men were grabbing suitcases from a cart and tossing them into the plane's underbelly. All that baggage, all these people. One day they would all receive the tap.

"I'm going to take a guess about something," the handsome man said over the empty seat. "You're not too keen on flying."

"Huh, what?" Maya said, shocked out of her grim reverie.

"I don't mean to pry," he said, "but it looks like you're trying to squeeze that book in half."

"Oh, no!" Maya exclaimed, looking at the journal in her hand. She flattened it out, smoothed her hand on its cover.

"I figure if something's going to happen," he said, "it'll be quick. Maybe even a thrill, if you want to venture out on that limb."

"I don't," Maya said quickly.

"Sorry, bad habit. Bluntness," he said.

Maya was dazzled, looking at him.

He stared back at her. "I'm Peter."

"Maya," she said.

"Are you from Chicago?"

"Maryland."

"Ah," Peter said. "The Chesapeake Bay. Soft-shell crabs. The Orioles. Great place. Me, I'm heading back to the City of Angels. Yeah, that's a laugh. Gomorrah by the Sea is more like it." He became thoughtful. "You know, it's funny. When I'm there I just hate the place. But when I'm anywhere else I'm practically a city booster. I could never figure that one out."

Maya looked at him uncomprehendingly.

"Los Angeles," he explained.

Ha! she thought with satisfaction. *Right!*

"What?" he said.

Maya flushed. "I guess I had a feeling you were going there," she said.

"Is it that obvious?"

"No, no, I'm sorry, I shouldn't have said anything."

"Hey, no worries," he said pleasantly. "If you're so psychic, what do I do for a living?"

"I'm not psychic."

"Prove it. Go ahead, take a guess. Anything. Be wrong."

A thought did come to her, a knowing. She really *was* on. "You're in radio. But not *on* it. Something behind the scenes. Helping, organizing, something like that. Producing."

Peter's eyebrows shot up. "Wow. That's good. That's very good. I'm a producer at a radio station in L.A. I was right about you, Maya."

She looked down at her hands, wanting to talk about something else.

He said, "What about this: married or single? That should be easy. Fifty-fifty." He covered his left hand.

"Do you mind if we don't do this?" Maya said.

"Sure," he said. He glanced at the journal in her hand. "What's that, your predictions?"

"No," she said, shifting it away from him.

The cabin lurched as the plane began to back up. Peter returned to reading his magazine. Relieved, Maya turned to the window and watched the terminal pass out of view.

The plane lifted off and began its climb. Maya pressed in her earbuds and set her music on shuffle, and opened the journal, even though she'd already been through it many times.

Consciousness brings the world into existence. Without consciousness, there is nothing—no thing. This is critical, Maya. Consciousness creates matter.

The world springs to life in every moment through the interplay of all the varieties of consciousness. We don't see it because we experience life through our senses, which limit what we can perceive. We're *built* to be unaware of what is really happening. Ironic, isn't it?

What force spins the Earth every twenty-four hours? What pushes creatures up the evolutionary ladder? What is behind every physical process in existence? It is this: pure, undifferentiated energy. That is the first level of

business. You must understand energy, Maya,
in order to understand the change.

Energy flows into the Earth at specific
locations around the globe. Such locales have
many names. I prefer the term vortexes. Some
native peoples call them power points. It is at
these places that the inflowing energy interacts
with the human mind, beginning the process by
which thoughts manifest into events.

If, for example, you deeply desire something
while at one of these locations, a momentum is
engaged that will bring your intention to pass.
Similarly, vortexes manifest the thoughts and
desires of *groups* of people. This is how social,
cultural and religious movements start.

As I write this, no manmade instrument
exists that can detect or measure pure energy,
and so science hasn't yet arrived at an
understanding of it. But Maya, energy is real. It
can be observed. The plants function in this
way. Be sure to ask Dr. Porter about this.

The plants, Maya thought as she watched the sunlight pattering
off the roofs of the houses whizzing by beyond the highway's
cement barrier. She was sitting in the backseat of a taxi speeding
into northern Chicago. She'd opened the window some and was
enjoying feeling of the breeze on her face.

Maya had learned nothing about Edgar Porter in her online
searches. Nor had she found his phone number. She had
considered mailing him a letter the old-fashioned way, but
decided that the glacial pace of snail mail wasn't just going to cut
it. She convinced herself it didn't really matter what happened
on the trip. She was hungry for a new experience and desperate
to get out of Plainfield, and even if the journey turned up
nothing, at least she'd get to see a new place. So why not just
take off and see what happened? Indeed, she was excited.

The late afternoon sun hung low in the sky—the *in-between time*, Maya once called it, when she could sense wonder stirring in the air. It was a time that hinted of transition and possibility, an opening when experience shifted and the mind could venture out of its well-worn tracks for something new, like a car leaving a highway for a shadowy exit ramp that appeared briefly and then vanished. She reveled in the feeling, stoking it, pushing into it as far as she could go.

The cab exited the freeway and entered a neighborhood of dilapidated houses and shabby apartment buildings, then made its way into a polished suburb. A few minutes later the scenery changed dramatically as the road ascended into a wooded area with many secluded streets.

Wealth was evident in every home Maya saw, each one surrounded by expansive lawns and well-tended gardens. It had been a warm autumn, and blossoms colored the views. Taking it all in, Maya felt certain the trip would be fruitful, that she would gain critical information about her father and maybe even learn what happened to him. It was as though the presence of wealth and beauty ensured success. She shook off the ridiculous idea, for truly that's what it was.

The cab made its way along a winding country lane and through the open gateposts of a low stone wall. A stately, enormous English Tudor mansion stood up ahead, built of cut stone, with many archways and patios. Magnificent old-growth trees threw complex shadows on the lawns. The cab rounded the circular driveway and stopped at the front door. Maya paid the driver and asked him to wait.

Standing at the massive door, she reached for the bell but stopped, suddenly anxious. What to say?

Tell the truth.

Right.

She rang the bell.

No answer. She rang again.

Still, nothing. So she rang a third time.

This time the door opened, but only a crack, just enough to reveal the pudgy face of a short man with furtive, darting eyes. He checked her out from head to toe.

"What do you want?" he said curtly.

"Mr. Porter?" Maya said.

"That's right. Who are you?"

She drew back, struck by his brusque tone. "My name is Maya Burke. I'm here about Ben Ambrose."

"Never heard of him."

Maya paused, confused. "You don't know him?"

His eyes narrowed.

"Ben Ambrose," Maya repeated.

"I'm not deaf," Porter said.

"You really don't know him?"

He stared at her.

Think.

Maya said, "It would have been a long time ago. Twenty years." She felt the dampness of perspiration on her neck.

"Describe him."

"I'm sorry, I can't," she confessed.

"Why not?"

"I've never met him."

"Who is he?"

"He's my father."

"But you don't know him?"

"No."

"Explain."

"Actually," she said, "He wrote to me—"

"I'd count correspondence as knowing someone, wouldn't you?" Porter's eyes bored into her. He gave a disconcerting smile.

Maya could feel her adrenal glands spring to life, pumping chemical discomfort into her body. She said, "No, I found something of his—"

"Hmm," Porter said. "And what would that be?"

Maya looked into his eyes, and to her horror, realized he was *enjoying* himself.

She opened her mouth to speak but couldn't get the words out. Her mind was painting. Images were arising on a hungry inner canvas. With the virtuosity of a Van Gogh, some disturbed part of her was busily constructing a detailed scene—troublingly unrelated to the matter at hand—in which she was a miserable failure. She was deteriorating, and heavy. So heavy she could barely move, her arms like granite blocks hanging at her sides. All she could do was summon her mother and ask—no, beg—for help. And maybe Muriel would come, maybe she wouldn't...

The door started to close. Maya saw it happening in slow motion, frame by excruciating frame.

"Wait!" she shouted, digging frantically into the pockets of her backpack. "Hold on!"

She took out the scrap of paper she'd found in the safe deposit box and read from it. "'Dr. Edgar Porter!' It's right here in his writing. Please, look! You must!"

The door opened further and the man's face came fully into view. "Why didn't you say so in the first place?" he said. "That's my father. I'm Jim. Jim Porter."

"Your father, yes," Maya said breathlessly.

"*Dr.* Porter."

"Yes, yes. Is he here?"

"Of course. He's in the yard, doing whatever he does back there. What was your name again?"

"Maya. Maya Burke. Tell him Ben Ambrose's daughter is here to see him."

"Wait here," he said, and shut the door.

Maya breathed.

"Come this way," Jim Porter said, motioning her toward a wide hallway that bisected the house. Maya had never been in a mansion before, and she almost tripped over her feet taking in the grandeur of it. She couldn't help but notice what lined the walls of the many softly lit rooms around her: art, and lots of it.

Of course she knew about the private collections of the wealthy, but she assumed their holdings were modest, maybe a few valuable pieces; certainly nothing compared to the bounty of the museums. But this—*this* was incredible. Here in the middle of an ordinary neighborhood—well, not quite—were walls of priceless oil paintings including two Monets she recognized. There were marble and bronze sculptures, one that was surely a Rodin, and walls with displays of tribal masks, spears and ancient jewelry. Maya saw even soaring modern art pieces. In all, it had to be worth a fortune.

Maya had once been obsessed with great art like this. It was a time in her life that seemed now like a past life. She'd spent too many afternoons to count wandering the museums in Washington, D.C., an hour's drive from home. The National Gallery of Art, the Freer, the Hirshhorn, the Corcoran, and others, too.

The masters' works pulsed with an energy that was palpable, and Maya had opened herself up to it fully. How did they do it? she had often wondered. How did they produce work that could incite so much feeling, that brought on transcendent and even ecstatic highs and could transport people clear out of their humdrum lives? Just thinking about it, without any idea of the answers, was stimulating.

Maya had never discovered her own art, though she had dabbled for a time in drawing, painting and writing. Was it simply living? She laughed at the idea. Although it was true she had friends who took pride in building their days creatively in speech and deed. Josh certainly could access the deeper dimension, which Maya felt sure made his life more adventurous than hers.

"Come, come," Jim said impatiently. "Yes, I know, father's art is fabulous. I used to come down here a lot back in the day. I don't have time for such distractions anymore. I have much to do, and I can't be detained."

"I'm coming, I'm coming," Maya said, not wanting to know what that might be. She hurried along, even as she tried to peek into all the rooms.

They came to a greenhouse at the back of the house just as the day's waning rays of sunlight were lighting up the tops of a few palm trees brushing against the glass ceiling. A gurgling stream flowed by Maya's feet, passing over moss-covered stones into a collecting pool where ruby and orange-flecked koi drifted lazily about.

Jim led her through a back door to a brick patio where an old man sat in a wheelchair. Wide-eyed, Maya surveyed the expansive property with its stone paths, gardens and fountains.

Edgar Porter looked as old and as interesting as his art collection. He had a large face dominated by deep wrinkles and a nearly bald head with a few wisps of white hair that danced when he moved. His thin legs were folded up into the wheelchair. His blue eyes were laser-sharp, and they were staring right at Maya.

"Your guest," Jim Porter said to his father. He turned on his heels and was gone.

"Well, well," Dr. Porter said, taking Maya in. "Ben Ambrose's daughter. You don't say." He pointed to a nearby chair. "Sit, please."

"Thank you," Maya said. "It's nice to meet you, Dr. Porter. I appreciate your willingness to see me."

"Not at all," he said pleasantly. He pressed a lever in the wheelchair's armrest and it rotated to face her.

He glanced up at the twilight sky. "You know, Maya," he said. "I come out here every day at sunset. Whatever it is I'm doing can wait. There's something deeply magical about this time of day. Do you know what I mean?"

"I do know what you mean," Maya said, feeling a kinship with him. "I love it, too."

"It's the time of the changeover," Dr. Porter said. "Maybe you are drawn to such things."

"The changeover?"

"When light becomes shadow and the invisible reveals itself," he said. "The subtle can rise up. When the day closes, a window opens into what can be a very different kind of experience."

Maya listened, examining him, noticing that his lips were ashen, the pigment bleached out by sun, or age.

"That is," he added with a conspiratorial wink, "if you believe what the shamans and mystics tell us."

Maya smiled politely, listening.

"Forgive me," he said. "I don't mean to lecture. I suppose it's in the blood. I used to be a teacher, once upon a time. Not that it gives me license to bore a lovely young lady."

"I'm not bored," Maya said.

"No, you're not," he replied, wheeling up close. "I can see that. You resemble him, you know. In the eyes, especially."

"You mean Ben?"

"Yes. And your manner. Ben also had a thoughtful way about him."

"I've never met him, Dr. Porter," Maya said. "I was hoping you could tell me about him. Or what happened to him. I don't know where he is, or even *if* he is."

"Then I'm very sorry to have to tell you this, Maya," Dr. Porter said. "But I haven't seen Ben in many years."

A darkness came over her, and she turned away. She wondered if coming here had been a mistake, that she'd been too rash.

"Surely you must know something," she said.

"Oh, I do," he said. "And I'll be happy to tell it to you. But first, tell me, how did you come by my name and know where I live?"

"He mentioned you in a journal he wrote."

"A journal? Really?" Dr. Porter said, interested.

Immediately Maya regretted mentioning it. The journal was the only piece of he father she had ever possessed and she wanted to keep it to herself. It seemed more special that way, like a gift. But so far she had failed miserably. Josh knew, and now this stranger did, too.

"What kind of a journal is it?" Dr. Porter asked.

"Actually, it was just a couple of pages, more like a letter," Maya said, backpedaling. "He wrote about using plants to perceive energy. He said you'd know about that."

Dr. Porter became thoughtful, looking right past Maya to the trees beyond. "Long ago," he said, "we taught at the university, your father and I. You might say Ben was my protégé for a time. He was quite the idealist, with this theories about what he called the post-scientific age. His work brought him some degree of notoriety. Ben was a futurist, and quite daring.

Or reckless, depending on your point of view. He taught only briefly. He left academia for a position in Washington, I think."

"D.C.?"

"Yes."

"Do you know where?" Maya asked.

"At one of the government agencies. I don't know which."

"Do you know anyone who might?"

"Let me think on that," Dr. Porter said. "It's possible."

"Thank you," Maya said.

She looked around. Night had fallen and she hadn't even noticed. Floodlights had come on, illuminating the tall trees. The drone of crickets was in the air, a dense blanket of sound that reminded her of home. The temperature had dropped, and she buttoned up her sweater against the chill air.

"I'll be happy to show you the plants," Dr. Porter said. "If that's what you—and Ben—want."

"Very much," Maya said.

"It's somewhat involved," he said. "It's getting late. Would tomorrow do? Are you staying in the area?"

"At a motel, I guess."

"You haven't settled anywhere? Why, you'd be most welcome to stay here. There's a wealth of guest rooms, more than we've ever used. That is," he added, "if you wish. You'd be completely comfortable, I assure you. Jim is quite harmless."

Maya offered a cordial smile. No, she wouldn't be comfortable sleeping in a house a thousand miles from home with two men who were, well, unusual, to say the least. Just the fact he'd offered gave her pause.

"Thank you, Dr. Porter. I've got a cab waiting outside."

"Of course," he said agreeably.

He led her back through the house to the front door, which opened with the press of a button.

"Come at ten," he said. "You won't be disappointed. I guarantee it."

"Goodnight," she said. "Thank you."

"Until then," he said, bowing his head.

Maya got in the cab and asked the driver to take her to a Travelodge she'd seen on the drive over, a half-hour away on the main street of a nearby suburb.

At the diner that adjoined the motel, she wolfed down a cheeseburger and fries, then settled into her room prepared for a long and sleepless night. Slowing the freight train of her thoughts had never been easy, especially amid new experiences in unfamiliar surroundings. But somehow she fell asleep quickly on the soft queen-sized bed.

She dreamt of her father that night. It was a dream she'd had many times, which she had once recounted to her mother's brother, Buddy, on the backyard swing-set one morning. Buddy was drinking coffee and reading the newspaper, the way he did every morning.

"Hey, what's with the happy face?" he asked, seeing her smiling. "Where's the usual morning grump?"

"I had a nice dream," Maya said.

"Well, if it's that good I need to know about it."

"It's private," she said, staring down at her feet.

Buddy laughed. "Come on, this is your uncle here. *Give*."

That expression of his always made her smile. "OK," she relented. She had trusted Buddy from the moment she met him. "It's about my father."

"Your father, huh?" Buddy said. He'd never met his sister's husband.

Maya climbed up onto the swing. "It always starts out the same way. I'm sitting on a picnic table under a shade tree. There's a lake with these long skinny things poking up out of the water."

"Those would be reeds," Buddy pointed out.

"Reeds, right," she said. "There's a nice smell of green grass. It's summertime."

"Summer is good," Buddy agreed.

"There's a dirt path that goes up into the hills. I don't know where, exactly. I don't know much of anything except I'm not supposed to turn around."

Buddy gently rocked the swing.

"It's like I've been sitting on that table forever, waiting," Maya said. "But I don't care. I know I'm in the right place. I mean, I *can't* be anywhere else, I have to be there, and this thing that's going to happen is really, really important."

"Hmm," Buddy said.

"There's a tap on my shoulder. It's him. He doesn't say anything, but if he did it would be something like, 'That's a girl, come on now. This way,' in this fatherly kind of voice. That's stupid, I know."

"It's not," Buddy said.

"He takes my hand, I stand up and we start walking on this path toward the hills. The thing I'm feeling is strange *and* good, and there's bright light and everything that's bad has gone away. Whatever I was, I'm not anymore. And this feeling is more than just him. It's like I'm a part of something else, something big. I don't know what. I ask him, 'Where are we going?' and he says, 'Home. We're going home.'"

"Home?" Buddy said, intrigued. "No kidding?"

"Uh-huh. And I get really happy when he says it. But I don't know where home is. Then I wake up."

"Right then?"

"Every time." She gazed at her uncle. "Weird, huh?"

He reached over and gave her shoulder a squeeze. "No, not weird. Interesting. Cool."

"When it's over I feel good. I still do."

Buddy said, "That's a whopper of a dream, Maya. A real beaut. I'd hang on to it if I were you. I'd hang on real tight."

"I always do," she said with a smile.

5

Visions

W hen I chose the location of my home some thirty-three years ago, it was not an act of economic speculation or a search for physical comfort," Dr. Porter said the next morning as he wheeled down a hallway toward the west side of the house. He stopped and spun his wheelchair around to face Maya.

"I knew the value was in the land, but not in the way most people think of it—not as real estate—but as an energy source, and a rare one at that. These grounds contain an indigenous feature of incalculable worth. Ben must have mentioned the vortex in this letter of his?"

"He did," Maya said. "Where is it?"

The old man's pale lips turned up in a smile. Though his face was blotched and pinched, and could be considered repugnant, it glowed with a young man's excitement when he talked about the mystical side of life.

He pointed down at the marble floor.

Maya said, "In the ground?"

"Under it."

"Where are the plants?"

"Downstairs," he said.

He led her to a door in a hallway that Maya had not seen earlier. It opened to reveal an elevator car of simple design. Maya stepped in and Dr. Porter rolled in beside her.

The descent was slow and dominated by the noise of grinding pulleys and motors hidden in the walls. When the door opened, Maya stared in astonishment at a cavernous room as large as a gymnasium, and she realized immediately what it was: a plant nursery, populated by hundreds of bushes and trees in long rows. A labyrinth of pipes and hoses snaked along the cement floor, reaching up into each of the ceramic pots, the bones of an elaborate irrigation system. Banks of ceiling lamps bathed the room in bright light. The air was warm and moist.

Dr. Porter made a grand gesture at the plants. "My instruments," he said.

To Maya, the plants looked quite ordinary, much like the ones she had labored over in the gardening section of Toby's Lawn & Garden Emporium where she had worked in her junior and senior years of high school.

"Come this way," Dr. Porter said, and wheeled up an incline toward a long desk stacked with glowing computer screens. He stopped at a panelboard of switches and dials, motioning for Maya to take the seat beside him.

"Are you ready to see something interesting?" he said, turning to her.

"Sure," she said. "I think that's why I'm here."

He turned a knob and the overhead lights started to dim until the room fell to complete dark—a dark broken only by a faint reddish glow emanating from a smaller set of ceiling lamps that had come on.

"Keep your eyes out there," Dr. Porter said, nodding toward the center of the room.

Out there?

Maya didn't know what to make of that. She decided it must mean to gaze out into the shadowy jungle and wait for something to happen.

Several minutes passed. Nothing happened.

"There!" Dr. Porter said, pointing. "Do you see it?"

Maya eagerly swept her gaze from one end of the room to the other but she saw nothing unusual, just a dimly lit expanse of plants.

"It's fine," Dr. Porter assured her. "It's perfectly fine. Just keep looking."

"Maybe it would help if I knew what I was looking for," she said.

"Energy," he said. "In its purest form. The way it exists before it inhabits something."

"Energy—what do you mean?"

"Just what I said," he said. "That which drives and animates all things. The fuel that powers us."

"You can't see it," Maya said.

"*Au contraire*," he said. "Of course you can."

Maya had always believed in energy—in theory. There had to be a base-level force at work beneath the animate and inanimate worlds. *Something* provided the power to move all processes. And maybe the intelligence, too.

The concept had come up in many of the anthropology courses that were a part of her history major. Traditional and indigenous peoples all believed in energy. Native American myths were rife with it. The Chinese claimed to have mapped its pathways through the human body right down to the finest detail. The Hindus had a host of gods to represent energy's many manifestations, and Sanskrit, a language that had a whole vocabulary about its properties. Why have words for something that doesn't exist? And why, Maya wondered, did the scientific West ignore all the ancient wisdom teachings that might be pointing to undiscovered truth? Thoughts were invisible, too, but nobody denied their existence.

So if energy was real, where was it?

Apparently right here in this strange bio-lab. And Maya was too dense to see it.

Concentrate.

She tried squinting and blurring and skewing her vision in every possible way. Still, she saw nothing.

"You're trying too hard," Dr. Porter said.

"Story of my life," Maya said.

"Listen, Maya. You don't *try* to relax. You allow it to happen. You make room for it."

"OK, I'll try that," she said and then quickly corrected herself. "I mean, I *won't* try…"

"I have a better idea," Dr. Porter said. He reached into a box down at his feet and brought up a pair of lightweight headphones which he handed to Maya. "These will help you get into an alpha state."

Alpha. Maya knew the term. Sarah Carter, the meditation teacher whose class Maya had attended on Monday nights at Breathe Yoga Studio on Falls Road had used it often. Alpha was the scientific term for the brainwave pattern of a kind of deep relaxation, a state of consciousness close to normal waking, yet just askew of it. People in alpha were resting *and* alert.

Maya had taken to meditation from the moment her eyes fell shut. She was surprised how natural it felt, as if she were already preprogramed for it. The sensation was one of floating, as if she'd discarded the heaviness of her body for an ethereal container. She had practiced on a cushion on her bedroom floor on many afternoons, blissfully releasing worries, riding the simple sound, her mantra, down into the quietude. Alpha came surprisingly easy. And the calmness that followed carried over into activity. Meditation had gotten her through the chaos of her first two years of college when she felt isolated and melancholy, and poured herself obsessively into schoolwork and let friendships slide. It was a lonely time. The peace she'd found in meditation helped a lot. But pinball mind always reasserted itself at some point after the meditations, with its exhausting barrage of thoughts and worries. For all of its benefits, Maya had dropped the practice, though she couldn't recall why.

The headphones played a simple tone, unwavering. Uninteresting.

"Close your eyes," Dr. Porter instructed.

Maya did, and a heartbeat later she was moving. It happened fast. She was moving and then she was falling. The floor dropped away and she was in free fall.

Frightened, her eyes flew open. She looked around. She hadn't gone anywhere. She was sitting in the chair, the room still and unchanged, with Dr. Porter right beside her. She was about to ask him what had happened, but she was distracted. A strange sight a few feet away was drawing her attention powerfully: shimmers of light crackling over one of the small trees. Quickly they disappeared.

"Hey!" Maya said. "What was that?"

"Excellent," Dr. Porter said. "Keep looking at it. When it returns, lock your eyes onto it."

The sparkles reappeared. Maya held her gaze on the unsettling sight, enduring the chills of fear and excitement ascending her spine, and a strange thought occurred to her, a preposterous idea: that she had *awakened* the plant and it was now aware of her.

Suddenly the whole room exploded in light and electricity. Where one sparkle had crackled, now hundreds erupted. Everything was on fire. Rivers of ruby, scarlet and emerald melted and shot out from the little trees, poured down to the floor, coursed along branches and leaves, climbed walls and spread across the ceiling in every direction.

"What's happening ..." Maya said, her mouth agape.

And with these words, the bizarre display abruptly ended. The high-ceilinged room and the dense life within it became dim and still again, bathed in the ghostly light. No movement or color, only silence. Silence broken by Maya's rapid-fire breathing.

"Where did the colors go?" she asked, turning to Dr. Porter.

"They're still there."

"I don't see them," she said.

"I want to try something else, Maya," Dr. Porter said. "Give me the headphones. Let's do it naturally, no props. Sit quietly and try to return to the feeling you had at the moment you saw the colors. You'll have a memory of it. Just bring it back."

"OK," Maya said.

She tried that and it worked. The psychedelic fast-moving colors returned, again enveloping every visible surface. Maya turned to Dr. Porter, who was awash in color, too...

"No, no, *out there*," he said, pointing an undulating orange finger toward the center of the room.

Now Maya glimpsed something she had not seen before, back near the rear wall: a small tree with a powerful violet light blazing around it, its luminescence so intense it blotted out most everything else around it.

"What is it?" Maya asked, mesmerized by the sight.

"It's what you came to see," Dr. Porter said excitedly. "That is the vortex."

The violet light was attracting Maya so powerfully that she could not pull her gaze from it. Nor did she want to. What she did want was to get closer to it. She began to rise. *Just a few steps—*

The assault of bright light from above was almost like a physical attack. She raised up a hand to shield her eyes and turned angrily to Dr. Porter, who had switched on the ceiling lights.

"Why did you do that?" Maya said.

"You were being seduced by the vortex," he said.

"Seduced?"

"We need to be careful of that," he said. "That's why you need a control, a guide. Someone to direct you. That's my role. Come, there's one thing yet to do and it's important."

He rolled rapidly down the ramp into the main aisle and Maya followed behind him, absentmindedly brushing her fingers against leaves and branches as she walked.

She was atremble with excitement. This was incredible. It was the confirmation of theory. She'd seen things that weren't actually there. And the colors … they had somehow come from the *trees*. How? It had to be pure energy. What else could it be? A crackling mysterious realm that existed beyond the observable world. Belief and theory were well and good, but this was direct experience. Maya wondered what else was beneath the surface.

"An ordinary ficus," Dr. Porter said, fingering the leaves of the tree that had glowed so brightly.

"Pardon?"

"This flora here. It's a ficus. But it could be anything. Look, it's just a normal tree."

Maya nodded, hardly hearing him. Her mind was reeling, trying to grasp the implications of what she had just experienced. If she believed in energy, *really* believed in it, then wasn't all of life and the natural world up for reevaluation? Anything was possible—like the possibility that she would have to alter her worldview to accommodate this new data. And the data, which was not yet organized, was likely the tip of the iceberg.

"Hello...?" Dr. Porter said, snapping his fingers in front of her face.

"Sorry, I was drifting," Maya said.

"Of course you were," he said knowingly. "It's easy to get lost down here. You see, Maya, proximity to a vortex affects thought. People act differently around them."

"How so?"

"Well, there's quite the difference growing up in, say, the Middle East versus here in Chicago. The great vortex of Jerusalem is one of the most powerful in the world. It's helped birth religions that shaped cultures and wars that devastated whole civilizations. Psychic activity runs incredibly high in such places. Passions are stirred up. People are incited to act in ways they would never even contemplate elsewhere. That's why it's so hard to maintain the peace, or at times, sanity itself."

"Where exactly is the vortex—your vortex?" Maya asked.

"It's deep in the Earth," he said. "It reaches up."

"How did you know it was here?"

"I search for them. It's a hobby of mine."

"How?"

"You're curious," he said. "Again, like Ben. There are two ways to locate vortexes: directly and inferentially. Inferentially, you look for ruins. Some of the more advanced ancient civilizations knew about the power of vortexes, which is why many of their structures have endured for so long. You know some of them. The pyramids. Stonehenge. Easter Island. There are many. Now, the more direct method is through clairvoyants. Psychics. People who can sense energy. That's how I mapped this one."

He wheeled up close. "There's something I must tell you, young lady."

"What's that?" Maya said, drawing back, suddenly uneasy.

"You were excellent."

"Excellent?"

"Most people—no, I dare say, just about all—could not do what you just did, see what you saw. They'd need training, and lots of it, and even then probably wouldn't get those kinds of results. I had a feeling about you. Here, take a look at this."

He grabbed the edge of the pot that held the fichus tree and wheeled backward, sliding the pot away to reveal an "X" painted in white on the cement floor. There was a chair nearby which he pushed over the spot.

"Sit," he said.

Maya didn't move.

"Sit, please," he insisted.

"Why?"

He thought for a moment. "Why are you here, Maya?"

"I told you. I'm looking for my father, trying to figure out what happened to him."

"Right. You want to find your father."

"Yes."

"And now you have an opportunity to do just that. One, incidentally, that may not come along very often."

She said, "I don't understand."

"By using your innate gifts, with the help of the natural energy here, we can seek information about Ben. You'll 'work the vortex,' as we say. If you succeed, images will come. Or they won't. There are no guarantees. All I'm talking about is a simple exercise in visualization. You may be able to *see* him."

Maya thought about that. Now, there was a concept— seeing her father, right here in this oddest of places. She stared at the simple wooden chair. Sitting in it would mean interacting with the vortex in some way, being subjected to a power that affected people psychically, mind-bendingly, and who knew what else.

And yet, here was an opportunity. She had determined to stop playing it safe. Wasn't this a perfect time to prove those weren't just empty words? She could almost see an invisible doorway materializing before her that led into the unknown, beckoning. But where would it lead?

"Is it dangerous?" she said.

"As dangerous as daydreaming," he said. "You get uncomfortable, you simply stop."

She nodded. "All right. Let's do it."

"You're sure?"

"I am."

"Then we'll start," he said.

She lowered herself into the chair and placed her feet flat on the floor. He wheeled in close. "Everything will be fine," he assured her. "It's actually quite easy."

"What do I do?"

"We'll start with some visualization. Close your eyes."

She did so, and again felt her chest tighten up, her breaths shorten. She brought her mantra to mind, repeating the simple, soothing sound she'd intimately experienced in meditation. Within seconds, her breaths lengthened and deepened. A faint red tint lit her eyelids from without; the ceiling lights again had dimmed.

"Place your father's image in your mind's eye," Dr. Porter instructed.

Maya had no image of him to place anywhere, except perhaps that distant memory of the old photo she'd found when she was a child.

"I don't know what he looks like."

"Just maintain the thought of him."

"OK."

"Let your mind drift," Dr. Porter said.

"Drift?"

"Keep the idea of him alive in it. When thoughts come, don't grasp onto them. Let them float on by like flower petals on a river."

She felt lightheaded. She heard something.

"A guitar! I hear a guitar!" she said, struggling to keep her eyes shut.

"Good," Dr. Porter said. "What else?"

"I don't know where it's coming from—"

"Don't analyze," he said quickly. "Just report what you see."

"Someone singing! I can't believe this! I'm really hearing this. It's a folk song, something about a country girl."

"A country girl?"

She nodded vigorously.

"Do you see anything?"

"Well, no, I don't exactly see it, but—huh, this is weird. There's a baby. Wait. She—it's a girl. God, I'm usually not this visual."

"What else?"

"A dark-haired man. Her head is on his shoulder. Wait, it's changing!"

"Good. Let it happen."

"It's a room. There are lots of people. Cement walls. It's underground. Uniforms—no suits. Men in suits. Someone is giving a talk. There are no windows, just thick concrete. I'm scared. Oh, God. There is something here I don't like." She paused. "Wait! It changing! It's a field! Sunlight. Something sweet in the air, I can smell it. What is it? It's familiar. I know it. Right …Honeysuckle!" She paused. "I see mountains. People are running. What's happening? Am I looking through someone's eyes? Is it him?"

"Do you see him?" Dr. Porter said urgently.

"There's a sign," she said. "A road sign. *Wicklow*. What's that?"

"A town," he said. "What else?"

"A settlement, like a camp. People cooking. Children. A blond girl with freckles. She's looking at me. Oh, God! She's staring right at me!"

"Steady now," Dr. Porter said. "Do nothing. It will change."

The image of the girl faded and disappeared. Maya slumped back in the chair.

"Quickly," Dr. Porter said. "Imagine yourself with your father."

Maya was finding it difficult to draw a full breath.

"Do it, please," Dr. Porter said.

She gasped.

"What do you see?" he insisted.

"Nothing," she said weakly.

"Let it happen."

"Wait! There's something."

"What?"

"The planet," she said.

"Which one?" he said.

Which one?

"The Earth. A drawing of it."

"You don't see him?"

"No. Just the Earth with a kind of web around it."

"A web?"

"Yes. I'm tired ... have to stop ... I'm going to ..."

She felt herself losing consciousness.

"One more thing," he said.

"No, no, can't ..."

"OK. Come back. Open your eyes."

"Yes ... back ..."

The bed was soft and welcoming and felt almost like a caress from beneath her. Sunlight was streaming through the window a few feet away. Maya lifted her head up off the pillow and peered outside, relieved to see Dr. Porter's chair parked on the patio. He was reading a book.

Maya stood up but weakness quickly overcame her and she almost fell, but she managed to reach out and press her palm against a wall. She was dizzy. This had to be one of the guest rooms, but how had she gotten here?

She shook her head vigorously and straightened up and shuffled down the hallway to a door that led outside. Squinting in the sunlight, she made her way over to Dr. Porter.

"Hey there," she said.

"How are you feeling?" he asked, concerned.

"Like I had three Margaritas and then got hit by a car," she said. "How did I get inside?"

"You walked."

She rubbed her eyes. "That's funny, I don't remember that."

"I led you, under your own power. You were fading fast."

"How long was I out?"

"Less than an hour. Come, walking helps."

"Helps what?"

"The disorientation."

"OK," she said.

He led her along one of the brick walkways as she breathed deeply of the sweet-scented air and struggled to recall what had happened. Slowly it came back to her.

She remembered the disjointed images that had played out in her mind like a string of film clips. They seemed like memories, only not hers—about people she didn't know and places she'd never been. As hard as she tried, she couldn't recall how it had ended.

She looked around. The day was certainly beautiful. The trees shimmered. The leaves were the greenest she'd ever seen. Colors vibrated. Sounds popped. Sparrows traced paths through the air that she could almost see. Overhead, clouds drifted like great white mountains through the bright sky.

A fountain was nearby shooting long arcs of water into a circular collecting pool, and Maya dropped onto a bench beside it, transfixed by the splashing of the water, which sounded like the music of flutes. Flutes! She almost laughed. Her senses were remarkably acute.

"Congratulations," Dr. Porter said, beside her. "You've seen energy in its purest form. If more people could do that, it would probably start a revolution."

Maya wanted to respond to that but she forgot what she wanted to say. Her thoughts were hard to grasp, like slippery fish that escaped through her fingers when she reached for them.

"Revolution?" she said.

"If more people understood energy it might start one."

"Why do you say that?"

"Our culture is based on a very different view of the universe," he said. "Are you OK, Maya?"

"A little woozy but starting to feel better," she said. Indeed, clarity was returning, the world coming back into focus. "What is this about a revolution?"

He said, "Most cultures—certainly we here in the West—favor a mechanistic view of things rather than one based on the interplay of unseen energy forces."

Maya stared at the fountain. The water no longer appeared magical. The flutes were gone, too. Probably a good thing.

"So what of it?" she said.

"A lot, actually," Dr. Porter said. "If people started thinking in terms of energy, they'd be facing a pretty big paradigm shift. Societies tend to look askance at radical changes to their underlying belief systems. You only have to look at history to see it. Imagine how Copernicus was received when he suggested the Earth wasn't the center of the universe but merely one planet among many circling the sun. Those poor devils must have had a tough time with that one. They believed right down in their bones they were God's gift to the universe, their civilizations his chief concern, and every celestial body existed for them and them alone.

"How would you feel if you found out your belief system was basically worthless, that it was rooted in monumental error? Copernicus started a chain reaction that brought down a centuries-old way of life. What I'm saying, Maya, is that people aren't all that comfortable with change. They want today to look pretty much like yesterday, tomorrow like today. They prefer to advance slowly and predictably, if at all. Life's vicissitudes go down a lot easier that way."

"Where is Wicklow?" Maya asked, recalling the road sign she'd seen in the vortex vision.

"It's a town in Wyoming, near the Big Horn Mountains."

"You know it?"

He smiled. "I have been around the block once or twice. It's near Jackson Hole."

"Is that where he is?"

"I don't know," the old man said. "You see, when you focused on him you received an image of the Earth rather than a physical location on it. That's when you should have seen an actual place."

"So all that was meaningless?" Maya said, disappointed.

"Oh, no," Dr. Porter said. "Far from it. You need time to digest it, let it stir you. More will come, naturally, of its own accord. It's a process."

"Why did he stop teaching?" Maya said.

"What?"

"Ben. You said he was a teacher."

"That's right," he said, pausing to retrieve the memory. "Actually, he was forced out."

"Really? Why?"

"He ruffled feathers. Ben didn't always teach what he was supposed to. His classes often came around to his own pet theories. He had very specific interests: the mass psyche, Carl Jung, the collective unconscious, the *I Ching*—"

The *I Ching!* Maya knew all about the Chinese Book of Changes, had used it many times, tossing the coins, trying to divine answers to her questions. But the cryptic remarks of the sixty-four hexagrams spoke a language she did not understand. But even so, she pursued it, for it was as compelling as it was inscrutable, even if it did respond to the simplest questions with statements like, "Hoarfrost underfoot betokens the coming of solid ice." To her surprise, words like that attracted her. She had decided not to pressure herself to understand them, but just wait. And sure enough, answers and ideas would pop into her mind.

"The *Ching* summed up what Ben believed," Dr. Porter went on. "That change is circular and therefore predictable. By properly using the book, he believed that the evolution of a culture, a life, a planet or any system could be mapped. Ben wanted to make predictions in a mass context. He wanted to know what the next global event, disaster, cultural shift, or even religion would be."

"I'm sure he did," Maya said with a doubtful laugh. "The world's just too complex. That's impossible."

Dr. Porter smiled his pinched smile. "You never know," he said. "If a person could accomplish something like that, well— you talk about a useful skill."

Maybe Maya was still off-kilter from the vortex experience, but when she looked over at Dr. Porter's face, it seemed somehow different, as if its lines and wrinkles were moving, stirred by a force beneath the surface of his skin. She blinked. She looked again. Something was happening.

Then he laughed. But it wasn't mere mirth. Hidden within his pleasant manner was a darkness she had not seen earlier. His personality had shifted into a wholly different gear. She shivered, and was overcome by the urge to stand up and run. Something terrible was about to happen. *I'm imagining it*, she thought. Maybe so, but she couldn't deny the overwhelming nature of the experience. When the fear reached a fevered pitch, she stood up.

"Dr. Porter, I appreciate everything you've shared with me," she said urgently.

He peered up at her. "Are you leaving, Maya?"

"Yes," she said. "I'm sorry. I have to go."

"I understand," he said pleasantly, appearing now as friendly and as welcoming as ever. "It was nice meeting you. I know you'll find what you're looking for."

I will, she thought. *And I know just where to look for it.*

6

A Most Unusual Community

The snow-covered peaks of the Rocky Mountains provided a jaw-dropping backdrop for anyone renting a room at Wicklow's ramshackle Pinewood Motel on West Turner Road. It was exactly the same view available from rooms at the elegant Hanford Lodge two blocks away, which cost three times as much to rent a room, an amount Maya could not afford—or rather, *would* not afford—since she did now in fact have the money, thanks to her father's late-in-life child support payment. The five thousand dollars was the most she'd ever had, and letting go if wasn't all that easy to do. The Pinewood would do just fine.

The flight to Wyoming's small Jackson Hole airport had been uneventful, to Maya's relief. From there she had caught a taxi to Wicklow, and now, a half-day after she had started out from Chicago, she found herself sitting on the edge of a springy motel bed beside a wide open window, and feeling very alone.

Maybe it was hearing Muriel's voice message when Maya had called to leave word that she'd be home a day or two late, trying to sound calm and convincing as she fabricated the details of the camping trip. She wasn't even sure why she lied in the first place. But she didn't want to change her story in mid stream. When she had hung up, uneasiness set in.

The situation, to be sure, was bizarre. *Wicklow*. A word that Maya had plucked out of the aether, yet very tangibly around her and underfoot. She had never even heard of the place before she'd "seen" that sign. That alone was bizarre enough. In fact, the whole situation hinted at threat psychologically, like a hairline crack that just creeping and extending along the bedrock of her foundational beliefs, a structure that had always been tenuous. Many of her recent experiences had been so unfathomable, and packed into such a short time, that she could barely believe it all.

There was no doubt she had seen that highway sign in her vortex vision. And it wasn't a dream, for she had most certainly been awake. Still it lingered in her mind like a flashing sign in a store window: WICKLOW in white letters on a green background.

For a moment she considered that it might be the remnant of some forgotten scene from a movie watched long ago which had lodged in the backwaters of her mind, coughed up by a neuron roused by the vortex. But she decided against that. It was real. It had to be. Or else being in Wicklow made no sense. What should she do?

She would look around, investigate, and hopefully find the connection to her father, the reason she was here. *Let the process unfold*. Trust in the process. Surely there had to be one taking place.

But maybe there wasn't, she thought, because hadn't that often been the case? Didn't things usually *not* work out? *Think about it, Maya*. What if the whole of life was what it seemed at times, a series of random events lacking in meaning and purpose, and all her grand striving for happiness, for relationships, for friends and self-actualization ultimately came to nothing because nothing was pretty much what was behind it.

What if Ben Ambrose wasn't anywhere to be found? What if he was dead, or he was a homeless schizophrenic wandering the streets of Detroit? What if life was just a fruitless search for solace and satisfaction that was never to be found because it wasn't there, and that all one had to look forward to was more of the same? Oh, sure, it was broken up by a few highs here and there—moments that probably existed for no other reason than to distract a person from the horrible mess of it all—but in the end, wasn't it just a lot of—

Stop, Maya told herself. *The voice! Stop! Don't go down that road. It's too easy. Don't put the pain out there when it's really in here. It's yours, yours alone, born of a brain that is always working. Prowling, stalking, devouring. Like an animal. Like a wolf.*

Even in the midst of the descent, she smiled. Despite everything. That was it exactly. *A wolf.*

The image fit perfectly. Her mind was like a predator. It had to be watched. Managed. She couldn't let it roam free. If she didn't point the wolf in a constructive direction, it wreaked havoc, on herself and those around her.

She began to pace across the worn, carpeted floor of the motel room. *The wolf.* Ha! That was definitely it. And it was trying to take her over right now.

She had come to understand a few things about the creature over time. She'd been watching it her whole life. Trying to abide it. Failing, mostly.

In college, it had practically destroyed any sense of normalcy in her life, though in some ways the university had been a godsend, for it occupied the wolf on a daily basis. The creature loved intellectual challenge. Maya had counted her study time by the minutes, not the hours, often hardly caring yet making the dean's list every semester. The wolf had graduated *magna cum laude*. Its expertise lay in the storage and retrieval of facts. It understood logic. It loved logic.

But the satisfaction of facts and logic had peaked and faded. Rationality, Maya came to believe, had little to do with happiness. In fact, it was often antithetical to it.

She recalled one especially tumultuous semester when she had kept regular appointments with a campus psychologist to see if she could channel the wolf's energy and aggressive nature into some productive use. Why was it able to possess her so thoroughly? Was there a way to stop it? Was it responsible for the plummeting of her moods to unfathomable depths? Or was that her fault? And why was she referring to herself as *two*—it and her?

Psychotherapy had answered few of these questions. All those hours were mostly spent in search of memories—of her mother, her childhood, of what was really going on during all the swaths of life when she had done nothing but read novels and watch television. The shrink had wanted to hear about Muriel and her drinking binges. He wanted to know how Maya felt watching her mother sobbing in a heap on the living room floor or in the presence of some random uncaring guy. What was it like, he had asked, enduring Muriel's wild behavior, the way she would gush out her love for Maya one minute only to call her a worthless loser in the next breath.

Maya's early childhood was hard to locate. Instead of going deep in, as Dr. Jobrani had urged, donning the hip waders and slogging down into the muck, Maya would raise herself up high and direct herself toward lofty ethical and moral issues. How much of the blame for her issues fell to Muriel, herself a lost soul mired in illness and unconsciousness, and what was Maya's to own?

The wolf pounced all over such examinations, analyzing them from every possible angle. In the midst of its nimble arguments and complex theorizing, Maya would check the good doctor for signs of awe, noticing instead that his face had gone vacant. He wanted gut, not mind. He probably hated the wolf as much as she did but for completely different reasons.

As much as Maya had wanted to hold Muriel accountable for her own pain, she just couldn't do it. It was a cop-out, an abdication of responsibility. People weren't responsible for deeds done in ignorance, and ignorant Muriel surely was. It wasn't her fault. She wasn't even there.

The therapeutic process had also touched upon the missing parent, the man now known as Ben Ambrose. In her childhood Maya had deified him. He was a great man, a humane man, a loving man, a man who would surely return to claim her—when he wasn't a low-life deserting loser.

In her teens, Maya had poured her fantasies of him into the molds of idealized men and he would come alive for a time. He was Atticus Finch, George Bailey, Tom Joad, Neo. Maya had communed with each of them in her private way, sometimes to extreme, speaking aloud in discussion, confiding secrets, and falling off to sleep with their constructed speeches playing out in her mind.

Eventually she wearied of the strain of pumping life into those burndensome and transparent fantasies. It was foolish, tiresome. When had she last read a novel? A year ago? Two? In years past she had gobbled up Castaneda, Vonnegut, Wells, Borges. Now the thought of absorbing hundreds of pages of artifice just brought on fatigue. The books were lies. Movies and television, the same. Perversions, shams.

Maya looked down at her hands, balled tightly into fists. *What is happening to me?*

She exhaled forcefully as if to blow such thinking clear out the open window, and recalled where she was, for she had forgotten. Wicklow. Why? What could possibly happen here?

Then nature intervened. It was subtle: a breeze blew in. A breeze with a particular scent on it. Maya sniffed at it, knew that it was significant. *So fresh, so clean, so pure.* And sweet. Yes. She recognized it but couldn't quite place it. Then she had it.

It was honeysuckle.

Her eyes widened and she grew excited. She ducked her head out the window and stared at the mountain peaks that were visible from this spot, recognizing them. It was them! *The very ones.* The familiar jagged outline standing imperiously beneath the darkening sky.

She examined the peaks more closely now as her excitement grew. The shapes exactly matched those she'd seen in the vortex vision. Tracing her finger along the outline of ridges, she noted them: tall peak in the center, mesa-like plateau beside it, skull-shaped rock on the right—exactly as she had seen.

But with a difference.

The image that had developed in the darkroom of her mind in Dr. Porter's forested basement had been an abstraction, a paper-thin representation, a mental snapshot that fell far short of the imposing eons-old reality that now stood in plain sight. And there was more. The mountains seemed to be transmitting a message. Not only to her but to all who would listen. It was this: Stretch yourselves. Expand yourselves.

She did not know why this was happening nor what it could mean. Entranced, she gripped the window pane tightly, as though to keep from being sucked out into something immense and primeval, a plan set in motion in ancient times that dwarfed her puny little life the way the sun outshines a light bulb. Something was happening. It was a feeling of separation, of falling away, of moving beyond the familiar toward the mysterious, of leaping head-long into the unknown. It was happening right here, right now. She recalled a passage from the journal.

> Only by accepting the impossible as possible
> will your path fully open to you and the
> meaning of your life come into view. Don't wait.
> Do it now. It's just a decision.

Perhaps, she thought. It was exactly what she was feeling.

She awoke the next morning shivering, clutching at herself beneath a blanket that was too thin to offer much warmth, the heavy wool comforter haven fallen to the floor. She snatched it up and spread it out over her, and glanced at the clock on the bedside table. Six-thirty. She pulled up the blinds for a look outside. The western sky was still inky black; in the east, a pale blue signaled the first light of day.

By the time she had showered and dressed, the morning sky was brightening. She stepped outside.

All was quiet. A hundred yards down the road a traffic signal hung from a high cable, swaying in the breeze, its glowing green dot the only color in sight. Beyond it was a storefront, with cars pulling in and out of its parking lot. The other buildings scattered along the road were dark and still.

Plunging her hands into her pockets, Maya strode along the roadside shoulder to the store. Men and women in jeans and cowboy boots nodding hellos to one another as they ascended the wide wooden steps of the porch. Maya followed them inside.

An imposing bushy-bearded man with an enormous belly that strained the fabric of his flannel shirt stood behind the counter, his hand resting on the ivory lever of the soda fountain. He smiled at Maya.

"Morning, miss," he said.

"Hi," Maya said, doing her best to return his good will. Even in the excitement of the journey, she hadn't fully awakened. She set a plastic-wrapped blueberry muffin on the counter and ordered a large coffee.

"One size fits all," the man said, reaching for a Styrofoam cup. "You get one refill free."

"Thank you," Maya said.

She watched the coffee pour out of the carafe and splash down into the cup. She stared at the muffin. Caffeine and white flour—two habits she badly wanted to break. Two substances that made her feel worse right after they made her feel better. Her blood sugar had always been wacked. Probably thanks to Grandpa Burke, who'd been diabetic. Somehow Maya had never quite made the needed appointment with the doctor to check it out. After the morning coffee lift, it was fifty-fifty she be rewarded with a headache. Yet each time she had tried to quit, she couldn't manage it.

Habit. Uncle Buddy had a theory about that. He believed that habit was the strongest force in the universe, bar none. Just about every process, small and large, he said, was stuck in grooves of varying depths, which was why real change was so rare. He even went so far as to claim that habit held the very *fabric* of the universe together, keeping natural laws like gravity and electromagnetism in place, which was why they had remained unchanged since the dawn of time.

According to Buddy, stars, buildings, tadpoles and people all shared the same tendency: to keep doing what they were already doing. The best chance you had at altering a habit, he said, was through persistent, willful effort. Only then, after a "suitable period of time"—which he never quite defined— could real change occur.

The big-bellied man was staring at Maya. She fumbled in her wallet and handed him a couple of bucks.

"Nothing like a good 'ol cup of Joe in the morning," he said genially.

"Joe ain't all that innocent," Maya said to his curious stare.

She settled in at a table on the porch. She warmed her hands on the Styrofoam cup. She sipped at the coffee. An hour passed. The sun drifted up over the trees across the street. Cars and people came and went. Maya waited for a sign, something that might get her going, but nothing much happened. Sitting there, she started to feel stupid. *What am I doing? What am I expecting to happen?*

She set the cup down and sat up straight and resolved to take a different path. To wait was the old way, the old Maya—a habit that would change right here and now and to hell with Buddy's "suitable period of time." Maybe Josh had been right. You didn't discover what to do with your life. The answer wasn't *there*. It wasn't anywhere. You made it up as you went along, responding to the moment, just like he said. It was up to you. Maybe she would share this brainstorm with Josh. He'd surely be surprised.

What the present situation required was a display of intention. *Decide what to do and do it.* She would get up off the porch and search, probe, inquire and ultimately push herself to discover how Wicklow, Wyoming fit into her quest.

And so she walked.

And walked.

By dusk the aching in her feet had spread up into her calves and thighs. She had strolled the streets of Wicklow, meandered through its parks, visited its gift shops, real estate offices and cafes, peeked around the corners of the quaint downtown searching people's faces for a sign, a spark, a recognition—anything that would start the conversation that would change everything. She had asked dozens of people if they knew Ben Ambrose. None had.

The following day, more of the same. More picturesque walks she didn't enjoy, more anxious searching the faces of strangers, and more asking about a man no one seemed to know. Only now the townspeople had started to notice her, walking alone, looking upset, sighing a lot.

Dispirited, Maya decided to leave Wicklow the next morning. She had done her best, hadn't she? What else could she do? She could always return, if necessary. The universe obviously had its own timetable for long overdue family reunions.

She circled back to the store for another dip into the brew pot, settling in again at a porch table. The afternoon sky had grown heavy with clouds. The scent of a storm was in the air.

A young girl, towheaded, ear-to-ear in freckles, bounded up the stairs and shot into the store like a missile. Watching her, Maya smiled. The pre-teen's alert eyes and bouncy manner reminded her of herself of a decade ago.

But there was something else, Maya thought, and she couldn't quite put her finger on it. She watched the girl through the storefront window, wandering the aisles, reaching for a pack of bubble gum, plunging her hand into her pocket for money.

Maya's mind—her wolf—engaged. Maya could sense it sniffing in the underbrush of her memories, pawing through thoughts and experiences, searching for a connection. *Who was this girl?* Why was she familiar? An image took shape, and Maya understood. Stunned, she gazed through the window in disbelief at the blond girl she'd seen in the vortex vision.

She came out to the porch. Maya could have reached out and touched her. Their eyes met. The girl grinned as if greeting an old friend. Maya, unnerved, dropped the cup in her hand, which hit the floor. The lid shot off and coffee splattered all over the bottoms of her jeans. The girl laughed impishly, hopped down the stairs and jumped onto a bicycle that was leaning against the side of the building. Before Maya knew what was happening, the girl was pedaling furiously down the road.

Maya found her voice and called out, "Hey, wait!" and started to run after her.

The rider turned her head briefly but picked up her pace.

"Wait, please!" Maya begged. "Hey!"

But the girl was too fast. The distance between them opened up and the bike became smaller and smaller until it disappeared below a rise in the road. Maya's long strides petered out. Baffled, she retreated to the porch to try to fathom what had just happened.

That girl was the reason she was in Wicklow, the connection to Ben Ambrose. So why had she fled? The girl had obviously recognized her, which was impossible. But so were visions and energy vortexes and plants that shot off fireworks and—

"Hi."

Maya spun around there she was, grinning.

"Did you really think you could catch me on foot?" the girl said. It was a challenge, delivered defiantly and with folded arms.

Maya fumbled to respond. "Clearly stupid of me," she said.

"Damned right," the girl said.

"Where did you go?"

"Down the road a piece. I circled around back." Her eyes seemed to darken. "Why are you here?"

"W-what?" Maya said, shocked. "You know me?"

The girl rolled her eyes and laughed. "How would I know you if I never saw you before? It's just the tourists are gone. And you don't look like one anyway."

"I'm not a tourist," said Maya. "I just thought … the way you were looking at me. Never mind. What's your name?"

"Gathering."

"What are you gathering?"

"Ha, ha, never heard that one before."

Maya stared at her.

"My name is Gathering."

"Ah," Maya said. "Sorry."

"That's OK. Some people think it's weird."

"I don't," Maya said. "Listen, Gathering. I'm looking for a guy who lives here in Wicklow. His name is Ben Ambrose. Do you know him?"

Gathering shook her head.

"Are you sure?" Maya said.

"Yeah."

"It is possible your parents do?"

"I doubt it. They're in Idaho," Gathering said with little care or emotion.

"Who do you live with?"

Gathering's eyes narrowed. "Oh, people. Some are old, if that's what you're getting at." She pointed in the direction she had taken off in earlier. "We live over that way. You can come over if you want."

"I do," said Maya quickly. Maybe the path to her father was opening up.

Gathering retrieved her bike and they started down the road, arriving a few minutes later at a brick ranch house separated from the road by a small lawn. Two cars were parked in the driveway: a sleek black Audi with California tags and a rusty old pickup truck that may have once been red but the paint was badly disintegrated.

Gathering tossed down her bike and yanked open the screen door, which almost hit Maya in the face. She led Maya into a narrow hallway girded by floor-to-ceiling pegboards on which dozens of pots, pans and skillets hung. The floor was old and scuffed up, the air rich with the scent of cooking food.

A man and a woman were sitting at the kitchen table poring over blueprints and architectural drawings. Pots were boiling on the stove, steam rising from the rattling lids.

The woman, who looked like she was around seventy, was large-boned, with a wide leathery face and long silver hair that flowed down her back in a single braid that almost touched the chair. She had tremendous vitality, Maya surmised, just watching her face and movements. Her gestures were grand and exaggerated and demanded to be watched. She peered at Maya over the top of wire-rimmed glasses that rode low on her nose.

The man, who looked much younger, perhaps in his forties, had dark, wavy hair and a slender, intelligent face.

"The old people," Gathering announced with a flourish.

"Hello," they said in unison.

"Hi," said Maya.

"She's looking for someone," Gathering said.

The woman set the papers aside and leaned back, sizing up Maya. "Isn't everyone?" she said with a laugh.

Instinctively, Maya liked this woman, who introduced herself as Georgia Roussey. The man's name was Brandon McGowan.

"And you are?" Georgia said.

"Maya. Maya Burke."

"That's a beautiful name. Please, Maya, sit."

"Thank you."

"Now, who is it you're looking for?" Georgia said.

Maya considered telling the actual truth, but something very strange happened. The phenomenon presented itself at the exact moment Georgia Roussey had asked her question. A week earlier, such an experience would have sent Maya into an all-out panic, but now, after the vortex, reality-defying sights didn't carry quite the shock value they may have in the past.

The older woman's words had faded from hearing, like the whoosh of a car speeding away, and a thin band of gossamer light appeared around Georgia's head, blocking a portion of the wall and a corner of a framed print hanging on it. The lower corner melted away into a whitish blur.

Maya's thought maybe she was witnessing an optical illusion caused by the play of sunlight coming in through the window. Only there *was* no sunlight. The day was solidly overcast, threatening rain. Then she wondered if she might be experiencing a flashback from the vortex, like what had happened at the stone fountain where the splashing water sounded like flutes.

Then it was gone. The phenomenon had lasted only a few seconds. The space around Georgia's head resumed clarity again, as did the bottom of the framed print.

"Are you all right, dear?" Georgia asked with a look of concern. "You look like you've disappeared into the fifth dimension."

Maya shook her head, wanting to purge the experience as quickly as possible. "That was weird," she said.

"What was?"

"I don't know," she said.

"Well, that's not much to go on."

"I guess I'm tired. I didn't get much sleep last night. I must have drifted off. I'm sorry."

Georgia's said, "Gathering, fetch Maya a glass of water, if you would." She turned to Maya. "So, what can we do for you?"

"I'm looking for a man named Ben Ambrose," Maya said. "He lives here in Wicklow."

"A wayward friend of yours?" Georgia said. "Whose address you presumably don't have?"

"That's about right," Maya said, offering no more.

Georgia pinched her chin and became thoughtful. "The name doesn't ring a bell," she said. "Brandon?"

"Sorry, me neither," he said.

"But if he is here," Georgia said, "finding him should be a snap. This town is barely a microbe on the map, if you haven't noticed."

Again Maya felt deflated, staring at another dead end. Gathering had obviously been the link, and this place had to be her lead. She looked out the window, noticing several buildings she hadn't seen from the road. The house was part of a complex of some kind. Lots of people were walking around.

"What is this place? Apartments?"

Brandon laughed. "Not exactly," he said. "It's an intentional community."

"A what?"

"A kind of village," Georgia said. "Only one that didn't evolve naturally. It was designed, intentionally."

"I've never heard of that," Maya said.

Brandon leaned forward. "Mostly we're a collective farming settlement," he said, and Maya noted in his voice the hint of a Southern drawl.

"Listen, Maya," Georgia said, "I wasn't exactly prepared to give our presentation, but you stumbled onto an interesting place. We're a community in the traditional sense—a group of people who share common values who've chosen to live out of the mainstream. Thus, our locale in the wilds of Wicklow."

"You could think of us as a kind of democratic ideal," Brandon added. "On a very small scale."

Maya smiled politely. The wolf—her critical inner voice—perked up, thinking, *cult.*

Brandon responded as if reading her mind.

"This place isn't about religion or anything like that," he said. "Far from it. There are no imposed views here. People believe whatever they want to. This is simply cooperative living. It's satisfying and economically advantageous. We pool our resources. Everyone participates in decision-making and governance. Housing, health services and food are bartered. We run a few small businesses. We're not ideologues in any sense. In fact, quite the contrary. If anything, we're anti-organization, anti-belief."

"But in a way, we *are* extremists," Georgia interjected. "But so what? Think about it, Brandon. Every group that's ever tried to live out of the mainstream has been viewed that way. Extremists? Maybe. So were the founders of this country, not to mention the progenitors of many great cultures."

Georgia turned to Maya, seeing her puzzled look. "Our charter is simplicity itself, Maya. To help each other blossom individually and collectively by creating a microcosm of trust in our little corner of the world. That's not such a bad idea, is it?"

Gathering, who was leaning against the refrigerator door, twirling her blond locks, said, "We're moving, right?"

Georgia began collecting the papers on the table into a neat pile. "We're expanding onto more land down the road," she said. "That's what these plans are all about."

"Impressive," Maya said uncertainly. She had no idea what to think of the place or the people, or even why she was sitting there with them. But she would have to stay open-minded, no matter what. Somehow, they were the key.

"Let me make a few inquiries about—what was his name?" Georgia said.

"Ben Ambrose," Maya said.

"Right," Georgia said. "In the meantime, why don't you have a look around? I have a feeling you'll find us interesting."

7

Something is Wrong
with this World

Following along with Gathering on the paved paths, Maya began to see the community as a fascinating and curious place, a vibrant small town that may not have shown up on any map. A gently sloping hillside hid much of it from view from the road.

They passed cottages, cabins, industrial buildings, orchards, gardens, a dining hall, stores, a dormitory, and a large cobblestone plaza, all connected by roads and paths. They paused at a playground where children scampered on jungle gyms and swings beneath the watchful gaze of two young women on a nearby bench. People were everywhere—in cars, on bikes, on foot, engaged in a variety of tasks—hauling supplies, moving machinery, taking deliveries, cleaning up.

"What's that over there?" Maya asked of a barn-like building that hummed with activity.

"A factory," Gathering said. "I think they make parts for tractors."

Maya had never been anywhere like this, and to her delight, found herself enraptured by its busy thrum of purpose. She'd never been around close-knit groups of people who lived and worked in such intertwined, continuous proximity. In Plainfield, Maya drove everywhere she needed to go, hardly ever escaping the sprawl and usually trying to avoid interacting with strangers.

What would it be like, she wondered, to *want* to be around the neighbors? The people she saw going by looked very tight. Everyone here seemed so integral. So needed. It was a depressing reminder for her. Maya had always thought of herself as optional in the world.

As a teen, she had expended a lot of effort in trying to escape that feeling of extraneousness. A sibling would have helped. But she had grown up as a latchkey child who returned home from school to fix her own dinner and figure out what to do with herself. When she was Gathering's age, she would rush over to Rachel Stein's house in the afternoons, blissfully losing herself in her friend's sprawling eccentric family, playing gin rummy with them at the kitchen table and listening rapturously to their stem-winders. Some guests stayed on for weeks at a time, ensconced on the plastic-sheathed living room sofa. Everyone was always talking, always happy. For a few precious hours, Maya would escape Muriel and the brooding silence that awaited her at home.

Thunder struck far off and wind shook the trees, springing a shower of leaves free. The women on the bench stood up and called out to the children. "Spencer! Tyler! Justine! Let's move it! Rain's coming!"

Just then, the Audi that Maya had seen earlier bumped across the grass and stopped right beside her. Brandon leaned out of the driver's side window.

"Thoughts?" he said.

"I'm liking it," Maya said.

Brandon said, "I'm heading over to the new site. Why don't you come along and have a look?"

Maya turned to Gathering, urging her to come along. But the girl frowned. "Rats, I've got to work."

"You work?" Maya said, surprised.

"Yep. Kitchen, as usual," Gathering said with a practiced groan. She dashed off, calling out goodbyes.

"Sure, I'd love to," Maya said to Brandon. She hopped into the car.

He pulled out onto the main road and accelerated rapidly, leaving a road sign vibrating in the car's wake. WICKLOW it read, in white lettering on a green background. Maya gasped as the sign shot behind them. Brandon turned to her, but she just shook her head.

"Don't ask," she said.

"OK," he said agreeably.

Brandon was open and friendly. At times, as he spoke, his voice slowed down as if he were busy processing lots of information. Or maybe he was just carefully choosing his words. Maya pegged him as the type who could devise complex plans and follow them through to completion with total confidence. It was a quality she had never thought about until this moment.

He lived in California. He had moved there from Atlanta to run an export business, shipping sporting goods and electronics to countries in Eastern Europe. He visited Wicklow every month and was active in building its community.

"What exactly *is* this community?" Maya asked.

"It's an alternative," he said.

"To what?"

"To the way you live," he said. He slowed the car down and pulled onto the road's shoulder. "Come on."

They got out and walked to a ridge overlooking an expansive valley. Tall grasses stirred in the breeze in a landscape dotted sparsely with trees. At the bottom of a hill stood a cabin with a pyramid of firewood stacked beside it.

Maya spotted some rocks peeking out of the grass a few feet away. "What's that?" she asked.

"Let's have a look," Brandon said.

They stepped over an extinguished campfire in a cement pit, filled with burned wood, ash and cinders.

"Some of our people practice tribal rituals," Brandon said.

"Really? What kinds of rituals?" Maya said, interested.

"Honestly, I have no idea what this was about."

"Why do stuff like that?" Maya asked.

"Because it's useful."

"How so?"

"Rituals done right can reconnect you with parts of life you may have lost touch with," Brandon said. "They remind you there's a lot more going on than meets the eye, that you're a part of a larger story. You know—the greater human story. The universal story."

He squinted up at the sky, sizing up the coming storm. He turned to Maya. "I'll tell you what this community is really about," he said. "It's about life. Your life."

"How's that?" she said, taken aback.

He thought for a moment, then said, "Have you ever had the feeling there's something wrong with this world—intrinsically?"

"Whenever I watch the news," Maya said.

"I mean," Brandon continued, "have you had the feeling that something important, some essential piece, is missing from our culture, and without it, things can't really make complete sense? Have you been to the mall lately? Watched any TV? Did you know the average 14-year-old has already watched twelve-thousand murders on the tube? It's a symptom, Maya. It's a sign that we've lost our connection to the world, and even to ourselves. You tell things like that to people but does that raise any eyebrows? You get inured to it. Are *you* surprised? Right, exactly. At a certain point, you don't that even know something's wrong. We've been immersed in it so long, you start to feel nothing. That, my friend, is the beginning of the end."

He reached down and picked up a woodchip off the ground and chucked it at a nearby tree. It arced past, sailing off into the tall grasses. He said, "What's happening is we're losing what makes us human. It's a drip, drip, drip. We're less than. We're becoming *consumers*, getting our meaning from things. You talk about it and most people will look away. They don't want to know. They go turn the TV on."

"What about you?" Maya objected. "You sell things for a living. You support consumer society."

"You can't fight swords with plowshares," Brandon said. "You have to work within the system to get power."

Maya considered that. "Can anyone actually change anything? I mean, haven't things been this way since the first caveman clubbed his buddy over the head and took all his stuff?"

Brandon arched an eyebrow. "You're young for that point of view."

"That's presumptuous," she said. "I'm just awake, or trying to be."

Brandon lowered himself down to sit on the grass by the fire pit. Maya sat on the other side, facing him.

"Do you know how this country was founded?" he said.

She laughed. "I majored in American history."

He held out his hands in mock surrender. "Tell me then, in simple terms."

"You want to hear about the founding of America, seriously?"

"Give me the abridged version."

"Why?"

"Humor me," he said.

"OK," she shrugged. "Back in the seventeen-hundreds, a bunch of guys—our legendary Founding Fathers—did something that was rare in the history of the world. They designed a society from scratch that was based on fairness and freedom, rather than going with the usual M.O.: servitude to aristocrats. It's a long story and I have a feeling you already know it, but the idea was to give regular folks some freedom.

"They wrote everything up in some enlightened documents, which, even to young me"—she gave Brandon a look and a wink—"tell you that people can occasionally rise above the usual pettiness and greed. England—Mom and Dad—tried to stop them. That was the Revolutionary War. The parental units lost, which meant our guys could proceed however they pleased. They decided democracy was the best thing going. Is that short enough?"

"That's perfect," Brandon said. "Now, this 'bunch of guys,' the legendary Founders. What do you think of them?"

"They had brass, man."

"Why?"

"They made the ultimate sacrifice. If they'd lost, they would have been hung from the rafters."

"And if that had happened, where do you think you'd be today?"

"At a pub, hoisting a pint? Long live the King!" She broke up in laughter.

Brandon waited for her to settle down, then said, "Consider for a moment how dangerous it is to do what they did, to rebel against the powers that be, to fight leaders backed by a military and the weapons of an empire."

"I have," Maya said soberly. "I've wondered if great leaders who can change things, really change things, are born every so often and are killed off, like Martin Luther King and the Kennedys. Maybe guys like that are being eliminated and we don't even know it. Maybe that's why things don't change."

Brandon stared so intently at her that she felt herself draw back. "What?" she said.

"Maybe things *can* change," Brandon said. "Maybe a revolutionary war like the one you've described is happening, right now."

"What are you talking about?" Maya said.

"A revolution that's happening now—through the land."

"The land?" Maya said, not following.

"The power of the Earth."

"The *what?*" Maya said uneasily.

"Change is occurring through the planet's own energy. Its power centers, or vortexes."

She turned away. She could almost feel her heartbeat start to race. The events of the past weeks rushed at her all at once—everything that had happened to bring her to Wicklow and this moment. The discovery of the journal, Dr. Porter, the vortex vision, Gathering, the synchronicities, and now Brandon uttering statements that could have come right out of the pages of the journal. Change. Vortexes. The land.

"That's why I'm here," she said, her voice rising with emotion. "I was at a vortex. I *saw* this place. It's impossible, I know, maybe it was a hallucination—"

"What?" Brandon said. "Where?"

"That guy I told you about? Ben Ambrose? He's my father. His teacher was this old guy in a wheelchair who had a vortex right on his land—"

"Edgar Porter," Brandon said.

"Right! Do you know him?"

"Sure. He's a researcher."

"I can't believe this is happening," Maya said, looking away. "My father was into all this. How can you not know him? You must know him."

Just then the wind kicked up, a welcome distraction. Ash from the pit swirled and blew off.

"You saw something back there in the kitchen," Brandon said. "Around Georgia."

Maya could only stare at him.

"How do you know that?" she said.

"Because I saw it, too."

Then that was real? she wondered. Again the boundaries of her beliefs stretched to a near breaking point.

Breathe.

"Listen to me," Brandon said, meeting her gaze. "There are George Washingtons and Thomas Jeffersons alive today. Human instruments of change. Do you understand?"

"No," Maya said, not sure she wanted to.

"Change is afoot," Brandon said, unaware or uncaring of her discomfort. "Great change."

Change. Great change. Incredible change. Uncontrollable change. Monstrous change. *Why is it happening all around me?* Maya wondered.

Suddenly the twilight sky was lit up by consecutive lightning flashes, and for a few flickering moments the day looked as bright as noon on a sunny day. Thunder roared. The rain was just moments away. Still, it held off.

"Tell me about this change," Maya said.

"The rain—" Brandon said, looking up.

"Hasn't started. *Please.*"

"I don't know where to begin."

"Anywhere."

He looked away for moment, thinking. "I'll try to explain," he said, gathering himself. "Consider the way cultural change happens. For example, take rock and roll music, the way it started out slowly, energizing a few young people and then caught fire and grew so quickly the country and the world came onboard. Cultural change begins just that way—as *an idea* in the minds of a few."

"I get it," Maya said. "Go on."

"No one can predict if it will catch on. Many fall flat. So then, where does the growth spurt, the fire, start? In the depths of individual human minds, before it spreads out into the collective mind.

"It's like that for all cultural change. We don't *know* on a conscious level if the human race 'wants' a period of peace or of war, or an invention that will change our way of life. But deep down, in the collective mind, we do. It's a group gestalt. That's where the energy comes from. Whether or not a change will be viable long-term, that's another story. It depends on whether it has built up enough collective psychic momentum.

"Here's another example: The Vietnam anti-war movement of the nineteen-sixties. It began with the protests of a small, inconsequential group but grew large enough to affect a country of millions. At a certain point, critical mass for the change was reached. Or, go back further to the Civil War and the abolition of slavery. An astute politician like Lincoln can read the collective mind presciently and with virtuosic skill long before others even have an inkling of what's brewing in it. *He knows.* Freeing the slaves at that point in the war was politically unpopular, but he understood that the collective support was there. So it worked."

Maya said, "But isn't that just normal change? Why are you putting the metaphysics into it?"

"It happens *because* of the metaphysics," Brandon said. "Come on, let's get out of here before we get soaked."

"What about now?" Maya said, not budging from the grass. "What's this revolution? How you know anything is happening at all?"

"Just look around," Brandon said. "The evidence is everywhere. Look how fast technology is advancing, how quickly political systems are shifting, how different the world is today from the way it was just a few years ago. There's been more change in the last few years than in the hundreds that preceded it. And it's going to speed up even more. Nothing like this has ever happened. Do you know why that is?"

A bolt of lightning flashed in the fields, followed by an ear-splitting thunder bolt.

"Why?" Maya said, feeling the urgency of the both the imminent storm and Brandon's words.

"Because cultural, social and political change is being— helped along."

"How's that?" Maya said.

"In much the way you did it," Brandon said. He waved at the surrounding land. "Why are you here?"

"I told you. I *saw* this place."

"Right. You saw this place. Think about that. And who do you happen to be talking to? Someone who knows about energy, who understands what's happening, out of all the people you could have run into. Do you think that's an accident? You created this meeting back at that vortex. I just came along for the ride. Right now your mind is working to manifest the intention you set in motion at Porter's house: to find your father. You're moving things energetically to make that happen."

She said, "Who are you, really?"

His voice softened. "A concerned citizen," he said. "Someone who wants to see us survive the coming years."

Survive the coming years. More words that could have been written by Ben Ambrose.

"You must know my father," Maya said.

"What I'm telling you is no secret, Maya. There are lots of people aware of what's happening—"

Suddenly a jagged line of lightning appeared overhead that connected with the topmost branches of a nearby tree, there was an explosive *crack* and a thick branch broke free and crashed to the ground, trailing a rain of sparks. Thunder followed. The first raindrops pinged against Maya's face.

Brandon stood up.

"Right," Maya said, and they dashed for the car, reaching the shelter of the front seat before the deluge started. Brandon revved the engine and swerved onto the road.

On the way to her motel, Maya stared through the swinging wiper blades at the rain-blurred road ahead, barely visible in the headlights' beam. *Maybe he's right.* Perhaps a change was coming. Maybe that persistent low-level anxiety, that sense of foreboding that loomed just out of reach, which most everyone felt, wasn't something to just accept and shrug off. Full-moon craziness was peaking. The news purveyors trumpeted it daily. The center *wasn't* holding. Maybe the stress that permeated modern culture was not only real but warranted, the chilling prescience of a radical shift to come.

Maya couldn't shake the feeling that the answers could be found in the journal. Her father's writings seemed to be eerily predicting much of what she was experiencing. Clearly she had not read it with enough attention. When she got home she would plumb its depths and bring to the surface the secrets she had missed. In the process, she would come to understand him better. What was a book but a topographical map of a psyche, a guided tour of a writer's mind? She would travel beyond the words on the page to divine their deeper message, and in so doing, begin to know the man.

Brandon waited in the car as Maya ran into her room to gather her things. She was exhausted, overextended and desperate to get home.

On the drive to the airport, Brandon went on about cultural change until Maya was so burdened with information and theory that all she could do was nod in agreement at the appropriate times and stare out the window the rest of the time. Brandon was connected to her father, somehow. Even if he didn't know it. And she was going to find out how.

"Tell Gathering I said goodbye," Maya said at the curb of the departure area, beneath the overhead structure that blocked the rain.

"I will," said Brandon. "Take care, Maya. I hope we meet again."

"I have a feeling we will," she said. "Goodbye."

An hour later, sitting on a chair inside the terminal, waiting for her flight to be called, Maya stared at a TV hanging from a nearby wall. A few feet away, occasional travelers strode down the long central corridor. She sipped orange juice from a bottle she had bought at an airport store, the tanginess burning away the stale taste of hunger.

Wicklow had certainly opened her eyes. There were other ways to live in this world, far different than the urban-suburban scene she knew so well. The media seemed to be lost. They were obsessed with reporting on the extremes: the far right and left, the gangs and militias that they milked for ratings. Maya had soaked up the carnival-like coverage of those disturbed countercultures from the comfort of her living room sofa, like so many people. But she was more interested in the expansive and positive philosophies, like the one she'd just experienced. Perhaps these would be at the fountainhead of the future.

The TV news confirmed that plenty of change was happening on planet Earth. Disputes among nations were erupting like brushfires in a parched backwoods, as usual. But something was different. It was no longer *them*. It was us. The planet's neighborhoods were blending together. Information that had been hidden from view was now out in the open for all to see. The shift was as real and tangible as the rain pouring down the terminal windows a few feet away.

Maya knew that throughout history, catastrophic events—earthquakes, geological upheavals and cosmic disasters—had been seen as precursors of change. Was the discord of the modern world a prelude to her father's "change?" He saw it this way:

> Such predictions are metaphors. The
> physical shaking of the Earth *symbolizes* change.
> Not geological change, but internal change.
> Change in people. The world will be
> "disturbed," life as we understand it will "cease
> to be." Physical reality as a whole is a metaphor
> for that which is internal. The true definition of
> apocalypse is revelation.

Maya had studied many of the storied civilizations of the past, learned how the corrupt and indulgent ones had collapsed from the weight of their excesses. She wondered if America and the West were sliding down that same slippery slope, with its growing shadow side and suffocating materialism, and its alienation, spiritual hunger and ever-widening gap between haves and have-nots.

At times she envied her mother's generation which had come of age when an individual's voice could still be heard over the drumbeat of corporations hungry for growth at any cost, when old America still existed and people weren't stressed out all the time. What would it feel like to be hopeful about the future? She'd never known the warm comfort of optimism, the soothing belief that tomorrow could be better than today. Maybe this change of her father's, of Brandon's, was real. Maybe things could be different.

8

Theory and Fact

Maya arrived home at two a.m., padded softly to her room and got right into bed, falling into a deep sleep that lasted late into the morning, despite the sun blasting in and lighting up the walls. She awoke bleary, and shuffled down to the kitchen, but stopped suddenly, startled to glimpse a lone figure sitting on the living room sofa. The shades were drawn, the room nearly dark.

Her mother was holding a glass and slowly swirling the liquid in it, the ice cubes clinking rhythmically and without pause. She looked as if she hadn't moved in hours. Maya wondered if she had been in that very spot, ghost-like, when she had arrived home last night.

Muriel switched on a table lamp and looked at Maya and smiled, but it wasn't much of a smile. It was a pained line drawn thinly across her face. When she spoke there was coldness in her voice.

"You could have said something," she said.

Maya wondered if Muriel had run into Josh somewhere and learned that the camping trip was a lie. Or maybe she'd somehow found out about Ben Ambrose. She said nothing.

"How long were you gone?" Muriel said.

"Does it really matter?" Maya said. There must have been hundreds of the times she had answered questions like this to the sound of ice cubes clanking in a tumbler. There were never any right answers. "Three days," she said.

"Did you say you were going to be away that long?"

"If you're so worried, why didn't you just call?"

"I was busy. I was distracted."

Why was she even asking? It had to be the booze talking, as usual.

"I didn't think we'd be that long," Maya said.

"You didn't think," Muriel said. "Exactly. Now, listen to me. I don't care what you do or where you go, but as long as you're living in this house I want to know if you'll be gone for the better part of a week. Is that clear?"

So she didn't know. At least there was that. Maya wanted to say she'd been away *less* than half a week. But why bother?

"Forget it," Muriel said. "Just forget it."

"No problem," Maya said.

Muriel reached up and ran her fingers through her bleached-blond hair, pushing a few strands behind an ear. "Well, anyway, look at you. You look exhausted."

Was that it? Maya wondered. What about the lashing out? The accusations? The rage? She shrugged, and made her way to the kitchen and returned with a heaping bowl of Cheerios. She settled into an easy chair.

"So, how was the trip?" Muriel asked.

"Great," Maya lied. "You know, hiking. Flies. Fish. Tent. Hard ground. It was a blast."

"Try selling real estate," Muriel said. "That's hard ground, too."

Maya ate some cereal. She had no idea why she was sitting there with her mother.

"What about work?" Muriel said.

"What about it?"

"Are you even looking?"

No. And I don't know why.

Maya's eyes were fixed on her mother's hand, which was shaking so violently the liquor was practically jumping out of the glass. Muriel had had tremors before, but not like this.

"What?" Muriel said, eyeing her.

"Nothing," Maya said, lifting a heaping spoonful of Cheerios into her mouth.

"What is it? My hair? My makeup? What?"

"You look, well, different."

"Different? Different how?"

"I don't know. Just—different."

"Now that's a big help. Are you messing with me?"

"No."

"My goodness. Here I am, enjoying the morning and I get stared at."

"In the dark?"

"The sun's going to be out all day."

"OK, OK," Maya relented. "I'm tired. I'm going back to sleep."

"It's eleven o'clock."

"What about you? How long have you been sitting there?"

Muriel thought about that but didn't respond. Maya kept silent, which was the best course at times like this. Her mother's emotions moved in unpredictable ways, like river currents that wound through fast-changing terrain, disappeared into caves, went underground, spilled down unseen waterfalls and shot up in powerful waterspouts. Maya had expended enormous energy trying to tack to those currents and hated doing it, but it seemed to happen automatically, siphoning off precious life force.

"This sucks," Muriel said, staring at the glass in her hand. "This just really sucks."

"What is it?" Maya said.

"Iced freakin' tea is what it is."

"That's *iced tea?*"

Muriel gave Maya the dead-eyed stare that usually meant trouble. "What of it?" she said.

"Nothing."

"Why don't you go find something to do? Look for a job. Clean your room. Buy some decent clothes. Wash your hair. Get a hairstyle for once. I mean, look at it."

"Sure, I'll do all that," Maya said, rising.

Back in her bedroom, Maya leafed to a passage Ben Ambrose had written about relationships. There wasn't much on the topic, just a couple of paragraphs.

> You needn't decipher all of the tangles, nor even understand them, to do what's right. Act from the noblest possible place in your interactions with others and you will create a momentum for positive outcomes. Use that exquisitely powerful tool, your imagination. Imagine you are loving, even if you think you're not. Come from that place and watch what happens.
>
> When you are angry, it may be because you're reacting to an aspect of a person or an event that does not conform to your expectations. Anger also can be a plea from a repressed (perhaps hated) part of yourself that seeks expression, which may come to the fore when someone displays a behavior similar to this shunned aspect. The trapped energy is like a caged animal, desperate for freedom. Free it. The bars on your cage are of your own making.

Maya's cell phone rang at noon the next day.

A man's voice said, "Is this Maya Burke?"

"Yes?"

"Hello, Maya," the man said. "My name is Albert Fiske. I'm an associate of Edgar Porter's. He told me who you're looking for. I think I can help you."

"You know my father?" Maya said, grabbing the back of the kitchen chair.

"I worked with Ben," Mr. Fiske said. "I know quite a lot about him, Maya. I'd be happy to talk to you."

"When?" she said. "Where?"

"My office is in D.C., just off the Mall. Do you know the area?"

"Absolutely," she said.

Of course she knew the National Mall, Washington's most famous destination. She knew it intimately. In fact, she knew every historic monument, museum and memorial that stood on it. Without the Mall she may not have emerged from the Crash, as she called it, that bottomless pit she'd fallen into a few years ago, which had swallowed her up like a sinkhole. Those were the darkest days of her young life, ones she did not long to revisit. Curiously, her salvation had taken place at the very location Albert Fiske suggested meeting.

Peacefulness emanated from the gardens at the Sackler Gallery museum. Curving brick walkways wove through flowerbeds and fountains like pathways through a corner of Eden. It was a bucolic oasis that was far from the countryside, since just a few feet away was Independence Avenue, a bustling Washington, D.C. street on which morning traffic hummed and honked as morning commuters converged on the city for the workday ahead.

Maya had arrived early, found a bench and sat, munching on a doughnut and watching tourists pass through the museum's monolithic entrance, the only part of the structure aboveground. She sipped coffee out of a paper cup, which she set beside her on the bench. A gardener smiled at her, singing softly as he watered the flowerbeds. On the wide sidewalk across Independence Avenue, Maya watched people march toward an enormous office building that spanned the length of the block.

Beyond the garden stood the Smithsonian Castle, and beyond that was the lengthy, grass and dirt pedestrian path that connected the many buildings of the National Mall, from the U.S. Capitol in the east to the Lincoln Memorial in the west. In between stood the formidable Smithsonian Institution complex, a city within a city, with its vast and priceless collections of art and historical artifacts.

Maya was excited to be around those treasures again. She had been fascinated by history since she was a pre-teen. She had watched the History Channel rapturously, soaking up its dramatic reenactments of ancient Egypt, Rome, the New World and the settling of America by Europeans. She experienced a titillation—and an odd comfort—in imagining herself living in the past, participating in the historical dramas of bygone ages. When Uncle Buddy was living at the house, she had her first encouragement for her geeky interests from an adult who wasn't a teacher. All of Maya's interactions with Buddy Burke thrilled her. Buddy was her mother's older sibling, an Air Force captain who had piloted B-52 bombers in the Vietnam War. He stayed on with Muriel and Maya for six months, a period which affected Maya profoundly.

Many a summer evening saw the handsome, amiable Buddy sitting with his niece on the backyard swing, regaling her with stories of foreign lands, translating complex political dramas into terms she could understand, at times interrupting his discourses with the whack of a mosquito or a quick jog to the kitchen for a can of Pabst Blue Ribbon beer. Maya would hang onto his every word, eager to escape Plainfield for the great cities of Europe and Asia.

It was only later, when she was in college, that she would come to see Buddy's interpretations of historical events as highly creative and at times far-fetched, though often more fascinating than what was commonly understood. In fact, her professors' lectures paled in comparison to Buddy's theories, which he carefully and painstakingly laid out for Maya between slugs of beer.

To Buddy, countries possessed personalities and temperaments, just like people: innate, unchangeable qualities that formed the basis for their decisions and actions. America, he told her, was an adventurous, brazen young explorer, brimming with potential and able to create truly new things in the world. Buddy believed that every country had a gender leaning as well. India, for example, was a feminine force, a nurturer and a keeper of secrets, a place that welcomed strangers. Mother Russia and Germany's Fatherland had their obvious leanings.

Every land mass, Buddy believed, infused its qualities into the psyches of the people who lived on it. America's case was unique. Whereas the collective psyche of most other nations had become entrenched over the centuries, the ink on America's story was still damp, making it more malleable. Considerable good—and bad—could come of it.

Buddy and his theories. Oh, how Maya missed him! She loved Buddy as she would have loved her father, if only she'd had the chance. But he was not a happy man. His cheerful front could not hide an existential pain that simmered beneath the surface, and his obvious efforts to suppress it made her love him even more. What had happened to Buddy?

He disappeared into New York or Philly, she'd last heard. He was a salesman of some kind, a hustler who lived on the edge. Plainfield had been a sanctuary for him. But he hadn't written or called in years. And Muriel had no idea where he was. Maya imagined that whatever had happened—and maybe it was the worst—wasn't his fault.

When the meeting time approached, she tossed the empty cup and the doughnut bag into a trash can and wound her way out of the garden onto the Mall's pedestrian path. The day was beautiful, sunny and mild. Maya stopped at one point to watch an Asian man snap a photo of his smiling wife and children, with the U.S. Capitol building as its backdrop. People of all nationalities filled the area—twenty million a year, Maya had once read—making the tourist's pilgrimage from monument to museum to historic site.

Her gaze followed the direction of the man's camera lens up toward the dome of the Capitol. High up at its apex stood a bronze statue of a Native American woman. Maya knew the sculpture well, since she'd written a paper about it. Even now she could feel the piercing irony she had experienced then: the very men who had treated the Indians so brutally chose to crown their prime legislative building this way. They called the statue *Freedom*.

"Go ahead, believe the historical record if you want to," Buddy had told Maya. "You do so at your peril." History wasn't always what it appeared to be, he said. It was neither set nor stable, but ever-changing. The past *evolved*, just like the present. Though the deeds of yesterday could not be undone, Buddy said, they could be rewritten, and were.

As Maya approached the National Museum of Natural History, she wondered if he had been right about things like that. Some of what she learned seemed to bear it out. In grade school, she'd been taught about a heroic visionary named Christopher Columbus, a ship's captain who discovered a new continent. Then, in her teens, amid changing times, Columbus had apparently changed, too, becoming just another European plunderer with ignoble aims. Though he had been dead for half a millennium, he had begun to act differently. Evolution.

Maya had learned that Europeans brought civilization to a continent of savages in a place they called the New World. But in truth, the indigenous peoples were treated like weeds in a field that needed to be cleared, their cultures deemed worthless, or nearly so.

Buddy said that recorded history was mostly a lesson in perspective. "One guy's colony is another guy's graveyard," he told his niece. Maybe he was right. Maybe everything came down to perspective.

Maya hesitated as she neared the museum's entrance. Long queues of tourists crept in through the doors, slowed by a security check inside. Behind her, children poured out of school buses idling at the curb. Pigeons bobbed on the pavement, and the scent of fresh-popped popcorn from a sidewalk vendor filled the air.

As she stared at the doors, the role that this building played in Maya's own history hit her with full force. She now regretted the choice of meeting place.

The Crash had struck when she was seventeen. Dr. Yanikowski, the psychiatrist whom Muriel had recruited for help, offered a diagnosis of clinical depression. Maya didn't care much about the label; all she knew was she was in some serious pain. Her mind had become a self-loathing machine, and her body possessed of a molasses-like torpor. She took up residence in bed, weeping at all hours without knowing why, feeling so physically weak that it took effort even to move at all.

It had started with Uncle Buddy's departure. He'd given no real explanation, just said a quick goodbye and was gone. Just like that. After all they'd shared. She was upset for two days, but nothing out of the ordinary. But the next day she was immobilized. Her attempts at even simple tasks were a strain: fixing a meal, showering, walking, reading. Whenever she would exert herself, she would immediately lose energy, as if her life-force was draining out through a hole in her body.

Her thinking process became muddled, her memory porous. The things and people she cared about mattered less and less until they hardly mattered at all. She began to detest inconsequential, ordinary things: a bus going by, a young mother pushing a stroller, a man picking up trash on the sidewalk. She hated herself for feeling this way. Mostly she felt victimized. By whom? No one had harmed her. Who, then, was to blame?

The organ of thought, the brain—her wolf—that indefatigable miracle of evolution that could solve the most complex of problems, that could figure out how to send a man to the moon and discern subatomic particles—*that* was the very part of her that was ill! Without her problem-solver, how could she emerge from this mess? Compulsively it looped over and over with the same bleak thoughts, the same insufferable questions, the same agonizing complaints. Her mind seemed intent on destroying her, and itself in the process. She could stop it no more than she could stem the flow of clouds across the sky. And so, she waited for it, or her, to end.

The hellish agony lasted two weeks, a brutal fortnight that would change her forever. The horror would always be lurking in the background, lying in wait.

But she did outlast it, won the war, and her strength began to return. At first the best she could manage was to shuffle around the house like a weary foot soldier who had survived a terrible battle. Complex or difficult tasks were out of the question. If her to-do list filled up, anxiety would chase away her newfound energy, bringing her crashing back into bed. Slowly she made gains. Dr. Yanikowski had prescribed antidepressant medicine, but Maya didn't want to go that route; she kept the bottle in a drawer. If she found herself hovering at the edge of the abyss, leaning into it, perhaps then.

One of his ideas interested her very much. It was a kind of mental *jujitsu* that could disperse negative thoughts before they could gather enough momentum to initiate a descent. Maya had taken to the technique immediately. It was simple. It consisted of writing her negative thoughts on a piece of paper along with their opposites. Beside, "I am weird and no one will like me," she would respond, "Everyone is strange in their own way, so I am really normal." Next to, "I will get depressed and hurt myself," she would retort, "I will live in the moment, and the future will take care of itself." Amazingly, it changed her mood instantly. It was called cognitive therapy.

Also around this time, she found herself thinking often about the National Museum of Natural History, the building she stood before now, which she had first visited on a field trip with her fifth-grade class.

In the wake of the Crash, Maya came here many times. When she first set foot inside, she understood why. Her bruised soul sought convalescence in a place unrelated to anything in her present life, or, as it turned out, in the modern world. It needed a completely neutral locale in which to be curious and interested and let the scabs of her wounds fall away. The distant past served this purpose well.

Maya would happily drive the hour on I-95 to visit this building, spending long afternoons wandering through its halls, often finding herself standing at the dinosaur exhibits, where she would travel back tens of millions of years to a time that the world she knew was undreamed, for people had not yet arrived to dream it. Her voracious mind, her hungry wolf, swam happily in a waterfall of facts and theories.

She took the audio tours. She learned the scientific terms. Her vocabulary grew with words she would never use. Mesozoic. Brachiosaurus. Iguanodon. Such terms became the lyrics of her new anthem. Names and places and dates washed over her in a cleansing ablution and she grew stronger. But even if contemplating the life of the dinosaurs satisfied the wolf from moment to moment, Maya often had to suppress a cynicism at the certainty implied on the exhibit signs.

When it came to knowing when Triceratops stomped around the countryside, how it spent its days and what it liked to do, there were theories. Theories that changed. New ones rose to dominance as old ones fell away. That was the way of science, as Maya well knew.

How much certainty, she wondered, could one accord to a theory? The very *idea* of it was uncertainty. It *meant* you didn't know. So didn't it then follow that whichever theory you chose as true today could be tossed aside by a totally different "truth" tomorrow? What, then, constituted real Truth?

Years ago, when Muriel attended Plainfield Elementary School, dinosaurs were believed to have been slow-moving reptilian clods. When Maya sat in that same classroom, they were thought to be quick bird-like creatures. Which was it now? What, she wondered, would be "true" tomorrow?

Wasn't all knowledge just theory? How could you know anything for certain? Every so-called fact upon which you based your understanding of the world was, in reality, shifting, changeable, not at all rock solid, not something you could bank upon. Weren't you then just standing in quicksand?

Maya could no longer feel the concrete beneath her Converse All Star sneakers, nor the gentle breeze sweeping across her face, so entangled had she become in these thoughts. Somewhere deep inside of her the wolf's eyes glowed with a red, hellish fire.

Let it go.

She took a deep breath, calmed by the knowledge that she knew exactly what was happening. That awareness made all the difference, for then she could do something about it. She would turn her attention to something in the actual *world*: the glass and metal doors of the museum's entrance a few feet away. Pulling her attention away from the wolf grounded her in reality.

She stepped into the queue and soon she was standing inside the museum's expansive high-ceilinged atrium, smiling, feeling the old titillation, which oddly was tied to the familiar reek of the place, the all-pervasive musty stuffiness of it. It was the intermingling of decades-old exhibits, preservation chemicals and perspiring humans, a complex scent Maya had come to attach to natural history. And healing. Actually, she liked it.

The room was packed with tourists. Every step brought another body close. Corridors radiated out from this central hub to the exhibit halls—sea life, rocks and minerals, mammals, reptiles, native cultures, the dinosaurs.

A soaring display of an African bull elephant dominated the room, its trunk reaching permanently for the sky, sealed in place by the taxidermists of 1955. THE MODERN WORLD'S LARGEST LAND ANIMAL. A throng of chatty children gazed up at it, pointing and laughing.

Maya walked around until she spotted a man with a gray umbrella under his arm. It was the only one in sight, given the sunny weather. That was how Albert Fiske had said she'd know him. She waved, and he started toward her.

He was in his late fifties and youthful looking, with bushy black eyebrows, close-cropped hair and a solid chest. He was wearing neatly pressed trousers, a shirt and tie, and loafers. He was only a couple of inches taller than Maya.

"Hello, Maya," he said, and pointed toward the exit doors. "Do you mind if we walk?"

"Sure, that sounds fine," she said.

Outside, they headed in the direction of the Washington Monument, the five-hundred-foot-tall marble and granite obelisk that Maya, as a child, had called the big pencil.

"I've lived in D.C. for twenty-five years and I've never been up in it," he said. "That's downright unpatriotic wouldn't you say?"

Was he joking? Maya looked closely at him but couldn't tell. She surprised herself when she said, "Was my father patriotic?"

"I'll let you be the judge of that," he said. "My office is just over that way."

A few minutes later they passed by the garden of the Sackler Gallery where she'd been earlier, and the massive building across the street, then continued on. Maya slowed momentarily, considering what was to come. She felt the pull again, the one that told her she was on the path that led to her father, which brought with it the sensation of passing through a doorway she could sense but not see.

9

Psychic Spy

Your father was a remarkable man," Albert Fiske said as he settled into the squeaky chair behind his desk and leaned so far back in it that Maya braced herself, certain he was going to topple over backwards. But he just hovered there, perfectly balanced. For her part, Maya scooted forward in the guest chair in front of the desk, trying to hike herself up to eye level with him, but she couldn't quite get there.

He had led her into an unassuming two-story office building a few blocks from the Sackler Gallery. She had seen no signage or name on the front of the drab cement structure, just a small metal plate with a street address engraved on it.

Mr. Fiske had strode into the lobby with authority, flashing an ID badge at each of the three guard stations they passed, leading Maya down the stairs to an underground level. Uniformed guards had waved them through the checkpoints with a deferential nod.

"By the way, you have a conditional security clearance," he to her across the desk.

"Why do I need that, Mr. Fiske?" Maya asked.

"Please, just *Fiske*," he said, tilting his chair forward, finally, to a normal sitting position. "Everyone calls me Fiske."

She nodded, though she wasn't sure she was comfortable with that.

"The clearance is so I can speak to you frankly. It's why you came here, I guarantee it," Fiske said. "Can I offer you something to drink?"

"Do you have a Diet Coke?"

"Sure, I'll be right back," he said, heading for the door.

While he was gone, Maya examined the office. Clean and institutional. Nothing much caught her eye except for two posters tacked to the walls. One was a street scene of the Champs-Elysées and the other a whale leaping out of the ocean. Curious choices. There were framed diplomas, awards and certificates. Fiske's desk was piled high with papers.

He returned and handed her a can of Diet Coke, and shut the door.

"So, this the government?" Maya asked, popping the top of the can.

"Correct," Fiske said.

"Which branch? There's no sign outside."

"Defense Intelligence Agency," Fiske said. "We're part of the Department of Defense. This unit doesn't advertise."

Maya had a sip of the soda and set the can down.

"First things first," Fiske began. "I've got something here you'll want to see." He reached into a drawer and pulled out an 8-by-10 photograph and handed it across the desk to Maya. "You probably know who that is," he said.

Maya looked at it—and almost stopped breathing. The black-and-white image showed a young man standing at a blackboard, surveying an expanse of chalk-scrawled equations. He had dark, angular features, piercing eyes and a shock of disheveled longish black hair that spilled over his forehead, a dash of irreverence in an otherwise neat appearance. He was wearing jeans and an untucked white shirt. His expression was composed and yet excited, too.

Maya stared long and hard at the eyes, as if trying to rouse them, get them to transmit some badly needed information to her. She suffered a pang of discomfort on seeing her father for the first time in a room with a guy she didn't know or feel comfortable with. She kept her reaction in check.

"When was his taken?" Maya said.

"About twenty years ago. I'll make you a copy."

"I'd like that," Maya said. "I'd like that very much." She knew there software out there that could age a person's image, show what he would look like now. She wanted to do just that.

Reluctantly she handed the photo back, staring at it until the last possible moment. Fiske slid it back into the drawer.

"Just out of curiosity," he said, "why, after all these years, are you looking for him?"

Maya gave him a hard look. "You're asking me why I wouldn't want to know about my father?"

"Yeah," Fiske said. "Why all the effort now?"

"Like I told Dr. Porter, I found a letter of his. That's what started all this. I never had anything to go on."

"What about your mother?"

"What about her?"

"What does she say?"

"She doesn't know what happened to him."

"She must know something."

"She knows he left."

Fiske thought a moment, then nodded. "OK," he said. "Fair enough."

He picked up a cup on the desk and drank whatever was in it—Maya assumed coffee—while his eyes never left hers. "Actually," he said, "I'm looking for Ben, too."

"So, then, he's alive? I mean, he's somewhere."

"Oh, yes."

"How do you know all this?"

"Hold on a minute," Fiske said. "There's something we need to talk about before we get into that."

Maya waited, staring at him.

"Do you know what remote viewing is?" Fiske said.

"No."

Fiske became thoughtful, then looked over at Maya and smiled. "Make yourself comfortable," he said. "I'm going to tell you a story that's like nothing you've ever heard. It'll answer a lot of your questions. Do you know what the Cold War was?"

Of course Maya knew that. She recited as if reading from a textbook: "A conflict between the United States and the Soviet

Union that lasted from the forties until 1991, called 'cold' because there was no actual military conflict."

Fiske nodded, impressed. "Wow. That's very good."

"So, what about the Cold War?" she said.

"You're right, there was no *open* conflict," Fiske said, "but there was a hell of a lot of covert conflict. The Soviets had their fingers in a lot of pies. One of them was extrasensory perception, or ESP. They employed psychics to spy on us. You know what ESP is?"

Maya looked at him quizzically, realized what she was feeling. Not only was the man patronizing, but he didn't know it. But there was more, and it bothered her. She was attracted to him. He had a primal, macho kind of allure that hinted of power and unpredictability, qualities she'd rarely encountered in the guys she knew, most of whom were soft. She decided the best course was to ignore it.

"ESP is the ability to see things without being there," she said.

"It's being aware of things without using *any* of the senses," Fiske said. "In other words, perception that's totally nonphysical. That was the capability our Russian friends were developing when your father worked for me. The Ruskies were training teams of psychic spies."

"Psychic spies?" Maya said, stifling her disbelief. If that type of spying were possible, why bother with the real kind, the kind got people tortured and killed?

Fiske said, "The Soviets were acquiring intel on our military targets—locations, bases, tech, things like that."

"So, it actually worked?" Maya said.

"Oh, hell yes."

"Then we got into the act," she said.

"Correct," Fiske said. "Now, this was back in the eighties. And since they'd had a head start, when our budget came through we had some catching up to do. The Soviets called their technique remote viewing, which is kind of like 'throwing' your consciousness, the way a ventriloquist throws his voice. A remote viewer transports himself mentally to a location, receives impressions and reports on what he's seen. Physically he hasn't gone anywhere. He's just a guy sitting in a room with his eyes shut, following a detailed regimen."

Fiske leaned back, and again the chair squeaked and groaned, and Maya braced herself for the fall. Again he balanced perfectly on it. He came forward quickly. "I was director of the agency's remote viewing program," he said.

"The one doing the ESP?"

Fiske nodded. "Our early viewers were psychics, just like the Russians had, guys hand-picked for their abilities. We started out small on simple tasks like working to identify the contents of sealed boxes. We spent a lot of time fine-tuning the techniques."

"OK," Maya said, interested.

"It starts with a prep routine," Fiske said. "Like a lot of this kind of stuff, you need to relax the mind. The viewer is given coordinates—a pair of numbers that correspond to a real location. They're meaningless to him, but of course significant to us. When he's ready he carries out the protocols and goes into trance. Then, *voila.* He 'travels.' He takes his pencil and draws what he sees on a piece of paper. Pretty simple.

"A viewer in one of the early trials reported a moving gray mound at the target location. What was it? A mouse in a box on a table across the hall. *Boom.* Direct hit. That's how it works. The observations are correct but don't always happen the way you'd expect. Shapes and colors come in strongest. Sometimes a viewer gets details, other times he doesn't. It depends on the viewer, the situation, and who the hell knows what else. The phases of the moon, for all I know. This is strange stuff."

"I'm betting it gets stranger," Maya said.

"It does," Fiske said. "We moved in stages from the sealed-box trials to real locations, starting with rooms in the next building, then going farther and farther out, to other buildings, other states, distant cities—statistically successful all the way. There were plenty of misses, to be sure. We expected that. But the hits! It was incredible. The images would float in and the viewer drew them. Now, this is a subtle process, Maya. The instrument is the mind, which can be unpredictable as hell. A bad dinner can skew things. Or a bad date. Even the thoughts of the person guiding the viewer can screw things up."

"Thoughts?"

"Yep," he said. "Like I said, strange. Now, one day—I remember this like it was yesterday—someone says, 'How about an extraterrestrial target?' Ha! We laughed. When we'd settled down, I thought, why not?

"We chose Jupiter. That's right, the planet. Now, stay with me. There was a NASA satellite due there on a fly-by so we knew we could check our data against theirs. We didn't expect anything. The day comes, and our viewer does the protocol and reports, of all things, a ring around Jupiter! Which is ridiculous. Jupiter has no ring. Maybe, we joked, he overshot and bumped into Saturn by mistake.

"When the data came back, it showed a ring around Jupiter that was previously unknown. The joke was on us. Boy, did we have a few drinks that night. After that, funding flowed into our little project in a torrent. We were in business. We recruited psychics, trained a team of viewers and made discoveries every bit as incredible as the ring around Jupiter."

Maya edged forward. "Such as?"

"That future events might not be a complete mystery."

"What?" Maya said, unbelieving.

"Here, I'll show you," Fiske said.

He riffled through some papers and found a sheet with a diagram on it and placed it on the desk in front of Maya. There was a tree-like illustration on it with branches extending out from the trunk. They were labeled POTENTIAL FUTURES.

"The 'future' doesn't exist, of course," Fiske explained. "But the probable future does. Think about it. Time moves forward, and one of many potential futures becomes the present. The question is, which one? Many potentials exist at any one time. Nobody can see the future, per se. What you *can* see is the construction site, so to speak, the skeleton that's being built for it. What's likely to happen."

Maya said, "You're telling me the government is into all this?"

"You bet," Fiske said. "Initially, the CIA and Defense Intelligence Agency. Nowadays many independent groups do remote viewing."

"You said it was secret."

"Not anymore," he said. "Everything I've told you has been declassified. You can read about it at any bookstore. Just look up 'psychic spies' or 'remote viewing.' There's plenty written on the topic."

"Then why do I need the security clearance?"

"For this," Fiske said, reaching into the desk drawer.

He brought out two folded-up sheets that opened into maps, which he laid on the desk. One was a map of the United States, the other a Mercator projection of the Earth which appeared like an orange peel cut into sections and flattened out. He laid the U.S. map on top.

It was peppered with blue and red dots. Maya counted a dozen of the blues, which were larger than the reds. Most of them were in the Southwestern states and along the West Coast. Red dots were sprinkled throughout the country, too many to count.

"Any idea what these dots represent?" Fiske said.

Maya had no clue. She shook her head.

"I'll give you a hint," he said, touching his finger to a red dot in the upper Midwest. "This one's near Chicago, where your friend Edgar Porter lives."

"Vortexes," Maya said immediately.

"Correct," Fiske said. "The blues are majors, the reds minors—in terms of power."

He refolded the U.S. map and set it aside, revealing the Mercator projection beneath it. It, too, was covered in red and blue dots. He slid a finger to a blue dot on a strip of land east of the Mediterranean Sea.

"Jerusalem," he said.

He moved his finger south to Egypt. "Giza."

And further east to the Himalayas, stopping again on a blue dot. "Tibet."

Then to Central America. "Guatemala."

Maya's brow wrinkled as she looked on.

"Any idea what these places have in common?" Fiske asked. "Let's see how smart you are."

Maya stared at the map. She tried to recall the societies that had developed in those places. She had studied many of them.

Her face brightened. She gazed triumphantly at Fiske. "Influential societies," she said. "The Egyptian pyramids are in Giza. The Mayans, also pyramid builders, lived in what's now Guatemala. And Jerusalem is home to Judaism, Christianity and Islam. Religions started in all those places. The vortexes are about religion?"

"Broader, even," Fiske said. "Belief systems."

Maya considered that. She recalled Dr. Porter's lecture on how energy "flows" into certain locations, stirring people to new ways of thinking. Fiske was showing her the actual locations where it happened. It was fantastic. If this were true, she asked Fiske, why didn't people know about it?

"Some do," Fiske said. "The mystics of certain indigenous cultures do. Many others as well. But why share the wealth? There's an old saying, 'He who doesn't know, says. He who knows, doesn't say.' These people don't say."

"Then how do *you* know?"

Fiske smiled. He folded up the Mercator map, then leaned back in the creaky chair and again Maya winced, waiting for him to crash down. This time, though, she realized what was happening.

He was tipping back like that on purpose! He knew exactly how far he could safely go and was enjoying watching her reactions, like it was some kind of perverse game. She'd been stealing glances at his powerful chest most of the time and had missed it all. She felt like an imbecile. Plus, it was just flat-out weird. Watching her, Fiske quickly leaned forward and became serious. Maya decided to just let it all go.

"The vortexes have always been there," he said. "The difference is that now we have people who understand them. The guy who saw the mouse in the box? That was your father. Ben was the first remote viewer."

"He was psychic?" Maya asked, taken aback.

"Was and still is," Fiske said.

Maya thought about that, her mouth wide open. She herself had abilities like that, or suspected so. Maybe now she knew why she could often sense people's moods, or know events in advance. At times she became so overwhelmed with mental impressions she'd have to hide out in her room with the shades drawn just to calm down from those deluges of information. Was she psychic, too?

"Ben was the best of all my viewers," Fiske said.

Maya absorbed that as she sipped nervously at the Diet Coke, which was starting to irritate her stomach. She set the can down on the side table.

Fiske said, "The vortexes form a communications network. Each one is a node connected to all the others. If you want to know what happened to you in Porter's basement—why you received those mental images—here's your answer: it was a message."

"From him?"

"No," Fiske said. "From a group in Wyoming. That was the reference to Wicklow. Wicklow is a rural town."

Wicklow! Maya was about to tell Fiske about her trip there and all that had happened, but she decided to keep quiet about Georgia and Brandon's "intentional community." She didn't know why. It was just a hunch.

Fiske said, "This group calls themselves the Mandala."

"The Mandala?"

"It means circle," he said. "It's an ancient term. It refers to a sacred plan or a chart that shows cosmic or metaphysical relationships."

"I've heard of that," Maya said vaguely.

"They live on a kind of commune," Fiske said. "They know about the vortexes. They know how to use them."

"Use them? To do what?"

"To influence—people and events."

He gave her a moment to process that, then said, "What the Mandala is trying to do is use the vortexes to increase the likelihood that a certain future will come to pass."

Maya said, "The tree branches in that diagram."

"Each one of those represents a different outcome for our civilization," Fiske said. "Forks in the road, so to speak. We know what they are because our viewers have seen them. So have the Mandala's people."

Fiske picked up the cup on his desk, took another sip and set it down. When he spoke next, his voice was intense.

"Three distinct probabilities exist for the Western industrialized world," he said.

"You mean what might to happen to us."

"I mean what *will* happen," he said. "We call them Continuation, Low-tech and Breakdown. Continuation is the best case scenario: little change from today's world. Low-tech brings an erosion of critical infrastructure—technology, power, food production, trade, building, governance—but life goes on. It's impossible to know how it would play out but it's a big step backwards. Breakdown is the scary one, what we want to avoid it at all costs. It's the end of our way of life, with a small, surviving population retreating to outlying areas, urban areas savaged, law and government and communications decimated. It's centuries of progress, gone. It's *Mad Max* and *The Stand.*"

Maya was stunned, hearing this. She said, "What's the probability of that happening? What would bring that about?"

"Hard to say," Fiske said. "It would be nuclear war, famine, plague, economic collapse, natural disaster. We're unable to see the domino chain of events, only the aftermath."

Maya sipped at the Coke, but still it offered no relief. She thought about her father's warnings of change. Fiske, it seemed, had worked out the details. Still, a part of her objected. *No one can predict the future.*

"Our job is make sure the scenario is Continuation," Fiske said. "Our team is working on that around the clock. Breakdown means collapse, Maya. That's what that group in Wyoming, the Mandala, wants."

"Why?" she said. "That makes no sense."

"They want it because they believe it's necessary," Fiske said. "'The old must be destroyed to make room for the new.' They see it as a required step for their spiritual renaissance to occur. That's their term. *Spiritual renaissance.* The irony is that their goal is a peaceful world. That would be nice, right? No more war, cooperation among all peoples. We could all live with that. The problem is, the change they would see would be too great a strain on the group mind. The subconscious agreements upon which all societies are based will weaken and become dysfunctional. In the end, it will be anarchy. We'll have lost the ballgame—centuries of progress. We'll revert to the Dark Ages."

Maya, who had been slumping further and further down in the chair with each of Fiske's assertions, suffered an assault of mental images: cities decimated, food and shelter scarce, warlords and gangs reigning, women in constant danger; no electricity, laws or transportation. It was a brutal world in which nothing came easy and only the strong survived.

"Listen, Maya," Fiske said intensely. "The Mandala understand the vortexes. They know how to use them. Do you know what will happen when they set their plan in motion?"

Maya said nothing, just stared at him.

"The end," Fiske said with rising force. "They are no different from terrorists. They are psychic terrorists." He paused. "I need your help, Maya."

She stared at him with alarm and surprise. "Me? What can I do?"

"They've attempted to contact you."

It was true. But not only that. She had met them, spent time with them. She *liked* them. What Fiske was saying didn't square with what she'd experienced in Wicklow.

"Ben has a relationship with them," Fiske said.

"He does?" Maya said. "How do you know that?"

"Let's just say, for now, we know."

They knew her father? If that were true, then Georgia and Brandon had lied to her.

"They will contact you again," Fiske said. "When they do, I want you to let me know."

"OK," Maya said, simply because she could think of nothing else to say at that moment.

Fiske held out a business card. Maya reached over the desk and took the ivory-colored rectangle from him. There was no name on it, only a telephone number.

"Call me at that number anytime, day or night," he said.

"OK."

"Thank you, Maya. It was a pleasure to meet you. I'll have someone show you out."

A few minutes later, Maya stepped out into the midday sun feeling as though she'd just taken a trip to the moon. Mostly she was confused. Was her father on the wrong side of the fight? Was Georgia working toward a societal collapse? These were questions that needed answers.

10

The Inner Medium

A dull throbbing pulsed somewhere behind Maya's eyes. She pushed away the blankets, stretched out her arms and inhaled sharply, hoping to divert the headache that seemed surely to come, but all she was doing was sucking in more of the stuffy air, which had probably caused the problem in the first place. She stared up at Josh's ceiling fan. It was not cooling the room in the least, its blades turning so slowly she could see clumps of dirt and grime caked all over it.

A question had been nagging at her for the two hours now. *Why?* Why was she here? Why had she let Josh back in? Because *here* she most certainly was, prone in his bed, enduring his annoyingly rhythmic breathing while she struggled with an eye ache that was worsening by the minute.

The answer was simple. It was weakness that had brought her to him. She didn't want to be alone. She had caved and Josh had played his part well. He had apologized so profusely and groveled so convincingly that she just couldn't stay angry at him. She'd earned the bounty of her selfishness.

He had told her he was confused that night at the café, he'd been in a creative slump, having not written a decent song or even a passible riff in weeks, even though he'd been carving out huge amounts of time for it. He was going out of his mind and he had taken it out on Maya that night. What he did was unfair and selfish but he was scared. He was sorry. He'd been dealing with strong feelings, intense feelings, feelings that could turn a guy into a self-centered idiot. And then, suddenly, she was gone.

It's amazing, Maya thought, the things you'll do for someone who lies down and bares his belly, who admits to weakness.

Yes, she had let him in, but coming over to his apartment had obviously been a mistake because three a.m. had arrived and she was wide awake, watching the slow spinning of a filthy fan through eyes pulsing as relentlessly as a heartbeat.

Most of all she felt the frustration of their conversation of last night. How could he not understand what she had so painstakingly laid out for him? It wasn't that difficult.

She got up out of bed and stepped through the piles of clothes and shoes and magazines spread around the floor, and went over to the window. Looking outside put her at ease. *Beloved night.* She sensed its promise in the amber haze of the streetlamp that gave a magical middle-of-the-night sheen to the lawn of wild weeds.

Plainfield in the wee hours. Maya had known countless nights like this, from back in her emo teens when she would stay up into early morning hours, binge-watching old black and white movies, films her friends would surely have ridiculed. When she'd gotten her fill she'd emerge from the back door of the house into the quietude to stroll the block in peace, bathed in a clarity she rarely felt in the waking hours. While everyone slept, she reveled.

She turned her gaze back to the room, to the concert posters tacked on the wood-paneled walls, the guitars propped up on their stands, a crusty dish of something unidentifiable and oatmeal-colored on a side table. Maya and Josh's jeans intertwined in a heap on the floor. At this bewitching hour all seemed strangely animate, as though the music waiting within the guitars could be sensed, the service in the jeans felt. It was crazy, but these objects seemed to be alive.

She imagined the other renters in the old Victorian house asleep in their beds. The three-story structure was divided into apartments, each unique, yet possessing an essence of the whole, that same quality that holograms have. Josh's three rooms at the top were marked by a V-shaped ceiling and a woodsy aroma. The two other units were larger. A narrow stairway connected them all. Outside, the lawn surrounded the house like a moat.

Josh shifted beneath the blanket, and Maya walked quietly around the bed, slid in beside him. *I'm here.*

She had not held back about her adventures in the West. The story of Chicago and Wyoming had shot out of her with the force of pressurized steam, and to her surprise, Josh didn't, or couldn't, understand.

He had listened, to be sure, at first attentively and then perplexed, and finally doubtful, while Maya noted the involuntary shaking of his head with growing dismay. Only when it was too late did he understand what had happened.

"What time is it?" Josh mumbled, wiping sleep from his eyes.

"Three," she said.

"A.M. or P.M.?"

"A.M."

He smiled wearily. "You're upset," he said.

"It's OK, Josh. Really."

"No, it's not," he said, ever the good soldier. He slid up on an elbow, touched Maya's shoulder softly.

He said, "I want to understand."

"You're just saying that," she said.

"I'm not, honest."

Just then she got an idea. Her face brightened and she sat up. With an air of formality, she announced, "The hundredth monkey theory."

"The what?"

"It's an old story and no doubt spurious," Maya said. "But it relates, trust me."

"If it has monkeys, I'm in," Josh said agreeably.

"Many," Maya said. "They live on an archipelago."

"A troop," he said.

"Huh?"

"A *troop* of monkeys. That's what it's called."

"Right, a troop," she said. "A troop that eats bananas. Only they don't peel them, they just pop 'em in their mouths and spit out the peels afterwards."

"Skilled monkeys," Josh said.

"Right," Maya said. "They've been doing it that way for generations, until one day one of them says, 'I'm going to try something new. I'm peeling this banana before I eat it.' Which works out really well. Soon others are doing it, too."

"Everyone's peeling," Josh said.

"Months go by, as more and more of the monkeys follow suit. Then one day, when the number of peelers reaches a hundred, something amazing happens."

"They make smoothies?" Josh said.

"No, idiot," Maya said, playfully punching his arm. "The monkeys on the neighboring islands start peeling, too."

"Huh."

"Right," she said.

"So, some kind of communication is taking place."

"Correct—in theory."

"As in?"

"Well, nonphysical communication," Maya said.

"Like an evolutionary leap."

"Exactly," Maya said. "Which is what Ben Ambrose believes is happening to us. It's what Brandon and Fiske mean when they say you can create cultural change psychically. We're able to to somehow prompt the first 'one hundred' to do the new thing that starts the chain reaction going."

Josh nodded, processing. He did seem interested.

Maya went on, "Think about all the inventions and discoveries that happened in different parts of the world at the same time. Like Darwin. He published the theory of evolution the same time Wallace did, though neither man knew about the other's work. What are the odds of that? I mean, after all human history these two guys come up with the same incredible work at the same time?"

"I remember that from somewhere," Josh said.

"Or the way the same myths and rituals and gods appear in cultures that are separated by oceans, by people who could have never communicated any of that because they never traveled out of their backyards. Savior myths, fertility myths, harvest stories, stories of rebirth and the afterlife—tons of cultures have the same exact ones. Chance? Luck? I doubt it."

Before Josh could respond, Maya reached down beside the bed and brought up her backpack and plunged her hand into it. She took out the journal and started to page through it.

"So, that's it, huh?" Josh said, leaning in for a closer look.

"Uh-huh," Maya said.

"May I?" he said, holding out his hand.

She hesitated, then handed it over, carefully, as one might proffer a delicate porcelain vase, and watched tensely as he turned the faded pages and inspected a few passages. When her anxiety reached a fevered pitch, she snatched it back.

"Possessive, are we?" Josh chided.

"Maybe a tad. I'm sorry."

"No, no, it's fine. I just wanted to see it. Go ahead. You want to read some of it to me, right?"

"Is it OK?"

"Are you kidding? This thing rules you. Yes, read, please."

"All right," she said. She turned to a specific page. "He says we communicate telepathically all the time, only we don't know it, because it happens deep in the mind in a place he calls the inner medium."

"I'm listening," Josh said.

The inner medium is an environment, a landscape, a state of consciousness—all are true. It is where the unconscious desires of humankind coalesce into psychic structures which in time, become matter and events in the world.

The inchoate future lives in the inner medium. There are seers who can glimpse it even as it forms, the same way meteorologists see weather patterns as they take shape.

I'll explain it this way, Maya. Imagine we are at a seashore, curling our toes in the sand (a wonderful thought!). A wave laps in. Then another. And another. Though we can't see it from our vantage point, we know these waves originated far away, shaped by the currents, the weather, the ocean floor and the moon's gravity—many, many factors. If you fully understood them all, you'd be able to accurately predict the movements of waves.

Cultural waves are similar. They form the political, social, technological and even spiritual direction of humankind. The world's great expansions all started out as such waves. The Renaissance, the Enlightenment, ancient Rome, Greece, Christianity, even modern democracy— all originated in the inner medium, propelled by the unconscious desires of people en masse.

Does the human race want an artistic resurgence, a war (to shift the balance of power, perhaps), technological progress, a new religion, or maybe a population-reducing epidemic to open up space in overcrowded lands? Such questions are answered constantly by the species as a whole as we infuse our desires into the inner medium.

Every human being who walks the Earth contributes to this great endeavor. We are all connected, you see, collectively moving the inner medium, and so contribute to the vast undertaking of creating the experience of this world…

Maya closed the journal and turned to Josh. "Interesting," he said.

He lay back and stared up at the ceiling. He yawned. Maya waited to hear him tell her how fascinating that was, how compelling and how cool. She wanted to hear words like *fantastic* and *amazing*. But none of that happened. She knew he was doing his best, that he wanted to satisfy her.

"Josh, I'm sorry. Can you forgive me?"

"It's fine, Maya."

"Is it?"

"Yes. Tell me, what do *you* think?"

"About what?"

"The inner medium."

"Come on," she said. "You're just saying that."

"I'm not," he said. "I want to know."

"Well," she said. "I think people in different cultures have the same ideas because they're all fishing in the same ocean."

"What ocean is that?"

"The one in here," she said, tapping the side of her head. "The one beneath your thoughts."

Josh's face suddenly brightened. "Hold on a minute," he said. "Hold on just a minute."

"Yes?"

"Correct me if I'm wrong…"

Maya nodded, urging him on.

"The first monkey came up with the peeling idea all on its own, right? Then the others joined in. But not until a certain number started peeling that the trend gains enough momentum *in the inner medium* to start the chain reaction going."

"Right!" Maya said.

She leaned over and kissed him. "And nobody asked why or how. They just noticed, 'Hey, we're peeling!'"

Josh thought for a moment, then said, "We're creating laws!"

"Exactly!" Maya said. "We're driving cars!"

"We're buying tons of useless stuff we don't need!"

"We're working for companies we hate!"

"We're—"

"Wait, wait," Maya said, getting up out of bed. She dashed over to the window and then wheeled around to face him. "I know what's happening! The Mandala wants to use the vortexes to manipulate the inner medium. That's how they plan to influence large-scale events. Which means—"

"Yes?"

"It means—"

"What?"

"No," she said. "It can't be."

"What can't?"

"It means we're being controlled—to a degree," she said. "Manipulated. Things, events, aren't just happening."

"Whoa," Josh said. "Are you serious?"

"I don't mean the little stuff," Maya said. "I'm talking about cultural trends, mass beliefs, religious movements. They're into the large-scale stuff."

Josh looked at her doubtfully. "Maybe I could buy the hundredth monkey deal, but *that*? That's a leap, Maya."

"I know," she said. "It's a leap, all right."

It did sound insane. The world was not being manipulated by a few people with some mystical mojo. She, and everyone else, could do whatever they pleased. *Billions* of people were out there going about their lives however they wanted, their destinies in their own hands.

Right?

A wave of exhaustion hit Maya that seemed to come out of nowhere. She felt as if she were being dragged along the ocean floor in a strong undertow, scraped and beaten. She fell back on the bed and let out a sigh.

Josh wrapped his arm around her. "You OK?" he said.

"Maybe we'd better leave this stuff alone for a bit," she said. "Is that all right?"

"Uh, *yeah*," Josh said, barely able to contain his relief.

Maya nuzzled against him, pressed her cheek into his shoulder, felt the warmth of his skin, which meant she was cold. *Thinking* was cold. What she needed was less theorizing and more Be Here Now. Josh reached over and stroked her hair, the perfect move at the perfect time. It was the last thing she remembered that night.

She awoke in the morning wrapped in his embrace, pleasantly surprised. More than surprised. Shocked. *This is new.* She had not had to creep crept over to the far side of the bed, didn't need to break free of a cozy union in order to feel safe enough to sleep. She'd relaxed fully for once, fell asleep *with* him rather than despite him. She was thrilled.

She brought her face up close to his, near enough to see his eyelashes shiver in the dim light sneaking in under the window shade, close enough to feel his breath tapping against her lips. She grazed her mouth lightly against his.

"Too early," Josh said in a sleepy whisper. Maya smiled and drew back. He reached over and tugged the window shade all the way down. Soon he was snoring.

Maya looked up at the ceiling fan, its dirty blades still turning too slowly to do much more than remind her of their existence. The headache hadn't come, after all.

She was getting what she had asked for. The winds of her life were picking up speed. A gale force was gathering, in fact, that would soon build into a hurricane.

11

Material Things Don't Matter

Maya opened the front door of her house and stared wide-eyed at the remains of the living room, which looked as though it had been visited by a tornado. Muriel's beloved Chelsea sofa was ripped to shreds, its stuffing strewn about the floor like the entrails of a great upholstered beast. Chairs were slashed, tables broken and framed prints pulled from the walls. The TV was a pile of glass, splintered wood and ravaged cables. Even the wall-to-wall carpet had been yanked up in places at the baseboards.

Maya stood there motionless, taking in the disturbing scene. Then, to her surprise, a stillness came over her, and even a sense of serenity. She knew things would be OK, that the threat was well passed and that something good would come out of this, though *what* that could be she could not imagine. She felt she was visiting that moment just after the passing of a storm, when the first rays of sunshine peek through the clouds and all is calm and well.

What had happened? she thought, stepping through the wreckage. Who had done this? At first, Muriel came to mind. Had she finally leaped all the way over the edge, unleashed the full force of her pent-up frustration and anger—*on the house?* It didn't make sense. Muriel's eruptions, which could be volcanic, didn't cause much damage. The worst might be a dinner plate launched against a wall or a few knife-edged words directed at Maya. Any actual destruction was rare.

So where was Muriel? Was she all right? Worriedly, Maya dashed down the hall to her mother's bedroom and found Muriel in bed with her blanket pulled up to her chin. She was staring blankly at the wall. The floor was littered with balled-up tissues. When she saw Maya, she smiled wanly and dabbed at her damp, bloodshot eyes. Maya almost reached out to stroke her hair. Almost.

"Last night—" Muriel sniffed, her words punctuated by sobs. "I was out with Henry. We got home—you saw it—"

"It's awful," Maya said.

"It is," Muriel said.

"What happened? What did they take?"

"I don't know. I can't bear to look. My house, my wonderful house. Sweet Jesus, what am I going to do? What have I got now?"

Maya wanted to say, *You've got me.* But she didn't want to hear her mother's response to that. She said, "Don't think about it, Mom. Just try and get some rest. At least you're OK."

"I'm not," Muriel said.

Maya examined the bedroom, which had gone untouched. Then she realized she hadn't seen her own room. She ran down the hall, terrified of what she might find there.

At her doorway, she froze. Her room had suffered like the living room: total, savage destruction. Her dresser had been yanked and dumped, shelves pulled from the walls, the floor was a mountain of clothes. Everything that defined her—the things, anyway—had been abused mercilessly.

She reached down and started to gather up books, clothes, photos, stereo and computer, but she stopped, feeling suddenly sick to her stomach. She leaned against the wall and slid down it to the floor where she sat hugging her knees. She tried to console herself. It was all just *stuff.* At least no one had been hurt. She wondered if the perpetrators had been looking for something. What did Maya or Muriel have that could have brought this on?

She jumped up and ran to the living room in search of her backpack. The journal! Surely she had brought it with her. She looked everywhere but couldn't find it. Her anxiety shot up sky-high. "Where are you!" she pleaded, fighting back tears, as she ripped through the shreds of the couch and kicked random detritus across the room. Panting, she found herself staring nervously at the front door.

Muriel's voice drifted in from the bedroom. "What's going on out there?"

"Nothing!"

Think.

She had dropped the backpack inside the door when she arrived. Hadn't she?

No.

Idiot! She reached into her pocket for her cell phone, but stopped. Where was Josh? *Think.* He would not be home today. He was working the ten-to-six shift at the store. She did recall that. She dashed back to Muriel's bedroom.

"I've got to go, Mom. I'll see you later."

"Uh-huh," Muriel said as she reached for a glass of water on the nightstand. "You go right ahead, honey."

Five minutes later the front tires of Maya's Civic were bounding up on the curb in front of Josh's house. She turned the car back and crashed it down on the street with a jarring bump that stalled the engine. *Doesn't matter.* She got out and ran for the door.

She was up the stairs in seconds. At Josh's door she plucked the spare key off the top shelf, and with a shaking hand, slid it into the keyhole.

The room was exactly as they had left it: not as wrecked as her own, but not exactly tidy. And there was the journal, sitting right out on the nightstand! She snatched it up and collapsed in a heap on Josh's recliner. "Thank you, God," Maya mumbled to herself.

With the passing of the excitement came an awareness of the outside world, and of her body. The muscles in her legs were quivering. Her back was moist with perspiration. She counted off breaths in fours until she felt herself calming. The neighborhood noises drifted in—cars passing by, the drone of jets overhead, a leaf blower down the street.

She grabbed a can of beer out of Josh's dorm-sized fridge, cracked it open and had a long swallow. She disliked the taste of beer, but the occasion called for something mind-numbing. She plopped back down on the recliner. She would stay in the apartment a while. She had to think. Had someone really wrecked the house in search of the journal? Or was it one of her mother's boyfriends returned for some well-deserved revenge? Maya mentally catalogued all the people she had told about the journal. There was Dr. Porter, Josh, and Fiske. She couldn't remember if she had mentioned it to Mr. Hollywood on the flight to Chicago. What was his name? Peter. Right.

She heard the front door close down on the first floor. Then footsteps coming up the stairs and a shuffling outside of Josh's open door. Maya rushed to shut it but she was too late.

A woman stood in the doorway, small and slender-faced, with spikey blond hair. She stepped inside and walked right up to Maya and extended out her hand. In it was a letter-sized envelope.

"This is for you," the woman said.

Maya took the envelope. "Who are you?" she said.

"A messenger. With a special message. Go ahead, open it."

Obediently, Maya slid a finger under the flap, lifted it up and pulled out a sheet of paper that was in it. On it was a printed a two-column table that ran the length of the page.

Perplexed, Maya looked over at the stranger for help but found herself staring at an empty doorway. The woman was gone. Maya ran over to the window just in time to see the stranger get into a car parked on the street. It pulled away.

Maya examined the page. A long list of icons ran down the left-hand column: a windmill, a car, a house, a face, a gun, a book, the sun. And many others. In the right-hand column, beside each symbol, were city names: Amsterdam, Berlin, Buenos Aires, London, New York, Paris, Sydney, Tokyo …

The last icon, down at the bottom, was a tiny image of a webbed Earth, an outline of the planet covered by a web of lines—exactly what Maya had seen in her vortex vision. Here was yet another unfathomable synchronicity. Another event known only to Maya that was manifested in the physical world. The city name beside the webbed Earth was Los Angeles. What did that mean? Would she have to go there? She tapped her fingertips nervously on the bedpost, feeling adrift, and glanced over to where the mysterious woman had stood just moments ago, as if the physical space she had occupied might present some the needed guidance.

Maybe I'm not alone in this, Maya thought hopefully. It was a random, but comforting, notion. Perhaps there were others in predicaments just like hers, standing baffled in empty rooms, staring at mysterious printouts, knowing that somehow, some way, the explanations would come.

The next weeks were incredible, if not miraculous. After the shock of the break-in had worn off, Muriel's attitude changed in radical ways. The anger and sadness had lasted only a few days. The material losses were few—some old furniture, appliances, carpeting, jewelry and electronics—mostly items she didn't care about or had wanted to replace anyway.

At the height of the tumult, Muriel had availed herself of the support of Henry Rossmore, the same man Maya had heard outside her bedroom door the night she first read Ben Ambrose's journal. Henry was a heavy-set energetic gentleman with salt-and-pepper hair, and a veteran insurance claims adjuster. He had made a few calls on Muriel's behalf, and in record time a sizable reimbursement check was issued to the Burke household for losses suffered in the break-in. All Muriel had to do was figure out how to spend it.

Now that Muriel had regained her footing, she was a changed woman, a believer, even. She told Maya that the ransacking of the house had been a *good* thing. "Out with the old, in with the new!" she would declare with over-the-top cheer. Instead of losing herself in the bar scene or sweating through serial Zumba classes, she would sit at the kitchen table and expound to Maya about destiny and the benefits of hard work. Maya would listen in stunned silence. Muriel even went so far as to say that a higher power had been at work and that the destruction was an act of divine providence.

The most startling phenomenon of all was that Muriel did not seem to be drinking. There was no way for Maya to know for sure, but work seemed to have supplanted booze.

Starting daily at seven a.m.—as Maya would try to sleep with her head sandwiched between two pillows—Muriel could be heard barking orders to the workmen, micromanaging repairs, directing the placement of new furniture and overseeing the painters, and all many the details, with patience and fortitude. She was thriving in the compulsive activity, which was typically accompanied by the drinking of copious amount of Chai tea. And Henry had been spending more and more time at the house. Muriel had even taken to fixing him meals.

Muriel had selected the new furniture for Maya's bedroom, which was just fine with Maya. She knew the room was destined to become a guest room, and soon, though she had no idea how it would happen.

Things changed in late September. It often happened in the fall, when the temperature dropped. Maya did not want the search to be delayed, and she had an idea of what to do to derail the despair that threatened now, and get herself back on track.

She lay in the grass of Canyon Park beneath its tallest beech tree and stared up at the leaves that shivered in a light breeze. The events—or, unfortunately, *non*-events—of the past weeks drifted into her mind. The search for Ben Ambrose had stalled. She had nothing to tell Fiske, even if she had wanted to contact him, which she didn't. And her emails to the Mandala, whose website presented them as "an intentional community situated in the dramatic beauty of northern Wyoming," had brought no replies.

She had tried passing a few afternoons applying for jobs, emailing out her sparse resume and lackluster cover letter, but she had little enthusiasm for it and it showed. Reading over the requirements on the job boards, even for entry-level administrative positions, depressed her even further, and she began to understand the impracticality of a history degree.

Life, it seemed, had taken a turn for the worse. The warning signs of a descent were all there: the mental sluggishness and dulled affect, the lethargy and isolation. At times Maya felt as though she were watching the world through a thick slab of glass. Though a few dark spells had hit since the Crash, she could usually get back on track with a seven-mile run or some good TV or movie watching.

One of her most effective techniques for fighting off depression was Dr. Y's cognitive-therapy writing exercise. But today's attempt would be more sensory, more physical.

Her first task was simple: stare. Star at the leaves fluttering overhead. It was easy to do, for they were alluring, like a crowd of waving hands.

Do nothing else, no matter what.

The resistance manifested within seconds. That was no surprise. Her mind—her tireless, awful wolf—detested such folly. It wanted to do something more interesting than that. It wanted to get up off the grass, get in the car, drive away and find something to *do*. A movie, a café, a walk downtown, perhaps. Wouldn't that be better? Or maybe find a thorny problem and obsess upon it. Worry! Is there not much to be concerned about? If not personally, then certainly out in the greater world, a most troubled place. The last thing her mind wanted to do was watch a bunch of stupid leaves jumping around in a stupid breeze. Do something!

She knew it would go on like this. The wolf would never rest, never slow down and sit in the simple beauty of nature. Already it had latched onto something—a tangible, valid fact, and was communicating it vigorously to her. It was like a voice she could actually hear:

All of your precious leaves at this very moment are desiccating. Losing their color and vitality. Soon they will be hanging on by a thread. They will wither and die. It's that time of year. Have you forgotten?

One day you will die, too.

Everything dies.

All relationships end.

You are alone.

So typical. Maya could feel herself starting to sink. The black cloud began moving toward her, and she felt pulled into it. But she was smarter than it. She knew what to do. A few years ago she would have lost the fight at this point, for she didn't know it *was* a fight. Now she understood the wolf's strategies.

I won't follow, she thought. *I know where that leads.*

She stared hard at those leaves, mustered her resolve and focused every iota of her attention on what was happening in the sensate world. Not just on the leaves, but on the sky and the grass and the feeling of air on skin.

She stuck with it, even as her foe tried to derail her. It wanted to stoke the despair, the drama, the rush, the journey down that old familiar road.

I won't go, Maya thought. *I am in control.*

No—you are not.

I won't engage you. That's how you get your energy.

Give it some time. You'll see.

I'm stronger than you. I'm smarter. You're just a program.

So you think.

The dialog went on like this, the push and pull, the disappearing into mind and pulling out of it, for some time. It was always like this. Her own personal fog of war.

Soon it would happen. She could sense the stirring within her. The shift, the unraveling.

She pressed in her earbuds and clicked through the songs until she had found *Disintegration* by The Cure. It was old but it always worked. She wasn't sure why. She cranked up the volume and allowed herself to dissolve into the droning, consuming melody, where no thought could maintain a foothold.

She listened. She opened to it. She waited. She breathed. It always came on fast. It *wasn't* and then it *was*. She would feel as though she were being blown through a wind tunnel, there would be a fast movement in the release, and then, stillness. Just like after a run. As long as she didn't give in. She had to be vigilant. If she let up even for a moment, she wouldn't succeed.

It began with the faint chattering of voices—disembodied, imploring. Muriel. Josh. Friends. Teachers. Writers. Musicians. Filmmakers. Advertisers. All of them pushing, urging, manipulating, vying for life force, seeking for energy. They wanted her. They wanted her now.

I am not listening.

When she was hovering at the lip of the release like this, she often thought of tragic figures of the past. Van Gogh, Plath and Cobain were favorites. Though Maya did not think of herself as an artist, she felt she could relate to the challenges they faced.

Pass through me.

The voices wailed and beckoned and called for her. She gave herself over to the song. And to the sky and the leaves and the wind.

Stay present.

Music opened the channels through which the poisons could drain out. The natural world absorbed and recycled them.

It was happening now. The voices were losing energy, weakening, faltering, becoming hoarse … and … *gone!*

The vast space opened up and the fetid air whooshed out. Her mind was like a sky. All she could feel was stillness. Deep, unshakable calm.

She lay motionless, lost in that calm. She sat up and took a few deep breaths, tasting the richness of the air, and stared out across the park. The world looked brighter and crisper. She had accomplished something her friends would find puzzling, if they considered it all. She had beaten the wolf; she would have to be satisfied with that knowledge. *Use the mind to beat the mind.*

Traffic sounds floated over from Iris Avenue. Engines, squealing brakes, horns. She saw a maintenance man spiking trash on a pole on the other side of the park. She waved, and he waved back.

On the drive home she didn't turn on the radio, just rolled down the windows and let the wind wash over her. Everything would be fine. Everything *was* fine. Muriel, the house, Josh, the search for her father. If something was going to happen, it would do so in its own time.

That evening, Georgia Roussey called.

12

Body Consciousness

Maya knew the Seneca Lounge & Study Hall in the Towson University Student Union as well as anyone. She had spent hundreds of hours nestled in the beige couches in the enormous high-ceilinged room, studying for exams and writing papers, sometimes making her way over to the tall panoramic windows to stare out at the soccer fields for a change of visual focus. It was strange to be back here without schoolwork to do or classes to worry about.

She was sitting on a couch near the huge faux fireplace that dominated the center of the room, her gaze settling on a guy who was wearing a Hawaiian shirt. He was fast asleep in an easy chair, sitting perfectly erect. He wasn't even *leaning*. Maya chuckled, watching him. College. She wondered if the four years she'd spent here would mean much in a world that was about to undergo cataclysmic change, as some thought.

She hadn't gotten far in her musings when she spotted the sturdy, unmistakable figure of Georgia Roussey striding rapidly toward her through the labyrinth of mismatched furniture and cheap veneer tables. Maya rose, and Georgia came at her in a way that almost made Maya jump out of the way. But all Georgia had in mind was a hug, which she engaged without asking, practically lifting Maya off the ground in arms that were surprisingly strong.

"Hey, nice place you've got here," Georgia said dubiously. Maya and Georgia sat on the sofa.

"You said nearby," Maya said. "I'm just down the road."

"And this will do just fine," Georgia said. "I had business in D.C., so I was just a hop and a skip away. I figured you'd be comfortable on your old stomping grounds."

As Maya looked at Georgia, she recalled Fiske's warnings about the Mandala. *Psychic terrorists* he had said. At this moment she found that hard to believe. The great big bear of a woman beside her seemed about as dangerous as Santa Claus.

But you never knew.

"There's something I've been wanting to ask you," Maya said, eager to settle a question that had been on her mind since Wicklow.

"What's that, dear?"

"In the kitchen that day with Brandon, I saw a—I don't know how to describe it—a *halo* around your head. Brandon said it was really there, that I wasn't seeing things. What was that?"

"Didn't he tell you? That *was* my halo. I'm an angel."

She stared at Maya for a few seconds, then exploded in laughter. "I'm sorry! You left yourself wide open for that one! That was energy you were seeing, Maya. We all glow."

"But I saw it," Maya said.

"No doubt due to a recent experience you had at a certain vortex," Georgia said, her tone now serious.

"Can everyone see them?"

"Oh, no. Not everyone. Only the gifted."

The gifted. Maya liked the sound of that. She liked Georgia. Just being in her presence felt good. And yet, the image of Fiske's face kept flashing in her mind like a warning beacon.

Georgia seemed to know what she was thinking. She said, "You've heard from Albert Fiske, correct?"

"How did you know?"

"Simple. You visited Edgar Porter. Naturally, he would have contacted Mr. Fiske. Ours is a small community. And did Fiske tell you about the Mandala?"

Maya nodded.

"A dark and sinister organization, no doubt," Georgia said. "You're wondering about your father's connection to all this. And why I chose not to mention that we know Ben."

"I am," Maya said.

"All right," Georgia said. "But first things first. Yes, I do know your father. I'm sorry I had to withhold that from you in Wicklow, but we couldn't risk having you pass information on to Fiske. Did you tell him that you paid us a visit?"

"No."

"Really?" Georgia said, surprised. "Why not?"

Maya shrugged. "I didn't want to. It was just a feeling."

"A valid one," Georgia said.

"Why's that?"

"Albert Fiske is no friend of your father's."

"He said the same about you."

"Of course he did," Georgia said.

"What is the Mandala?"

"A way of life, as Brandon told you. A community."

"But that's not all."

"No," Georgia said. Quickly she changed the subject. "What did you think of your Dr. Porter?" she said.

"I liked him," Maya said. "At first. Then I wasn't so sure."

"You're observant, Maya," Georgia said. "Edgar Porter isn't some fuddy-duddy old professor. Far from it. He's an extraordinarily wealthy man with ties to more clandestine organizations and unsavory government officials than you could imagine. He speaks five languages. He owns land—not to mention politicians—in dozens of countries. He is a *very* powerful man. The only reason he has a relationship with Fiske is a common interest: the vortexes. He's a nut on the subject. Otherwise, he wouldn't touch Fiske with a cattle prod. Porter has been acquiring knowledge on the vortexes for years."

"Why?"

"That's the sixty-four-thousand dollar question," Georgia said. "No one knows."

"Why are they looking for Ben?"

"For his talent," Georgia said.

"Remote viewing," Maya said.

"*Active* remote viewing," Georgia corrected. "It's a technique Ben developed when he worked with Fiske. It's different from traditional remote viewing in that you don't just observe, you *do*. You influence—people, events. They experimented for years, even, at times, using psychotropic drugs to enhance Ben's abilities. Under Fiske, your father ventured far out of the box, doing things some would consider highly unethical. With the active viewing, they targeted influential people like business leaders and opinion makers. They manipulated them."

"How?"

"With great skill," Georgia said. "But that's a story for another time. Ben continued on with Fiske purely out of scientific curiosity. That's Ben. He's a trained scientist, but he's got a strong strain of the adventurer in him. He enjoys stretching boundaries. People like that don't always have their feet planted firmly on the ground. Eventually he refused to go on with Fiske's work. They parted ways."

—recently I left a project of great importance—

"It ruined Fiske," Georgia continued. "Ben was the best of the viewers and the only one who could do the active viewing. He was the leader, popular among the others. When he decamped, the team fell apart, decimating Fiske's project. The funding dried up. Humiliated and discredited, Fiske's career sank. It's only recently, after all these years, that he's managed to resurface, and with a vengeance. He's already built credibility in some of the covert agencies."

"Where is Ben?" Maya said.

Georgia's face softened. "I know, Maya. I understand. You want to meet your father. But I have to continue to ask for your patience."

"But you do know."

"I do," Georgia said. "Please, trust me."

Maya wanted to. It just wasn't easy. What seemed likely, though, was that the woman sitting beside her knew where her father was. And Fiske did not.

Maya shifted on the couch, accidentally kicking the table, toppling over a plastic cup filled with water, which spread out on the tabletop. "I'm sorry," she said, embarrassed, reaching for her backpack for a tissue, but Georgia stopped her.

"Never mind that," Georgia said, gently taking Maya's shoulders and turning her to face her. "Listen to me. I, too, can *see*, like a remote viewer can. Like your father can. Like you are beginning to. I can project my mind and receive images. You didn't stumble onto us, Maya. We called you. Porter didn't know that would happen but when it did, he tried to use it."

"Use it?"

Georgia said, "Tell me about your vision. I need to know what they know."

Maya recounted it all: the man she had seen whom she had assumed was Ben Ambrose, the blond girl who was Gathering, the scent of honeysuckle, the mountains, Wicklow, and the webbed Earth. Georgia listened attentively, remaining quiet long after Maya had finished.

Georgia said, "You received the printout, correct?"

"You mean the letter from that woman? That was from you?"

"Yes," Georgia said. "Did anything stand out?"

"The webbed Earth," Maya said.

Georgia smiled, satisfied. "That's very good."

"I don't understand," Maya said.

"That's part of a test we gave you," Georgia said. "We plant symbols in the vortex communications network—the icons on that page. Different ones can be observed at different levels of consciousness. The webbed Earth is seen at one of the deeper levels." Georgia looked intensely at Maya. "I need to ask you something, Maya. Will you help us?"

"Me?" Maya said, surprised. "What can I do?"

Georgia said, "I only need to know that you're willing. If so, I can guarantee you'll meet your father."

"Deal," Maya said quickly. The details didn't matter. Only that it would happen.

"Thank you," Georgia said.

Maya said, "I don't know what's happening to me. All these strange things. I feel lost. Everything's become so unpredictable. I feel so alone."

"You're not," Georgia said softly. "As the world grows more troubled, your keen awareness of it causes you no end of unhappiness. You choose, due to your youth and immaturity, to manifest the events of your life burdened by this handicap. Such thinking creates a loop—negativity reinforcing negativity. It's not your fault, Maya. One day, and soon, you will create more positive events, even on a canvas that appears to be dark."

She continued, "We don't have the luxury of time. We're approaching an opening, an opportunity ... when something truly new can happen in this world."

"Fiske said you want to disrupt society," Maya said. "He said you want to cause a disaster."

"It's true we once thought discord could result," Georgia said. "But now we understand that that stage is not necessary."

"What will you do?" Maya asked.

"What we've wanted to from the beginning," Georgia said. "Elevate the collective mind. Think about it, Maya—a world without war, where cooperation is the rule rather than the exception, where aggressive energy can be channeled into exploration, building and healthy competition rather than divisiveness and destruction. As a race we are capable of so much more than what we see! Let's do something about it, eh? Let's create a new destiny. I'm talking about the experiment that's never been tried. We're so close now."

Maya wondered how the Mandala might pull off such a feat. Even more, she wanted to know her father's role in it and why no one would talk about it. Where was he?

But before she could press Georgia again, there was an interruption. A towering, muscular man with a shaved head and a massive chest bulging under an untucked T-shirt filled Maya's field of vision, blocking the view of a sizable portion of the room. Georgia waved for him to wait, then turned back to Maya. She took both of Maya's hands. "You want to be a part of this?"

"More than anything," Maya said.

"And you shall," Georgia said. With that, she stood up, said goodbye and glided away with the muscular man at her side, leaving a confounded Maya to watch their exit from the end of the couch.

Air was necessary—cool, fresh air blowing in through four wide-open car windows.

Maya drove home on the back roads instead of the Beltway to revel in that air. Old Court Road wound through a rural, verdant part of the county and into Glendale, a small burg of a few hundred country people situated halfway between the university and Plainfield. Maya had always loved this drive, stealing glimpses at the fast-flowing stream that followed the road, passing beneath the small bridges only to reappear on the other side, back and forth, mile after mile, like a snake shadowing the car beneath the black tar surface.

She passed by Glendale's lone gas station, a still-operating relic a half-century old with red and white fuel pumps, small and rounded in the style of the period. A sign in the station window read, FRIENDLY SERVICE.

She drove past Norma's Kitchen, its large windows lit in the sunshine, shielding the restaurant from view where Maya had spent afternoons huddled in a corner booth, bleary-eyed from studying through the night, sipping coffee from Norma's "famous" bottomless cup and occasionally bolstering her energy with a slice of apple pie or a chocolate cake doughnut. Glendale was a deeply quiet place, the entire town a stretch of thirty sturdy old houses. An abandoned log cabin stood at one end, its windows shuttered up for as long as Maya could remember.

She approached the town's lone traffic signal at a reasonable twenty-five miles per hour when a sense of foreboding came over her. She squeezed the steering wheel tightly, suddenly frightened, certain something horrible was about to happen.

Stop.

The word gave her a start for she didn't know where it had come from. Had she heard that? Thought it? Whichever it was didn't make sense, for the traffic signal up ahead showed green. No vehicles were in sight.

She felt something unnerving happening: her right leg rising up off the gas pedal. *That isn't me*, she thought. Yet was happening—of its own accord. She feared to look down as the foot slid a few inches to the left and hovered over the brake. When the Civic had reached the intersection, the rogue foot stomped down on the brake.

The car's tires locked and began a skid. Maya's body shot forward, stopped suddenly by the seatbelt going taut. She slammed back into the seat.

The car was now still, just shy of the intersection, as if … puzzled. Maya's breathing came in rapid-fire gasps, her eyes opened wide in alarm. Here was another crazy event. The world—her world—had become bizarre, eerie and unpredictable.

She heard the distant sound of an engine, which grew louder until it had become a deafening roar. Maya looked up just in time to see a metallic flash blaze through the intersection, inches in front of the Civic's front bumper, sucking the air out from around the car and leaving it rocking as if in a high wind.

A *crunch* pierced the air, like a bomb exploding over peaceful Glendale. Maya turned to look, dreading what she might see.

It was a pickup truck, smashed head-on into a telephone pole and accordioned into a heap which now stood eerily still, the pole sticking up out of its crumpled engine like a stake. Its wobbling rear fender slowly came to rest.

The whole world was still. Then, slowly, the people of Glendale started to stream into the street, some running to the truck and its driver, others standing back with fearful looks on their faces.

Maya did not know what to do. But she found she could control her foot again. *Go!* Carefully she shifted it over to the accelerator, held her breath and pressed down softly.

She didn't turn to look at the wreck or try to see if the townspeople had noticed her there in the intersection. She stared straight ahead, kept her hands on the wheel, and pressed down harder on the accelerator. The car crept forward.

It gained speed, arriving at the edge of town, and then beyond, and Glendale passed from view. Ten minutes later Maya pulled into the driveway at home.

In her room, she ripped off her clothes and bolted for the shower and stood rocking under the hot spray, allowing it to massage her neck and back, sore now after the hard stop.

When she was done, she put on jeans and a sweater and walked out to the back patio with the journal in hand, and spread out on a lounge chair. She could see Muriel through the kitchen window, wrestling with a stir-fry, shaking the wok, tossing the vegetables and leaning out of the way of the shooting steam. Maya had passed by Henry on the living room, ensconced in the new curved sectional sofa, watching a football game on the even newer TV that filled a good portion of the wall.

Maya considered what had just happened. Somehow she had known of the truck's arrival in advance. How? It was impossible.

She went over and over it in her mind: if she had continued on through the intersection, the speeding truck would have crushed the Civic, and her with it. She had not been in control of her foot. A passage in the journal came to mind.

> Many layers of consciousness exist in the human psyche, from those that control the higher thinking processes on down to the lesser ones that maintain the body's functioning. This latter type, called body consciousness, controls the autonomic activities of circulation, respiration, digestion and other essential processes.
>
> Don't underestimate it. Don't demean it. Every cell possesses intelligence. Body consciousness can even act of its own accord, circumventing the higher functions of the mind, to save someone from danger, for example.

Years ago, when Uncle Buddy was staying at the house, he had almost been run down by a car speeding on McDonough Road. He had leaped out of the way at the last possible instant.

Maya, who was sitting on the front stoop, had seen the whole thing.

When she asked him how he had managed to get clear of the car so quickly, since he hadn't really been watching for traffic, he offered a response that didn't make sense, at least not then.

"I didn't get out of the way," he said.

Huh?

"It just ... happened," he said, which didn't help much.

He kept on insisting that *he* hadn't done it. One second he was in the street, and the next he was leaping lightning fast out of it. But it wasn't *him*?

Maybe now she understood. The initiator of his life-saving leap wasn't a who but a what—the body's innate intelligence, which could wrest control from the mind and propel a person to do something the mind wasn't even aware of.

Buddy had said the life-saving force wasn't him. But it *was* him. It just wasn't a part of him he was aware of.

Perhaps, Maya thought, her body, too, had sensed the approaching danger, shoved her mind out of the way and stomped on the brake. Body consciousness, then, had saved her, too.

It was a theory, anyway. If Buddy had been there on the patio with her, he might have asked for odds. "How sure are you?" he would have said. Maya smiled, recalling the way he always used gambling terms.

"I'd give it a ninety percent probability," she would have told him.

"Why not a hundred, if you're so sure?"

"Because I'm not," she thought. That would imply absolute certainty, which is impossible—at least where human knowledge is concerned. Again, a passage in the journal spoke to the moment.

> The truth seeker must revise his beliefs
> mercilessly over time, incorporating new truths
> as they emerge and letting go of old ones that no
> longer serve. Grasping a truth too tightly makes

you a slave to it. Without knowing it, you will
alter your perceptions to conform to it. Release
old truths as you outgrow them, just as you
have let go of the belief in Peter Pan and the
Land of Oz.

Maya opened the sliding glass door and went inside and sat
down to dinner with her mother and Henry. Muriel's fry was
surprisingly good, and Maya had to stop herself from piling on
a third helping. Amazed at her mother's changes, she thanked
her and excused herself. There was much to do to prepare for
the next day when she would try to discover the truth about
Albert Fiske.

13

Deep In

T he plan was ill-conceived and scant on details, but sometimes improvisational and open-ended could morph, or veer, into useful and enlightening. Other times it just meandered into crazy.

Maya peeked out from behind a wide concrete pillar and watched Albert Fiske step through the doorway of his office building near Independence Avenue. He stopped on the sidewalk and buttoned up his overcoat against the cool evening air. Watching him, Maya felt equal parts trepidation and excitement. She had been standing in place for nearly two hours and was eager to start walking, if only to generate some body heat. *Where* she was going she had no idea.

Fiske flowed easily into the rush-hour crowd that moved in a controlled march toward the Metro station on the next block. He was short of stature, so Maya had to frequently lean this way or that, or tiptoe and crane up her head to catch a glimpse of him among the throngs hurrying for the station entrance. After a day of work in the city, these people were on a mission: to get home.

Spy on the spy. The notion had appealed to Maya the previous night, but now she wasn't so sure. On the drive into D.C., she had considered U-turning for home, but she was glad she ignored the urge, for that would have meant quashing the most excellent buzz she was feeling, the thrill of doing something totally out of the box and titillating.

Focus.

Carried along in the crowd's peristaltic embrace, Fiske approached the escalator leading down to the underground station, as Maya looked on from a few feet back. He stepped onto the stairs, rode down, and at the bottom, turned right and pushed through the turnstile for the Virginia-bound side. Then he was gone from view.

When Maya reached the turnstile the line slowed and then halted when a man could not figure out how to slide his card into the slot. It was so simple, and yet it wasn't happening. Maya leaned into the back of the woman in front of her, struggling to keep an eye on the corner Fiske had rounded. Finally the man got his card in, and the line advanced.

Pushing through the turnstile arm, Maya hurriedly made her way to the Virginia platform where she saw Fiske leaning against a railing, reading a newspaper. Relieved, she stood back and out of view.

Relaxed for a moment, she observed the teeming crowds. Each person was immersed in his or her own world. Most of them looked tired or impatient. All were eying the train tracks, and a minute later when the approach lights flashed and a train pulled in and hissed to a stop, they gathered in groups eying the doors with the hungry purpose of animals collected at a feeder. When the doors slid open, they created a narrow lane for riders to exit. But few got off.

The waiting tide poured in, carrying Fiske along like a piece of driftwood. Maya hesitated, not knowing where to go. She decided to get in the next car back, and walked up to the front where she could watch her quarry through the forward windows.

The train started off. Soundlessly it sped across Washington. Fiske didn't budge from his seat nor look up from his newspaper. The stops came and went: Federal Triangle, Metro Center, McPherson Square, Farragut West, Foggy Bottom. Nearing Arlington, the first stop in Virginia, Fiske dropped his newspaper onto an empty seat and reached for a hand rail, his face strobe-lit by the tunnel lights flickering through the window. Handsome, yes, Maya thought, followed by *ignore it.*

Fiske got out at Arlington. Maya followed him onto the platform, keeping safely back as he walked along with the crowds up the long escalator and out into the street.

Arlington at night—a few square blocks of tall office buildings cut by a grid of streets. Across the Potomac River, the lights of Georgetown glowed brightly.

Fiske made his way to a street corner, while Maya, fearing being seen, turned to face a newsstand she was passing. The proprietor, a bearded Middle Eastern man, was pulling down his awning for the night. He smiled and began to say something, but Maya turned away, seeing that once again Fiske had escaped from sight.

She bolted down the block on a dead run as the newsstand man yelled out to her, his words falling unheard into the night. She arrived at the next corner out of breath and saw Fiske approach the front door of a church. He went inside.

Maya paused and took stock of herself. Her body was jumpy with energy, her mind hyper-alert. *Think.* Keep going? Turn and retreat? Fiske had arrived at his destination, a place she could not have come upon by chance. She wondered what would happen if he saw her.

She didn't care. It was all about the rush now, the thrill. The experience was too exhilarating to abandon. Whatever happened, she would find a way to deal with it. She bounded up the steps of the church and pulled open the door.

A brightly lit foyer. And an open doorway leading into a large meeting room. A sign on an easel read, PARENTS WITHOUT PARTNERS. Maya heard the sounds of a crowd inside.

Idiot!

Fiske was simply a dad in search of a date! In a deflating instant, Maya's high dissolved into an agonizing low. Standing against a wall she fumed at herself for engaging in such folly.

Down the hall, a door swung open—the men's room—and a short, solidly built man stepped out, smoothing his hair back.

Fiske.

Maya winced.

She was flush against the wall and out of sight. He hadn't seen her. He turned and walked down a long hallway as Maya leaned forward, watching him go all the way to the end where he turned a corner.

Her near humiliation now a memory, she hurried after him, arriving at the end of the hallway. *Why am I doing this?* Maya didn't know. She didn't know what she would gain if she caught up, what she would see. She peeked around the corner. No Fiske. There was a doorway leading into a classroom where child-sized wooden desks were lit by shafts of light coming through the blinds from the parking lot. A door at the far end of the room was ajar.

Where was Fiske?

Maya stepped into the room and walked to the doorway.

Another hallway.

She entered it. The overhead fluorescents were dim and the air dank, and she fought the urge to sneeze, clamping her fingers down over her nose and holding her breath until the feeling passed. Inching forward, she came to a set of double doors bisected by a slot of light. She heard voices coming from the other side.

She moved in closer. Her heart was racing. She tried to peek through the slot but it was too narrow. She pressed her ear up to it lightly, straining to hear. The voices were thin, tinny. She realized she wasn't hearing a live conversation but a recording.

She recognized the voices.

Georgia: "They're intercepting our communications. I'm certain of it."

Brandon: "Have you been able to raise Ben?"

Georgia: "No. Not yet."

Brandon: "What do you want to do?"

Georgia: "Go to Plan B."

Brandon (intensely): "Seriously?"

Maya pressed her ear flush against the slot, desperate to hear more. The doors moved. The catch hadn't been clicked in place and they inched open, then swung all the way out and Maya stood, squinting, in a bright light. Slowly a room came into view: table, chairs, cement floor, small window up on the wall, and

Albert Fiske standing directly in front of her. There was a table beside him with a digital recorder on it. He grabbed it and clicked it off.

"Well, well," he said casually. "Nice of you to stop by, Maya."

He held up the recorder. "Recognize anything?" he said, watching her expectantly.

Mortified, Maya could barely look at him. Slowly, she shook her head.

He smiled. "Do you get to Arlington much, Maya?"

"Boy, is this embarrassing," she said.

"You get an 'A' for effort," he said, giving her a piercing look that made her wilt.

"You could have said something," she said weakly.

"Where? On the street? On the train? At my building?"

"All of them."

Should have taken that U-turn, Maya thought.

"So," she said. "Am I in trouble?"

"That depends."

"On what?"

"On whether you'll let me buy you a drink before I send you packing. It's been a long day. I could use the company. Hey, what exactly did you think you gain by following me? I mean, why not just give me a call?"

"I don't know," she said honestly.

She considered his offer. He seemed safe enough in his suit and tie and penny loafers—a Washington bureaucrat on his way home from work. But then, he wasn't that at all.

"There's a place near here," he said.

"Sure," she said.

The Lookout was a gloomy tavern with wood paneled walls and rough-looking men sitting shoulder to shoulder at a long bar alongside military types and office workers. Maya could see no windows anywhere, though the bar was certainly above ground. Country music blared from a jukebox against a wall under a row of dartboards. It seemed impossible that such a place could be in Arlington, but here it was.

Fiske pointed to a table toward the back and they sat down. A waitress drifted over.

"Sam Adams," Fiske said.

"I'll have a glass of Merlot," Maya said.

Fiske sat back and smiled at Maya. "So, how are you, kid?" he said.

"Embarrassed," she said.

"Oh, don't sweat that. Like I said, I was impressed."

"By what?"

"You didn't quit," he said. "That's worth something."

Maya wasn't sure how to ease into what was on her mind, so she decided to dive right in. "Actually," she said, "I did almost call you."

"You've got something for me?" he said, leaning forward.

"Someone broke into our house," she said. "They wrecked the place pretty bad."

"Sorry to hear that," Fiske said. "What happened?"

Maya glanced uneasily at him. She was out of her depth and she knew it. Still, she wanted to try to get a few answers.

"They were looking for something," she said.

"Like what?"

"I don't know," she said.

"What did the police say?"

"They're investigating."

The waitress returned and set down their drinks. Fiske fingered the frosted mug, then lifted it and drank half the beer in a single swallow.

Maya said, "I thought you might know something."

"Why would I know about that?"

"Maybe it was the Mandala."

"You don't know about them, remember?"

"They obviously know about me."

Fiske had another long drink, nearly emptying the mug. He said, "I can't imagine what they'd gain by doing something like that. Scaring you isn't going to get them what they want."

"And what's that?" Maya said.

He eyed her, said nothing.

"Maybe it was you," Maya said, watching for his reaction.

A menacing look came over Fiske. Then, in a flash it was gone. Maya wasn't sure she had even seen it. She looked down at the wine glass and picked it up by the stem, sipped, and immediately felt lightheaded. She had some more.

"Sorry," Maya said.

"That's OK," Fiske said. "You get one pass. What did you think of that recording?"

"Who was it?" she asked.

"No guesses, eh?"

"I heard *Ben*."

Fiske gave a thin smile. "Nothing else stir your memory?"

"It was the Mandala, right?" she said. "You're recording them."

"That's right."

"You can do that?"

"Routine surveillance," he said. "Homeland security."

"That's for terrorists."

"Exactly," Fiske said pointedly.

Maya had more wine. There could be no better drink right then. She said, softly, "Can I ask you something?"

"Hang on," Fiske said as he waved down the waitress to order another beer. He turned to Maya "Do you want to ask me if it's OK to tell me what you know? If so, yes, that would be good."

Maya said, "I wanted to know where Ben went after he worked for you."

"He moved on," Fiske said. "He didn't say where."

"I thought you two were close."

"He went overseas, something like that. Asia, maybe."

A weary look came over Fiske. He smiled wanly. "You know, you remind me of someone," he said.

The waitress set down his second beer. She was a tall woman with thick eye liner and a languid way of moving. She looked at Fiske for a long moment before walking off.

"Don't take this the wrong way," Fiske said. "My brother. I'm just talking personality here. You're a lot prettier than Arnie." He paused. "Like you, Arnie was a lousy liar. It got him in a lot of trouble. Didn't matter to me. I had a soft spot for him. Do you want to know why?"

Maya tensed up, watching Fiske stare at her.

"Why?" she said.

"Because I liked him," Fiske said. "I like you, too."

Maya didn't know what to make of that. She twirled the stem of the glass, lifted it and drank more.

Fiske's look became hard. "Clueless, the both of you. But endearing. Clueless and endearing, that's the combo." He shook his head, angry at himself. "I didn't mean that. That's out of line. I'm sorry. It's been a long day. Sometimes I just speak my mind."

"What happened to Arnie?" Maya said.

"He's gone. He fell off an oil rig. Maybe he jumped. Who the hell knows."

"I'm sorry."

"Sure," he said. "Ancient history."

"Is it?"

"What do you mean?"

"Love," she said. "The love of a brother."

Fiske said, "I don't follow."

She flushed. "Never mind," she said. "I'm meddling. I have a habit of doing that. All I need is one sip of this."

"It's fine. Go on," he said, interested.

"Maybe you express your love for him by protecting others."

"How's that?" Fiske said.

"You protect people from harm. The work you're doing."

"That's very creative, Maya." Fiske's look became grave, his voice serious. He said, "Have you ever seen what happens in a war? A real one?"

Maya locked eyes with him. *Look at me*, she thought. *What do you think?* But she just shook her head no.

"Right—what can you possibly know about that," he said. "I was in Kosovo, Somalia, Iraq. I've seen crazy things happen on a scale that would knock your socks off. Riots, looting, rape, murder. When things go to hell, the scary people come out of the woodwork. Nice innocent girls get—well, it ain't pretty. Which is exactly what's going to happen if the people—those people you say I care so much about—aren't protected from your friends in Wyoming."

He leaned forward, put both arms on the table. "Like most dangerous people, the Mandala aren't evil. They're just misdirected. *Hitler* was an idealist. He thought he was doing the world a favor, killing the Jews, cleaning things up. The worst crimes are perpetrated with the best of intentions."

Maya stared at Fiske, feeling fear and revulsion. Things weren't going well. "What do you want from me?" she said.

"Just the truth," he said. "Stop playing games, Maya. What did Georgia Roussey tell you?"

"Who?"

"You're a lousy liar, kid. Who do you think you're dealing with here?"

In a quick motion, Fiske reached over the table and grabbed both of Maya's hands. She tried but couldn't budge from his grip. He started to squeeze.

"What are you doing?" she said with alarm.

"Why are you protecting them?"

"Let go of me!"

He squeezed tighter, mashing her fingers together. Nails dug into tender flesh. Across the room the jukebox blasted "Sweet Home Alabama."

"Stop it!" Maya said. "I'm going to scream!"

"What happened in Wicklow?" Fiske said.

Her gaze shot around the unfriendly surroundings. Now, even more men lined the bar, talking in whispers.

"Please, let me go!"

"Tell me what happened in Wicklow."

"You're hurting me!"

"Surely you remember. You were there."

"All right!" she said.

He loosened his grip.

"Nothing happened," she said.

"What did Georgia tell you?"

Panting with fear, she said, "I don't know. She didn't tell me anything."

His grip tightened.

"She talked about their experiment in democracy! I don't know what you want from me. Let me go!"

"Where is he? Where is Ben?"

"You think I'd be here if I knew that?" she rasped.

"What about Brandon McGowan?"

The grip tightened.

"I met him!"

"And?"

"He told me about the commune, if that's what it is. Why are you doing this? You're crazy!"

He released her. She yanked away her hands and fell back into the chair, massaging her aching fingers. She wiped her arm across her face, which was damp with perspiration, and stared hatefully at Fiske, watching her calmly from across the table.

His face softened in a practiced way. "I'm sorry, Maya. You have no idea how important this is," he said.

She stood up and almost fell down. She grabbed onto the edge of the table to steady herself.

"Know this," Fiske said, staring up at her. "They will deceive you. They will tell you what you want to hear. They will offer you your father, but you will never see him. Join them and you'll be caught in their net. You won't be able to escape it. You're in over your head, Maya. You need an ally. You can't possibly understand my urgency. Please, think about what's at stake. There's still time to do the right thing."

"Go to hell," Maya said and bolted for the door.

She sprinted for the Metro station on a dead run. The train ride to Rockville was spent in deep terror. As she pulled her car out of the parking lot, she wondered how much Fiske really did know. Did he know about the trip she was about to take, the one Georgia had said would be impossible to track? The one that would lead directly to her father?

14

The Message of the Trees

Rain pounded on the porch awning on the cold, gray morning, spilling in wide sheets onto the front lawn, which was to starting to resemble a marsh. Out by the street, the sidewalk was gone from view, submerged in puddles. The rain had been falling steadily since midnight—which was just fine with Maya, sitting on a plastic chair under the protection of the awning, spellbound by the nonstop and hypnotic pattering from up above. There was a comfort in unswerving uniformity.

She recalled the last downpour she'd been in: her short time with Brandon. How long ago it seemed. Now she was preparing for another journey. She mused for a moment that the rain had become an omen of transition for her. *A good downpour means I'm about to change.* She laughed at the notion. As if she were the precious heart of creation.

Today, the rain seemed to be a unifier, bringing together the disparate parts of the natural world, illuminating their common ground: water is the blood of all life on planet Earth, the glue of every ecosystem. Within the rain hides the promise of a new day for every creature, from the tiniest microbe to the most mammoth African bull elephant.

Maya zipped up her coat against the misty wind swirling up onto the porch. She felt at peace. *Weather.* It was a *good* thing.

Clouds and wind and rain may have been a problem for some, but not for her. If you didn't fight them, if you fully accepted them, they could totally relax you, lull your mind into a receptive and fertile state from which ideas and solutions could spring. One had only to let it happen.

She stared at the soggy grass at the base of one of the trees, imagining the vast networks of roots beneath the ground, snaking tendrils pulling moisture high up to branches and leaves through processes perfected over eons. It was a miracle, plain and simple. Anyone who didn't see that was not seeing clearly.

Beloved old souls, the trees. If they were people, they would be sought for counsel. The great woody perennials: tempered, dependable, steady. They watch, Maya thought, as we humans race madly on our treadmills. Where are we going? Why must we go so fast?

Perhaps, she considered, it is to blur the evidence of our eyes, the suspicion that we are actors in a drama that may hold no meaning, or may possess meaning we cannot fathom. We don't know where it will go from one moment to the next, or why.

Do the trees know this of us? Maybe. Their knowledge, after all, is far older than ours. Perhaps it is clearer, truer. They are wise, which is why they remain silent, like parents who smile knowingly at the antics of small children, withholding explanations that are too complicated for them.

But they watch, the trees. Of that Maya felt certain.

Someone had once told her that during the rain we can glimpse this, if we are quiet, if we allow ourselves to slow down to the speed of the trees. How? By sitting, by waiting. By allowing the mind to leave us and enter into the natural world. The rain's hypnosis, like the dance of a fire or the song of the surf, seeps into the psyche, a warm salve. During these times, we can come forward if we choose.

A car out on the street sped by, its tires spinning up water, its headlights distorted in the mist. *I am reaching out to it,* Maya thought. She let her mind relax, and yes, it did seem to reach out, even to something human-made.

She unfolded the Sunday newspaper on her lap and glanced at the headlines, breaking the spell of the rain and the trees, supplanting it with thoughts of industry and people and want. She sighed, mourning her error. The wall was restored, the magic yielding to the all-too-human message, that *we* are the rulers, and you who cannot stop us, are the vanquished. Then she thought, *No. I won't go there.*

She refolded the paper and dropped it onto the cement patio where it immediately soaked through—punishment for what it represented. Maya smiled with satisfaction.

Just then the front door swung open and Muriel leaned out, her face scrunched up in revulsion. "Nice day, huh?" she said.

Maya groaned. *No surprise there.* Here was a perfectly decent rainstorm, getting unjustly criticized.

"Well, I like it," Maya said.

"You would," Muriel said. "You're touched, Maya, always have been."

Maya glanced at her mother. She was holding the door open, as if equal parts of her wanted to step outside and retreat back into the house. Maya decided to do something she hadn't tried in a long time: solicit Muriel's opinion.

"Whatever do you mean, Mother?" she said, and braced herself for the response.

"About what?" Muriel said, stepping outside. The door slammed shut behind her. Muriel was wearing her bathrobe, which she pulled tightly around her.

"What you just said, about me being touched."

"You mean you haven't noticed?"

"I was wondering where it comes from."

"From your father, of course," Muriel said. "You probably figured that out by now."

Maya stared dumbfounded at her mother, feeling as if her body's thermostat had been cranked up to high heat. Despite the chilly air, she started to perspire.

"We weren't married," Muriel said, shocking Maya further, and shuffled her slippered feet to the edge of the patio, stopping just short of the sheet of rainwater pouring down from the awning. "You knew that, right?"

Of course not, Maya thought. *I know nothing.*

"Yeah, I guess so," she said.

An hour—or a year—seemed to pass before Muriel spoke again. She said, "You do want to know about him?"

"Uh-huh," Maya said.

"He worked over in Washington," Muriel said. "He came to the university here to meet with some of the professors. He gave talks. I was a secretary."

"What department?"

"Philosophy," Muriel said. "Imagine that."

Muriel lifted up her hand and pointed a finger right into the waterfall-like cascade in front of her, watching the runoff engulf it before splashing down to the patio.

"We jumped into something maybe we shouldn't have," Muriel said. "We both knew it."

Maya stared at her mother, watched her pull the wet finger back and wipe it on the sleeve of her robe.

Muriel said, "I guess I've been blaming him all these years when it was just as much my fault as his. Maybe you can change old ingrained feelings like that, I don't know. It's kind of like trying to turn a huge old ocean liner that's going full steam ahead. You see the iceberg coming at you, but you've got so much momentum going there's no way to get the damned ship out of the way. You're just ... stuck. So you just watch it hit."

Maya took that in, or tried to. She was frozen on the chair. The muscles in her throat were as tight as piano wire. She was afraid to breathe for fear she'd split apart. She watched her mother continue to reach her finger out into the waterfall and pull it back, again and again, each time holding her wet hand up to her face and staring at it as if she'd never seen a wet hand before. Maybe she was checking to see if the rain had washed the past off it.

"I know what you think of Henry," Muriel said.

"I like him," Maya said. It was true. Henry may have been a straight-arrow business guy, but if he made Muriel happy, it was fine by her. *Let's talk about my father*, Maya thought impatiently.

"Oh, is that right?" Muriel said.

"Yes, it is," Maya insisted.

"Hmm."

Muriel finally turned around to face her daughter. Her eyes were misty. "Not everything's my fault, Maya. Some of it is this—this—all right, I'll say the damned thing. This *illness*. You know what I'm talking about."

Confused, Maya said nothing.

"The drinking," Muriel said.

Maya wanted to acknowledge that but no words came. Instead, she tried to transmit thought waves of acceptance and love at her mother, if such things existed.

"Anyway," Muriel said, "after you came along we split up, if we were together at all. He went right, I went left. End of story. And no, I don't know where he went. I bet you're looking for some kind of fireworks. I'm sorry to say there wasn't much of that."

"Did he ever talk about his work?" May asked.

Muriel shrugged. "He worked in Washington, like I said."

"Doing what?"

Muriel held out her hand in a gesture of *enough*. A shadow of pain crossed her face. "I don't know, Maya. He was a scientist. We didn't get into every last detail about it."

"Did you love him?" Maya pushed.

Muriel stared long and hard at her daughter. Maya shrank back. Then Muriel's eyes softened. "Yes and no," she said, pulling at her wild, uncombed hair. "I wanted to. He wanted to. That was the problem. You can't *want* to love. No amount of wanting will make it happen." She paused, thinking. "I'm not sure he *could* love. He loved ideas, theories, abstract things. Me, I was a person, flesh and blood. He used to call me a human doing instead of a human being because of how I'm always on the run and such." She smiled wanly. "Oh, hell, I don't know, the past is past. You can't go around second-guessing everything you've ever done. That'll drive you straight into the loony bin."

She turned to leave. Maya sensed the incredible opening about to close. Muriel was reaching for the doorknob when Maya asked, "Do you ever want to see him again?"

Turning around, Muriel said, "A lot of water's flowed under that bridge, Maya. If he manages to surface, I guess I'll know what to do. Until then I'll just try to steer this old ship out of the way of trouble the best I can."

She smiled a kind of odd smile that seemed burdened by regret, or conscience, and squinted out at the storm. "I'll tell you one thing," she said, taking hold of the doorknob. "This damned humidity is just about making my hair stand on end."

As the door swung open, a loud groan erupted from the overhead awning, followed by a sharp *snap* as a support pole broke loose, overwhelmed by the weight of the rainwater that had collected above it. The released tension cracked the pole in half. The awning ripped loudly, sagging all the way down to the patio, pouring rainwater everywhere. The loose pole rolled into the grass. Muriel dashed inside the house.

"Look at that, the world's falling apart," she said, and shut the door.

Maya's chair was under the protection of the small section of awning still intact. Sitting there, she considered all she'd heard, allowing it to settle in her mind, as the storm grew louder.

An idea came to her. It was not rational in the least, but somehow that only made it more compelling. This is what she did: she stood up and walked over to the front of the patio where her face nearly touched the clear plane of water that had so hypnotized her mother. Grinning, she felt strangely, inexplicably energized. Was it because Muriel had finally opened up a crack? Probably, Maya thought. Just like Muriel had, Maya reached out a finger and watched the rain close around it, then turned her palm up, extending her fingers out to let the water wet her sleeve. Instinctively, she pulled back. That was her reflex—to pull away at the first sign of discomfort.

No more, she thought decisively. Instead of thinking or analyzing—for reason could be an enemy of action—she did something that was most assuredly and wonderfully illogical. She didn't know exactly why she did it, but she reached down and untied the laces of her boots and kicked them out onto the grass, almost to the sidewalk. She laughed at the brazen foolishness of that. Then off came her socks, which she tossed away, too. She took off her coat as well, flinging it to the back of the porch.

Laughing, she jumped out into the marshy grass, half-dressed—right into the arms of the downpour. The cold rain hit her hard. *But so what?* It soaked her hair and her sweatshirt and jeans. She dug her toes into the soggy turf and raised her arms up above her head. She saw Muriel watching her through the window, shaking her head with incomprehension. Maya grinned and waved. Then she extended her arms out and twirled and pirouetted in the rain and the mud as if in a primal dance, whipping her water-logged hair around and around and grinning like a mad woman. Maybe it was a rebellion against the routine, a rejection of the ordinary, using what was at hand. Perhaps it was preparation for what was to come. Maybe it was just an assertion of some needed unpredictability.

Joyfulness charged through her, and for a moment—for a tiny sliver of time—she broke free of the rut she'd been stuck in for so long, liberated herself from the dull predictability of a conditioned life she had adopted too easily and uncritically, and struck out against—what? She had no idea. Nor, at that instant, did she care. That moment, that insane moment, was *perfect*. Wrapped in the rain's embrace, she felt completely free.

15

Prelude

As Maya stared out the window on the Los Angeles-bound flight at the sparse cloud cover and the verdant land far beyond it, she tried to summon a memory that related to her father. There had to be something in her brain somewhere.

A recollection did come to her. She had been six at the time, an industrious youngster building castles out of Legos on the back patio, pausing every so often to gaze in wonder at the cigarette smoke rings her mother was sailing over her head from a lawn chair a few feet away.

"Where's my daddy?" Maya asked suddenly, looking up at Muriel.

Muriel straightened up and stared at Maya through her oversized sunglasses. She said that late one night long ago a magical airplane had touched down in the fields and picked up Maya's daddy and took him to a distant land of kings, knights and princesses. "It was a shame you missed it, Tater Tot," Muriel said. "But you were asleep, and sleeping children miss all sorts of neat things."

"When is he coming back?" the little girl asked.

"Never, probably," Muriel replied, puffing on her cigarette.

"Why not?"

"He's … busy," Muriel said, stomping out the spent cigarette on the patio, adding another ash burn to a surface that was already thoroughly speckled with black smudges. "What are you building there, Tater Tot?"

"It's a castle. Where's my daddy?" Maya insisted.

"He's gone and I'm glad of it!" Muriel snapped. "Just forget about it, OK? Forget I said anything. Go back to that house, or whatever that is. It looks like it needs a hell of a lot of work, if you ask me." She got up and left.

For weeks, the little girl wrenched her head up at the passing jets, squinting, waving, hoping to connect with her daddy. But not a single plane came anywhere near the fields, and she gave up, as the first seeds of futility took root within her.

Maya had spent much of her early life facing inward. Without a sibling, she was often alone. In middle school, shame had hounded her, for Muriel had often been the talk of the neighborhood with her boisterous parties and hard-drinking friends. Single-parent families were uncommon in those days in the conservative, former farming community of Plainfield. At fourteen, Maya had checked out of a relationship with Muriel, mostly. She became a renegade. She didn't care what people thought of her, and went out of her way to do the opposite of what was expected of her. For a time, she tried to imitate boys, dressing in baggy pants, buzz-cutting her hair, reading science fiction and comic books, even attempting, unsuccessfully, to join a boys' soccer team. To her amazement, her strategy had actually resulted in a brief period of high school *popularity*. It didn't last long.

In tenth grade, she discovered novels and obscure arthouse films, and her world opened up, and she began to fall secretly for the nerdy subjects of science and history. Socially, she was largely ignored and didn't much mind it. Her friendships were limited to the neighborhood kids she'd known her whole life. She was fine hanging out in her room or at the library, doing what she did best—being a bookworm and a decent track athlete who didn't do much with the fact that she was kind of pretty.

The cabin pitched in some turbulence, and Maya released her hold on the past for a white-knuckled grip on the armrest.

The sky outside was completely clear now, presenting an unobstructed view of the forests, farms and rivers of Maryland. Maya whispered farewell to all of it, her words swallowed up by the roar of the engines.

Lugging her backpack over her shoulder, Maya walked toward the baggage claim area of Los Angeles International Airport in search of her contact person. The terminal was so crowded she wondered how the connection would be made.

A woman did approach, and when Maya saw who it was, she could not hide her look of surprise. The mysterious spikey-haired messenger who had handed Maya the envelope in Josh's apartment now extended a hand again, only now it was one of welcome, accompanied by a warm smile. Maya noticed that her hair was now auburn and combed down in a conservative style. She was wearing a dark business suit.

"Maya, it's so good to see you!" the stranger said cheerfully, as if greeting an old friend.

"Hi," Maya said uncertainly, taking her hand, as she was pulled into a light hug. The woman whispered, "I'm sorry about that moment of drama at your friend's place. Georgia wants us to keep a low profile. I hope I didn't put you off. I'm Kira."

"It's fine, no worries, Kira," Maya said agreeably.

Outside, an SUV was waiting at the curb, one of hundreds of vehicles packed in the arrival lanes. The air was warm and dry, stinking of exhaust. Maya glanced at the driver, and to her surprise, saw the muscular man who had whisked Georgia out of the university's student lounge. He greeted Maya with a smile, which put her at ease since it was just dawning on her that she was far from home and in the hands of complete strangers.

"I'm Sergey," the driver said in a Russian accent. Maya sat in the passenger seat and Kira got in back.

"Where are we going?" Maya asked.

"Brandon's house," Sergey said. "It's a half-hour drive without traffic."

"How much *with* traffic?"

"Hour-and-a-half," he said with a laugh. "It's Los Angeles. It's a pretty drive. You'll like it."

Sergey drove through the morass of vehicles to a surface street and then onto a freeway ramp. The windows were rolled up tightly, keeping out the hazy heat, the air-conditioning blowing loudly.

Maya stared at the passing scenery, marveling especially at the rail-thin palm trees that reached beyond the tops of the tallest buildings, and noted that the land was flat and densely covered with houses and apartment buildings.

They rounded a bend and slowed in heavy traffic as a festive beach scene came into view.

"This must be 'traffic'?" Maya said.

"Oh, no," Sergey laughed. "This is piece of cake."

Maya took in her first southern California experience, which looked just as sunny and exciting as she had imagined. Groups of tanned, attractive beachgoers carrying blankets, towels and ice chests migrated across the multilane road at the crosswalks. Beyond the beach, far out to sea, sailboats appeared as tiny white triangles in the distance. Maya smiled, enjoying it all.

Soon the traffic thinned out and they picked up speed, passing more Santa Monica beaches, then making it into Malibu where beachfront homes were tightly packed on the ocean side. Inland, rolling hills sparkled with sun-drenched wildflowers.

Sergey veered onto a frontage road, leaving the whoosh of speeding cars behind, and made his way onto the quiet streets of a wooded peninsula neighborhood. A few turns later, they ascended the steep driveway of Brandon's home, a Spanish-style estate. Sergey pulled the SUV into its garage and the group made their way past the pool and into the house.

Maya stared wide-eyed at the living room, which was dominated by beautiful, handmade Asian furniture—tea tables, carved screens, bamboo bookcases and a large antique trunk with a vase of roses on it. A towering glass wall provided a floor-to-ceiling view of the ocean and sky. Kira slid open its doors and led Maya out onto the deck.

The house stood atop a high ridge, Maya noticed. From here the ocean didn't appear so much as a horizontal strip, but as an elongated oval spread out beneath the sky.

She felt a tap on her shoulder, and there was Brandon, looking far different than he had in Wyoming. The jeans, flannel shirt and cowboy boots were replaced with khaki shorts, a sporty pullover and deck shoes.

"So, we do meet again," he said with a smile.

"Your house is beautiful," Maya said.

"The fruits of capitalism," Brandon said. "May as well be comfortable while fighting the good fight. Are you hungry?"

"Famished," Maya said. "There's only so far one can go on Snickers bars and coffee."

"Let's fix that. Here, have a seat."

Kira brought out sandwiches and fruit, and Brandon and Maya ate at a table on the deck. Brandon seemed genuinely glad to see Maya and asked her many questions, following each of her responses with the next logical query. He never drifted in his listening, the way she always did when people went on and on about themselves. His attention was always unwavering and right there with her. She was impressed.

"I see you like the view," he said, noticing how often Maya's gaze was drawn out to the sea.

"It's awesome," she said. "I've never seen a sunset over the ocean."

"And you won't from here," Brandon said. "See those trees? Those, unfortunately, are my ocean sunset foil. But there's a nice place nearby. Interested?"

"Oh yeah," Maya said.

"Great. I'll show you."

Sergey and Kira joined them, and the group left the house and made their way to a trailhead across the street that led into a densely wooded canyon.

Maya marveled at the large houses perched atop the canyon's ridges, held aloft by thin poles that looked like stilts. When she asked about them, Brandon told her that even earthquakes had failed to budge those houses. In fact, the steel-reinforced pillars were designed to withstand the most powerful of quakes.

At a clearing, the woods thinned out and the bright blue sky filled the field of view. Just ahead, a chain-link fence blocked the way, coiled with barbed wire. Its gate was locked.

"This is a private beach," Kira explained. "Residents only."

That figures, Maya thought. *Hoard all the natural beauty for the chosen few.* But then she recalled the chaotic beach scene she'd witnessed earlier and wondered which was the better: generous access that threatened the natural aesthetic or limited access that preserved it? It was a question best left for another time, she decided.

Brandon pulled a key from his pocket and slid it into the keyhole and swung the gate open. They walked on.

Soon, Maya stood before the Pacific Ocean for the first time. It seemed darker and wilder than the Atlantic around Ocean City, where she'd spent many vacations. Gentle waves broke on the sand. The taste of salt was thick in the air.

Brandon kicked his sandals off and waded into the surf up to his ankles. Sergey and Kira remained back near the trees, urging Maya to follow him.

Maya threw off her tennis shoes and socks and rolled up the bottoms of her jeans, and trailed Brandon into the shallows. The water was stinging cold. He led her to a jetty of boulders and they rock-hopped out to the very end, past the shallows, and sat on the massive boulders, dangling their feet down to where they could be kissed by the spray from the breakers.

"So, Brandon," Maya said. "Exactly why am I here?"

"It's the next step on your journey, set up by you," he said. He tilted his head to indicate the cliffs back along the beach. "Look over there. Do you see that man?" Brandon said.

Maya looked. Indeed, there was a figure at the top, tiny from their vantage point. "Who's that?"

"One of Fiske's men," Brandon said. "Maybe even Fiske himself."

"*Spying* on us?"

"Lately, yes," Brandon said. "That's why we're sitting here. The surf cancels out their surveillance Here, turn back around, like this."

"What do they want?" Maya asked.

"They want Ben."

"Because you know where he is."

"And so will you. Soon."

"Honest?"

"Of course," Brandon said. "But you need some background first. That's why I brought you here."

"OK," Maya said.

"You've heard of the Anderson Foundation?"

"It's a charity," Maya said. "They sponsor public TV shows and stuff like that."

"It's a philanthropy," Brandon said, "an organization supported by big donors looking to spend money on important causes. There is a *lot* of that money out there looking for action. There are even foundations that exist solely to figure out *where* to spend that money. The lion's share goes to social programs, the arts and research."

Maya listened, watching the waves lapping down below.

"Back in the nineteen-eighties," Brandon said, "the Anderson Foundation poured millions into cancer research. The reason was that the family's oldest son, Roger Anderson, had lost his wife to cancer and became a fanatic about finding a cure. But what made him unique was his interest in unconventional treatments. Fringe stuff. Anderson hated the medical community, whom he saw as corrupt and beholden to special interests—big pharma and the insurance companies. He wasn't wrong about that. Whatever ideas they shied away from, he embraced.

"He hired a couple of researchers out of Harvard—a husband-and-wife team—who had made waves in the medical community by proving that malignant cell growth could be slowed and even reversed using visualization techniques. Their work was legit: peer-reviewed and published. They used no technology or drugs, just the human mind and its ability to imagine. Patients would visualize their white blood cells as sharks or imaginary creatures attacking the cancer cells. Statistically, it worked. So well in fact that it drew great interest, even in the mainstream media.

"Those successes prompted Anderson to expand into a wider range of disciplines. His team grew to include not only physicians and researchers but anthropologists, mystics and intuitives. He was obsessed with the healing modalities of indigenous cultures.

"As groundbreaking as all this was, his family saw his work as an embarrassment. They turned against him. A rift formed between Anderson and his two brothers. To keep the peace, he agreed to publicly sponsor conventional research, and bury his paranormal work deep within the auspices of the research facility, hidden from the world. In return, they agreed to leave him to indulge in his strange proclivities.

"Out of the way of scrutiny and with a lavish budget at his disposal, Roger Anderson quietly built a massive knowledge base on the subjects of subtle energy and metaphysical healing. This isn't public knowledge, by the way."

Brandon paused as a towering wave crashed into the rocks below, sending up a dousing spray. Maya, taken by surprise, jumped to her feet. Brandon laughed, watching her.

"Well, it's cooling," she said sheepishly.

"Anyway," Brandon said, "the reason I'm telling you all this is because Roger Anderson is an important guy around here. He's the major backer of the Mandala—and your father's primary benefactor."

Maya said, "How so?"

"Anderson met your father when Ben worked for Fiske," Brandon said. "It was a chance meeting, if you believe in that sort of thing. Anderson recognized Ben's gifts and tried to lure him away to his clinic. He didn't succeed then, but things changed when Ben broke with Fiske. Your father has worked with Roger Anderson ever since."

"What happened between Ben and Fiske?"

"Fiske framed Ben," Brandon said. "He falsified documents to give the impression that Ben had sold classified research to a foreign government."

"Really? Which?"

"China," Brandon said. "Not that it matters. The deceit was well-staged, elaborate, and screwed your father but good. Ben ran. He traveled, in Asia and Africa, using his unique talents as an entrée into certain circles. All these years—your whole life—he's been doing this. Roger Anderson has protected him from afar.

"The bottom line," Brandon said, "is that your father is wanted by the FBI for espionage. It's a phony charge, but that's the reality of it. Running away only made it worse."

Maya said, "But he's innocent?"

"Yes, of course he is," Brandon said, giving Maya a look.

"How can you be sure?"

Brandon said, "You'll understand when you meet him."

"OK," Maya said, relenting.

Brandon looked out to sea. His expression softened. The story of Ben and Fiske and Roger Anderson fell away. Maya didn't know what was happening.

"It must be in the DNA," he said, his eyes sparkling.

"What?" Maya said, confused.

"An appreciation of *that*."

She followed his gaze and saw what he was looking at: the orange ball of the sun, half submerged in the distant curve of the sea. She hadn't even realized it was sunset. Ribbons of clouds awash in crimson, amber and gold soared high in the sky.

"Oh my," Maya said.

"There's your ocean sunset," Brandon said.

"Indeed."

They watched in silence, as the weakening sun inched imperceptibly downward, until Maya could just about fix her gaze on it without feeling the burn.

All was still. So still. She was completely relaxed for the first time in days. The scene was idyllic. The waves pattering on the rocks below. The whisper of the salty wind. The dissembling light. Even the chattering in her mind had quieted. An image came to her, of a bridge forming across time, connecting her with the thousands of generations of coastal dwellers who had watched sunsets from this very beach, just as awestruck as she.

But to the ancients, the horizon into which the sun disappeared nightly was a mystery, the edge of the world beyond which only void existed.

All that remained now was an orange sliver trembling on the distant shelf, growing smaller and smaller, until it was a golden dot. Riveted, Maya stared at it until *blip*—it was gone. As if it had never been. Now only the twilight meeting of ocean and sky remained, fast becoming one. To the east, the sky was a deep indigo, pierced by the faint twinkling of a few stars.

Maya swiveled around and looked up at the cliff. The man was gone. The wind kicked up, and Kira and Sergey called out. Brandon waved at them and soon the group was retracing its path back through the ravine. Maya swore she heard sounds along the trail, but whenever she looked, there was only the quiet woods all around.

She awoke at seven the next morning, eager to see what the ocean looked like in the first light of day. But when she flung open the guest room curtains, everything, even the trees across the street, was swallowed up in a thick blanket of fog. *Oh, well.* There was much to be excited about today.

Standing at the bathroom mirror, feeling the cool of the stone tiles on her bare feet, Maya formulated a plan for the day. No, not just the day—the rest of the trip. Her strategy was simple. *Let. It. Be.* Let each moment take its natural course. Expect nothing, force nothing. Trust in the Big U, the Universe. She recalled a saying that described it perfectly. *There's God's way and your way, and your way doesn't count.* That would be her guide.

This did not mean she would not fight the wolf when it came or fight to achieve her goals against adversity. If she slipped in her resolve, if she tried to push—*when* she tried to push—she would do her best to release control of what couldn't be controlled, and flow with the moment. That was the plan.

Georgia arrived at noon, just as the fog was lifting, ruddy-cheeked, all smiles, bear-hugging everyone in the house, looking younger than her years in faded blue jeans and a fringed cowboy

jacket. She took a seat on the living room sofa beside Kira and
Sergey, opposite Brandon and Maya.

To Kira she said, "Are we all set?"

"As always," Kira said with a smile and a wink.

"Just don't speed," Georgia warned, as Maya looked on with
incomprehension. Georgia tossed a set of car keys to Sergey,
who deftly snatched them out of the air.

Kira and Sergey stood up, said goodbye and left through
the back door. Maya wandered over to the window and watched
them enter the garage. A moment later she saw Georgia's truck
back out and glide down the driveway and out of sight. Maya
returned to the living room.

"Where are they going?" she asked.

"Up the coast," Georgia said. "Did you notice anything?"

"About?"

"Kira."

Maya thought about it. She shrugged.

"Her hair?" Georgia said. "Her clothes?"

Maya shook her head.

"The wig?"

"Wig?"

"Yes, *wig*," Georgia said, disappointed.

Maya had been so preoccupied with trying to go with the
flow that she had missed it completely. She recalled little of
Kira's appearance.

Then it hit her.

"Oh, right! The wig. The clothes. The tennis shoes. I get it.
I'm as thick as a board. She was *me*."

"Kira is our lovely chameleon," Brandon said.

"The road trip is a decoy," Georgia explained, "to lead away
curious onlookers. They're going up the coast, to Oxnard."

"Where's that?"

"Someplace you're not," Georgia said. "Now collect your
things. We'll leave shortly."

"To see Ben?"

"That's right."

A few minutes later, they were in Brandon's car cruising
along Pacific Coast Highway, this time going south. Forty-five

168 | WARREN GOLDIE

minutes later, Brandon pulled up to the curb at the airport's departure area and wished Maya and Georgia well, then merged back into traffic and was gone from sight.

"It starts," Georgia said.

"But not here," Maya said.

"We'd better hurry. We're very late."

After the security check, Maya had to speed-walk to keep up with Georgia, who was racing through the crowded terminal corridors. They arrived at the gate only twenty minutes before liftoff. The destination: Albuquerque, New Mexico.

Before Maya could ask the question that was burning in her mind, Georgia answered it.

"He's there," she said. "We'll speak no more of it for now. Agreed?"

"Agreed," Maya said, feeling only excitement.

16

Into the Wilderness

Albuquerque's airport surprised Maya with its pleasant, sun-filled terminal. After the controlled chaos that was Los Angeles International Airport, she had been bracing for entry. But this was nice. She walked alongside Georgia fully grounded and ready for whatever New Mexico might bring. Probably, a lot.

There was a man up ahead walking directly toward them. He was tall and lanky, with long sandy hair flowing like a mane from the back of a tattered fedora. He was probably in his forties, Maya guessed, but as he came closer, she could see by his rugged, weathered face that he was probably much older than that.

Aging hippie described the man who walked right up to Georgia and embraced her without speaking a word. Hanging one arm over his shoulder, she introduced him as Keith Seputa, "the truest of the Mandala."

"We've been expecting you," he said to Maya in a voice somewhere between mellow surfer and world-weary traveler.

Maya took his hand and as she did so, she examined his facial features. A curious thought came to her. Is it *him*? Could it be? Georgia and the Mandala weren't exactly forthcoming at all times. But if he really was Ben Ambrose, he sure looked different than the man she had seen in Fiske's photo. Which might make sense, given the passage of time. As they walked toward the parking lot, she decided to wait and see.

"We'll spend the night at Keith's house," Georgia said. "Tomorrow we'll go see Ben."

So that was the plan. *One more day.*

They piled into Keith's Jeep Wagoneer. He took Route 25 north. Maya settled into the backseat and watched the blighted stretches of housing developments and business parks passing by. Then the landscape changed dramatically just out of town to vast, empty flatlands. Maya felt drawn to the open desert. The land seemed to roll on forever. And the sky—it was *huge.* As the miles ticked away, she found herself feeling increasingly light of spirit, unencumbered, and to her bemusement, even blissful, as if the weight of her life had blown off in the wind.

The sense of buoyancy grew, until she began to really wonder about it. Sure, she was about to meet her father for the first time. But there was more going on. A lot more. Was it the land? The air? Being somewhere new? Keith may have been on the same wavelength, expressing it in the speed at which he drove: a steady eighty-five miles per hour.

The boundless sky, the dusty browns and burnt siennas of the plateaus, the empty highway and the speeding car—it was intoxicating. If Keith had pulled over, Maya might have sprinted into the nearest field and turned cartwheels. She stoked the feeling, getting as much out of it as possible.

Afternoon gave way to evening, and with it the lights of Santa Fe came into view up ahead, glittering like a multifaceted jewel in the night. Keith sped past the trading capital of the Old West, continuing north. Maya rested her head on the window and closed her eyes, and tuned into the song that was playing, a droning band from the sixties, the Grateful Dead. It was a sprawling, random-sounding jam, strangely hypnotic.

Keith exited the highway onto a two-lane road, and Maya sat up and peered into nighttime Taos. The town was a skiing hub, she recalled. But otherwise a mystery.

Keith navigated through some residential streets and pulled up to a small adobe house in a neighborhood of many small adobe houses, parking right on the scrub grass of the front lawn.

Maya, Keith and Georgia got out and headed for the house, trailed by moon shadows. Piles of shoes and sandals greeted them in the foyer, several of them children's sizes. The house was low-ceilinged and very small but ingeniously organized with precisely sized modular furniture placed just so to squeeze every usable inch out of the space.

Keith bid Maya and Georgia goodnight and left to join his family, who were staying at a relative's house.

"So?" Georgia said, facing Maya in the hallway. "Are you ready for this?"

"I don't know," Maya said honestly.

"You are," Georgia said. "Get some sleep. Tomorrow's going to be a big day." She started toward the master bedroom.

"Hey, wait a minute," Maya said.

"Yes?"

"Keith," Maya said. "He's not, my, uh—"

"Your father?"

"Uh-huh," Maya said, holding her breath.

Georgia smiled, finding that amusing. "You could do a lot worse, but no. He's Keith. Tomorrow we'll go see Ben. Go get some rest." She walked into the master bedroom and shut the door.

Maya sat on the living room sofa, not even remotely tired. She was scared and feeling far from home. She wanted comfort, so she clicked on the TV and surfed through the channels, settling on familiarity: the History Channel. What was playing was a documentary about the Lakota Indian Chief, Crazy Horse, whose warriors defeated General Custer's troops at the Battle of Little Bighorn in 1876. The topic seemed appropriate, since New Mexico was home to a large Native American population.

The show completely absorbed Maya. It was just what she needed. But what was most interesting was that it told the story from the Indian point of view. Their lives had been made miserable by the white man. As the tale unfolded, Maya found herself growing increasingly troubled in a way that was *not* related to sad story onscreen. It was something else that was askew. She muted the TV and tried to figure it out. After a minute she sat bolt upright; she knew what it was. The show was inaccurate! The Battle of Little Bighorn hadn't happened that way at all. Many of the details shown, and the theories posited, contradicted what she knew to be true—what was presented in *Little Big Man*, a movie she'd watched years ago at Uncle Buddy's insistence. As with many of those classic old movies, its point of view was refreshing and different and counter to modern ideas.

Maya grabbed a bag of jelly beans off the coffee table and poured a steady stream into her mouth, chewing on the sugary mass as if to ground into oblivion the troubling realization that was dawning in her.

It can't be, she thought.

But it was true. She did believe the "facts" of the old movie over the newer documentary—simply because she'd seen it first.

She chewed more of the brightly colored pellets, leaned back on the cushiony sofa and wondered just how much of her "knowledge" had come from movies and TV—constructed fictions—and how much was really hers.

All those shows, all that data, poured into her like Kool-Aid into a bottomless pitcher, day after day, year after year, until she had absorbed it so completely she believed it was her own. The real and the fictional were blended together and often indistinguishable. Who was responsible for this devious undertaking? Who created these programs? She had watched their names roll down the screen at the end of the shows, and accorded legitimacy and authority to them all, simply because they were on TV. The idea was horrific.

What really happened at Little Bighorn? Was any account accurate? Maya didn't know and surely never would. Certainly there was a personal story for each Indian warrior and U.S. soldier, men long gone and unable to correct what was shown on the screen.

She clicked off the set, exhausted. The TV had served its purpose, after all. She shuffled down the hallway to the smaller of the two bedrooms, which, she could tell by the toys, belonged to two boys. She crawled into the lower bunk bed and felt something hard beneath the pillow. It was a book, *The Sword in the Stone*, which she tossed spinning onto the floor. She closed her eyes. A minute later she was lost in a deep sleep.

Georgia was obviously a morning person. She flitted and buzzed and chirped around the compact kitchen, collecting the ingredients for omelets. She cut up the vegetables, warmed the skillet, set out the dishes and gathered the silverware. Maya, who was rarely awake at seven a.m., looked on dull-eyed as she lifted a coffee mug to her lips as if it were a twelve-pound bowling ball. Mostly she was trying to stay out of the way of the sunlight streaming in through the window. But her torpidity surprised her, for on this day of all days she should have been bouncing off the walls with Christmas morning excitement. *Habit* and Uncle Buddy came to mind.

Georgia was waxing nostalgic about her years in Taos.

"Why did you come here in the first place?" Maya asked.

"I wanted to be near the mountain," Georgia said, her face aglow, the signs of age having fallen from it.

"Which mountain is that?"

"That one," Georgia said, pointing toward the window. "Taos Mountain."

Maya leaned over and peered outside, squinting to observe the area in daylight for the first time. The housing development was in a valley, the land between the homes wild and overgrown. Steep foothills towered nearby.

"What's so great about it?" Maya said with little care.

Georgia clucked reproachfully. "Now, here's a gal who wouldn't last long in these parts. You ought to show some respect, or else."

"Or else what?" Maya said. "What—do you have to pay homage to the geography around here? That sounds none too friendly to me."

"Geography, you say?" Georgia said. "Oh, boy. You'd better keep your voice down, young lady. Everyone knows you can't stay here unless the mountain accepts you."

Now, there was an idea. A judgmental mountain—geology with attitude. Maya couldn't help but wonder what a mountain's consciousness might be like, if that were possible.

It would be slow. Slowest on the planet, for it *was* the planet. The lives of Maya's beloved trees—even the Great Basin pine, which can live fifty centuries—would blaze past in comparison. A mountain's changes would be measured not by the years or the tens of years, but by the thousands of years. The millennia. Hundreds of generations of humans would have to pass before a mountain would even take notice.

"All right, all right," Maya relented. "How do you know if the mountain accepts you?"

"You don't," Georgia said. "You know if it doesn't. Little things go awry. All sorts of things. You start to lose stuff. You become accident-prone. You have car problems. You can't find work. You have trouble making friends. After a while you get the message. You realize the flow of your life is gone. If that happens, you'd better start packing."

Maybe such things were true. There were times Maya had been drawn to anthropomorphism. An odd comfort could be found in the idea that nonhuman life forms might possess consciousness. Maybe everything—cats, fleas, pin cushions, rocks—was aware, only operating at different frequencies, making communication with all others impossible. Perhaps each consciousness was like a radio receiver that could transmit and receive only one station.

She looked out the window at the rockface abutting the development. Her eyes brightened. She turned to Georgia.

"He's in those mountains," Maya said.

Georgia said, "That's right."

"Where?"

"Ah."

Georgia grabbed an apple from a bowl on the table and took a bite out of it. "There are networks of tunnels," she said, "built by the ancestral Puebloans, the Anasazi Indians who lived here centuries ago. This whole area is off-limits to outsiders. You can get into a lot of trouble messing around in there."

"So where is he?" Maya asked.

"Oh, he's there," Georgia said. "As you know, your father is unique. A group from one of the Pueblos invited Ben in. He's probably the only white man who's ever been allowed into that secretive part of their culture. He's working the vortex right now. He's working on the change."

"So, then, that's real?" Maya said. She reached for the coffee mug, then pushed it away, realizing that it was empty. When she gazed at Georgia, her eyes were met by a stern look.

"I'm sorry," Maya said. "I was just asking."

"It's fine," Georgia said. "The change hasn't happened yet. When it does, believe me, you'll know it. But smaller changes *have* happened."

"Smaller?"

Georgia said, "Choose something."

"Like what?"

"A field of human endeavor. An area of knowledge."

After a moment's thought, Maya said, "How about medicine?"

"Perfect," Georgia said. "What do you think of the human body?"

Maya wasn't sure how to respond to that. She watched as Georgia took another bite of the apple. Maya noticed now that the house was brightening in the high sun. It felt good. She was ready for the day.

"If you're like most Westerners," Georgia said, "you see the body as a machine. The parts pretty much do what they're supposed to do, like an engine."

"Sure," Maya agreed.

"Where healing is concerned," Georgia said, "that view works fine for straightforward mechanical processes like setting broken bones, controlling blood sugar and clearing blocked arteries. But then there are the more subtle processes which operate at higher consciousness and with more complexity: anxiety-related disorders, autoimmune problems, biochemical depression, trauma-related illness, chronic fatigue, cancer. That's where the mechanical approach often falls short.

"Mind-body healing practices have been around ages, though Western medicine has never taken them seriously. That's changing now. Soon, energy medicine will surge to move into the mainstream—practices free of instruments that rely instead on mind, will and touch. The body possesses all the healing power it will ever need to correct any malfunction. The trick is knowing how to channel it. For that, higher states of consciousness are involved. From there, techniques can be employed to direct the body's healing energy. Practices like acupuncture come close, but can be advanced even further. Today's surgery is often downright barbaric. Non-invasive energy healing and psychic surgery will replace it. The shift is already beginning."

Maya said, "What does the Mandala have to do with it?"

"Everything," Georgia said. "We engineered it."

Maya stared at Georgia, incredulous. "You changed the way medicine has evolved?"

"That's right," Georgia said.

"The Mandala?"

"Yes."

"Who, exactly?"

"You mean the individuals involved?" Georgia said. "Well, I know all of them. In fact, I'm one of them." She smiled. "It's a bit of a strain on the old belief system, eh? So was air travel a century ago. Or the heliocentric universe five centuries ago. Or the atom a hundred years ago. You have only to expand the mind beyond where it's already been."

She walked over to a bookshelf, scanned the titles and pulled down *The Archetypes and the Collective Unconscious* by C.G. Jung. She slid it across the table to Maya. Maya opened the weighty tome and took a quick look.

"Don't bother, I'll tell you what's in it," Georgia said. "It says we're all individuals, but each of us touches everyone else in the same way the spokes of a wheel meet at the hub. The hub is what Jung termed the 'collective unconscious.' It's a hidden part of the mind.

"Concepts such as soul, God and afterlife exist in every culture on the planet. Why is that? It's because each society draws from the same well. Those are archetypes. They exist for the peoples of Africa and China to discover and mold just as like for the people of Europe and the Americas.

"The glorious images painted in the Sistine Chapel originated in the collective unconscious, as did the work of

Mozart, Shakespeare and Rembrandt. That's why they carry such great power. Those geniuses all drew from the same source, translating what they found along the aesthetic guidelines of their art and cultures. They may have had no idea where the material came from and probably didn't care."

"OK, I get that," Maya said. "What I don't understand is how you changed the medical field."

"Simple," Georgia said. "You *use* the collective unconscious. You take away the 'un' and make it conscious."

Georgia tossed the half-eaten apple high up into the air and caught it—perfectly, skin on skin—then winked at Maya as if she'd planned it that way. She set it down on the table.

"You want to know how it's done," Georgia said.

Maya nodded, excited.

"I'll give you the broad strokes," Georgia said. "All work of this nature must begin with a still, unfettered mind. That's the baseline. You get nowhere in monkey mind. So, step one is meditation."

"I know how to meditate," Maya said.

"Then you have step one covered," Georgia said. "Of course, there are many forms. Ours is more than a relaxation or presence practice; it's an evolutionary tool. I learned from masters and practiced for many years, touching the deepest levels of mind.

"Think of the mind as an onion, with its many layers of skin," Georgia said. "The outermost layer represents waking consciousness, the state we know so well. Here, things are not terribly serene. Thoughts ping-pong around incessantly, chaotically. Try listening to your mind sometime and you'll see what I mean."

"Oh, I have," Maya said, understanding all too well.

"Meditation done right," Georgia went on, "allows you to dive below this level. If you're very skilled, you can descend all the way down to the onion's core. What will you find there? Pure being. Undifferentiated awareness. The unbounded. The land beyond 'I' where thoughts are born before they make their way up through all the layers to the surface where they go *pop!* This '*pop!*' is what we experience as a thought.

"As I descend deeper though the layers," Georgia said, "I approach this core, this source, this most powerful level. It is here where reality creation can be achieved. If you focus on a desire while maintaining awareness at this level, it will begin to take shape—at first in the pre-physical world, and then, if backed by sufficiently strong emotion, it will 'thicken' into an event in the real world.

"The closer you get to the onion's core, the faster it happens. That is, the faster your intention will manifest. Sound easy? Well, there's a catch, and it's a big one. It's almost impossible to hold awareness at this level. You lose focus, drift, fall into dreams and fantasies or simply fail to arrive there. You see, Maya, the psyche is *designed* to make it difficult to access this most magical of places. To enter it with full consciousness, you must learn the practice."

"The practice," repeated Maya.

"Which originated," said Georgia, "in an ancient culture and was adapted over millennia. So, to sum up, what I do is enter a state of supreme empowerment and simply ask for what I want."

"Do you get it?" Maya said eagerly. "Do you get what you want?"

"Yes. Today, tomorrow, next week, next month or next year, provided I harbor no conflicting beliefs or desires. Another catch. For example, if I asked for wealth yet believed myself unworthy of it, the intention would not come to pass. If I ask for love, yet fear intimacy, again I'd fail. Now, in order to achieve a *collective* change rather than an individual one, you need many minds working in unison—"

She was interrupted by the sound of a car arriving outside. Maya wanted to hear more, but Georgia was already on her way out to the porch. Keith had pulled the Wagoneer up onto the lawn, sending up a cloud of dust.

Georgia said, "Are you ready?"

"Since I was six," Maya said.

"Get your things."

Keith drove them through the downtown of tiny Taos, past its art galleries, restaurants, plazas and resurrected trading post. Then they were back on the highway, speeding through the wide open desert, and again Maya sat back and exalted in the sense of freedom that seemed an innate part of it.

They didn't remain on the flatlands long. Keith turned onto a narrow mountain road and shifted into a lower gear and started up a steep grade. Acacia trees sprung up on hillsides that sparkled with golden poppies. Maya looked out the window while Keith expertly handled the inclines and switchbacks.

The higher they climbed, the fewer the signs of civilization Maya saw, until she felt certain they were all alone in the world. Hardly a car shared the road in either direction. In an odd twist, the woods outside appeared *threatening* here, a dramatic difference from the plains which been so magical and inviting. Now "outside" portended danger. Maya imagined pre-historic hunters stepping soundlessly through the woods, gripping their spears, on the lookout for prey animals.

"This doesn't feel like the United States," she said. "This feels like *before* it."

Keith nodded his agreement. "Who needs government," he said, surprising Maya.

"I hate to tell you this," Georgia said, "but this state has been in the union since 1912."

"Not in spirit," Keith said, staring at the road ahead.

They drove on.

A dirt road appeared on the left, and Keith slowed to turn onto it. The Wagoneer bumped along for a few minutes before arriving at a small village carved out of a sloping hillside, far from main road. Several adobe shacks and mobile homes had been puzzled together into a small community.

Maya was amazed that people chose to live so remotely. It had to be about freedom. You could do whatever you pleased up here and no one would know about it, possibly ever. She tried not to dwell on that; it wasn't a comforting notion. She was deep in this world. She had placed her trust in her companions, even as she wondered why they had failed to mention how far into the wilderness they were going.

Keith parked the car beside a shiny Airstream mobile home and its door immediately swung open. A beautiful brown-skinned woman stepped out. Keith introduced her as Maria, his wife.

She greeted Georgia with familiarity and took Maya's hand. "This is my sister's home," she said, her accent Mexican-American. "When she is away, sometimes we stay here. The boys love it. Look, do you see them? Would you like something, Maya? Some water, maybe? It must be very dry for you here."

Maya thought about that. It was true. She had been guzzling glass after glass of water since she'd arrived in New Mexico. "Thank you," she said. "I think I will."

Maria had prepared a lunch of corn tortillas and green chili stew, which she set on a table in the shade of some trees. The group ate quietly and quickly. Keith explained that a hike awaited them. He stood up and grabbed a sturdy branch of desert ironwood that was leaning against the trailer and handed it to Georgia. He strapped on a weighty backpack.

"Let's go meet your father," Georgia said to Maya.

"Where?" Maya said, looking around.

"Not far," said Keith.

He led them onto a trail and into the deep forest, striding at a brisk pace. They climbed and descended many hills. Maya found herself crouched over often, her hands on her thighs, struggling to draw a satisfying breath, and she wondering what Keith had meant by "not far."

"Hey, hold up," she rasped. "What's going on? I can't breathe."

"I'd say you're a city slicker hiking at seven thousand feet," Georgia called back. "This is the southern end of the Rockies. We'll slow down. You'll be fine."

Embarrassed at falling behind her much older companions, Maya tried breathing slowly and deliberately and walking very evenly in an attempt to conserve energy. Nonetheless, over the next hour Keith and Georgia had to slow down many times for her. Georgia was bounding along like a teenager, touching the walking stick to the ground with each step. But it was obvious she didn't need it; she just liked it.

They arrived at a ridge that formed the outer edge of an immense bowl-like gorge. Thousands of treetops swept far down to the bottom in a gentle slope that climbed up the opposite side. Beyond, distant mountains rode one upon another to the limits of Maya's view.

The travelers sat on a fallen tree trunk, bathed in the warmth of the afternoon sun. Keith brought out water bottles from his pack and passed them around. The ground was covered in pine needles, which gave off a pleasant, toasty scent. Maya felt drawn to them. She felt an overwhelming desire to lay down.

"*Let's go,*" Keith barked, standing up, aware of the influence of the alluring scent.

They trudged on.

Descending the gorge wasn't difficult, for the grade was not steep, but when they reached the bottom, the path narrowed and became impassibly dense with growth. A solid wall of bushes blocked the way ahead.

"This isn't as hard as it looks," Keith said lightly, as he got down on his belly and crawled right into the underbrush, disappearing from sight.

"Watch out for snakes," he called back.

"Snakes?" Maya said worriedly to Georgia.

"Think nice of them and they'll do the same for you," came the reply.

Georgia said, "It won't be long now, I promise."

"We *are* going to see Ben?"

"This is necessary. You'll understand shortly."

"All right," Maya said. "Here goes."

She lay down on the ground and pulled herself forward into the dense growth, her eyes glued to the ground for signs of reptilian slithering. Three minutes later, trailing twigs and dirt, she emerged into a sunlit clearing. It was an unexpected, beatific sight. A field of saplings spread out in every direction. Then Georgia was standing beside her, brushing dirt from her clothes.

"This way," Keith said, up ahead.

They pushed on. The terrain changed from the dirt of the forest floor to an open field of rocks and boulders. Keith leapt confidently from rock to rock while Georgia and Maya kept pace behind him. Maya was surprised to find the rock walking easy to do.

Her stamina began to return. Each step brought more vigor. The aching in her legs was gone and she was no longer gasping for air. She felt … buoyant. How could that be? What had changed? She could hardly recall being bone-tired just minutes ago. Now she felt as if she could pick up a heavy boulder and haul it for the rest of the trek.

Keith made his way toward a cluster of rocks in the shade of some trees. Maya wondered why they were stopping, but followed along and sat beside him. He pulled a large plastic bag of trail mix out of his pack and again passed the water bottles. Maya scooped a handful of nuts, seeds and raisins, then took the bottle and drank of the cool water.

She looked over at Georgia, seeing that the older woman was grinning. Georgia opened her arms wide as if to embrace every tree and rock in sight. "Do you feel it?" she said excitedly.

"Totally," Maya said. "What is it?"

"It's the vortex," Keith said.

"You can *feel* it?"

"When you're this close, yes."

Gazes passed between them. Excitement was in the air. Maya turned to Georgia, her eyes saying, *I'm sorry I doubted you.*

"What you're feeling," Georgia said, "is the very energy the ancients used to build the great structures that time could not destroy. The pyramids, Stonehenge, Easter Island. All those places are near vortexes. Those cultures knew how to use the energy to hold the form and strength of physical matter."

Maya said, "I've always wondered about that—"

"*Shh*," Keith hissed.

Maya froze.

"They're here," he whispered.

"Who?"

"Look, there," Keith said in a voice that held no trace of lightness.

17

Faceoff

The boy was staring at Maya, his body half-hidden behind a tree trunk. He stepped out of the shadows and looked over the group imperiously. He was brown-skinned and small of stature, dressed in a simple white shirt and tan shorts. He was slender and muscular, and young, perhaps in his mid-teens.

Maya pressed against Georgia. "Who is he?" she whispered.

"He's the guy you're going with," Georgia said.

"Me? What about you and Keith?" Maya asked worriedly.

"Just you," Georgia and, and gave Maya a nudge. "*Go.*"

Maya looked over at Keith, hoping for a different response. He, too, urged her on.

Maya stared at the boy, who walked over and stood directly in front of her. "Hey, it's no big deal," he said casually and with an easy smile. "It's just a little walk."

Maya smiled back at him. She had expected to hear an exotic accent or broken English. Instead, his was the voice of an ordinary American teenager.

"Sure," she said, relieved.

He waved her to follow him and they started toward a nearby trail. Maya turned briefly to wave goodbye to Georgia and Keith, and then they disappeared from view.

Maya's guide didn't speak much; he was a boy of few words. When she asked where they were going, all he would say was, "Where he is."

That sounded fine, and she followed him. After a few minutes the trail narrowed and ascended, and soon Maya grew nervous, looking down over a hundred foot cliff.

She advanced slowly, grazing her fingertips along the flat wall of rock to her left and staring anxiously at the dusty trail without even a glance at the long drop-off. The boy, a few paces ahead, turned to check on her often, showing his impatience with her glacial progress, but she didn't care.

The path narrowed even more, to barely two feet wide, and the best Maya could do was inch forward in shuffling steps while leaning heavily into the wall, hardly lifting her tennis shoes off the ground. Up ahead, the boy ambled along untroubled.

They came to a three-foot gap in the path and he easily stepped across. Maya could have done so, too, had she not hesitated. But she had, and now she was unable to move, staring down to the ground far below and imagining the painful sting of sharp branches on her body as it fell.

"I'm not sure about this," she said uneasily, and weighed her options, which were three: forward, backward, downward. Only one made sense.

"It's easy," the boy assured her. "It's just one step."

"Looks more like three," Maya said.

"You'll be fine," he said.

She glanced over at him, seeking assurance. "You'll catch me?" she said, working up her nerve.

"I promise."

"OK," she said. "Here goes."

She readied herself, held her breath, and with the boy waiting on the other side, lifted her foot to step across. But she had missed a crucial detail: a small rock poking up out of the dirt, which caught her toe.

Not like this were the words on her mind when she toppled forward. Instinctively she reached for the wall but it was too smooth and yielded no catch. Her fingernails scraped long lines on the rock. She began to fall.

She screamed.

Images flooded her mind: the rapid hundred-foot plummet, far faster than she could have imagined; the *snap-snap-snap* of branches breaking on skin, and the puncturing of her body and the blood that would flow out of her; and then, the awful final thud on the hard ground, followed by silence but for her last wheezing breaths. Her life, all of its unlived years and unrealized potentials, finished, here in the middle of nowhere—

But instead, she found herself hanging in midair, swinging like a pendulum above trees that seemed to be calling out for her. Her wrist burned. Something had latched onto it, was squeezing tightly. She craned her head up to see, straining against the leaden weight of her body, saw the boy's hand welded to her wrist. He was belly down on the trail, lips tightly pursed, his face red with strain. Their eyes met.

Pull.

Maya reached up with her free hand and got her fingers on the ledge. Her toe found a catch and she pushed off mightily, while the boy struggled to pull her up. She scrambled up to the top and fell into a heap.

She lay there, arms and legs quaking, her abdomen rising and falling in powerful spasms. Breaths came only in intense gasps. She touched her hand to her cheek, surprised to find the wetness of tears. She turned to her companion, whose chest was rising and falling in unison with her own. She pulled herself up to a sitting position.

"You saved my life," she said, hardly believing the words she'd just uttered. "I don't even know your name."

"Tomas," he said.

"Thank you," she said.

"You're welcome, Maya."

"You know me," she said. "Of course you do."

They sat, breathing in their shared relief, and when they were ready, dusted off and began walking.

To Maya's relief, the trail widened and she was able to maintain a distance from the cliff. As they rounded a bend, Tomas turned to her.

"I don't know what you're going to do," he said and walked on. Maya didn't know what to make of the cryptic remark. She caught up with him.

"What did you mean by that?"

"You'll see."

"'You'll see'?" she said, bristling. "That's all you have to say? I'll see *what?*"

But he didn't answer. He looked uncomfortable, turned and started off again, only this time Maya didn't follow. He disappeared up ahead. A moment later he reappeared beside her.

"Please," he said. "We have to go."

"Listen, Tomas, I appreciate what you did back there, I really do, but there are a few things I need to know. Like, what's going on? Where are you taking me?"

"We're almost there," he pleaded.

"*Where?*"

"Where he is," Tomas said, struggling to hide his discomfort.

"You mean Ben."

"Yes."

"Then just say it," she said.

"Ben," he said.

"What else?" she said.

"Just him."

"All right. Let's go. I'm right behind you."

As she walked, she sensed panic rising in her. She considered turning back. If not for the gap in the trail, she may have. She didn't know what the real dangers were, and her only friends in the area—if they really were friends—were far away and getting more distant by the minute. And all she had for help was a strange kid who could walk a harrowing trail as if it were a wide boulevard, who was hiding something.

The trail descended at last, and they cruised along the easy grade to flat ground. Up ahead was an outcropping of massive eight-foot-tall boulders that looked like a cluster of giant beings huddled together in discussion.

Indiscernible sounds floated over from beyond the boulders. Tomas waved at Maya to follow him toward the other side, holding held a finger across his lips for silence.

They rounded the bend. What Maya saw caused her to freeze in fear. She had no reference for it. She could not comprehend it.

A dirt clearing was bathed in the shadow of an enormous vertical rock face. About ten feet off the ground was a ledge—a natural platform upon which one could stand. Footholds had been chiseled in the rock below it as a way up. Maya saw a dark hole toward the back of the ledge leading into darkness. A cave.

And there were men—a dozen Native American men sitting on the dusty ground, in a semicircle. They were dressed in brown shawls. One man caught Maya's attention in particular: a gray-haired, heavyset man who seemed to be watching everything, kneeling in the center of the arc.

To Maya, all this was unsettling enough, but what was in front of the men was shocking. It sent an icy chill all through her and made the hairs on the back of her neck stand on end. Twelve wolves were raised up on their haunches, one in front of each man. Their teeth were bared and they were primed to spring. The scene stole her breath away. It was an otherworldly standoff. Maya found it incredible that each man appeared expressionless and unafraid, surely due to some kind of superhuman effort.

Her stomach squeezed into a knot. Her thought was *run*. No—walk. Tiptoe around the outcropping as calmly as possible, take a few more steps, then sprint as far and as fast as her legs would carry her. To hell with New Mexico and Indians, the Mandala, the future of planet Earth, vortexes, and even her father—

Go!

But she continued to stand and stare. The wolves began to shift on the dirt and sniff at the air, searching. For what? Tomas touched her arm, startling her, and she jumped. And with that movement, twelve pairs of canine eyes fixed on her. Maya took a sharp inhale and held it.

She felt something at her waist. Tomas had placed his arm there and was slowly swiveling her around. He led her to the other side of the outcropping, where she found herself on the ground without knowing how she'd gotten there. Kneeling at her side, Tomas said, "Maya?"

"Yes?"

"Do you know why you're here?"

"What?" Maya said, lost, her mind having gone offline. She wiped away a tear. *Get control.*

Tomas said, "You have to go in."

"In?"

Tomas looked confused, like he was remembering something. "You don't know," he said.

"Know what?"

He stood up. "Wait for me. I'll be right back," he said.

"Tomas! Where are you going?" Maya pleaded, but he disappeared around the outcropping.

She sat in the scrubgrass and waited, absent-mindedly drawing lines in the dirt with her fingertip. She wondered why she was here. Was her father was really in that cave? She had no assurance of that. Maybe Fiske was right about the Mandala, maybe what they really wanted—

"Hello, Maya," said a voice beside her.

She turned and saw the gray-haired Indian who had been kneeling in the arc of men. He lowered his ample body down beside her, straining with the effort. His hair flowed past his shoulders. Dark rings hung under his eyes. He looked like he hadn't slept in days.

"I am Hania," he said. "You've met my son, Tomas. He means well, but he is young. Perhaps too young for the task at hand. How are you? You've been through a lot."

"I'm fine," Maya said, sensing a defensiveness in her response. She wasn't fine at all. Not in the least.

Hania leaned in close. Just moving his body seemed to pain him. "You are afraid," he said.

She stared at him.

A hint of a smile crossed Hania's face. "If it were me, I would be very scared. Those wolves are fierce. They could tear a person to shreds."

"What are you talking about?" Maya said.

"I'm trying to put you at ease."

"You've got a funny way of doing it," she said. But it worked. She was connecting to this man. She said, "Is he really in there?"

"Ah," Hania said. "You do not believe."

He grew quiet, then asked her, "Did you almost have a car wreck recently?"

Maya was stunned by the question.

"And did someone help you put the brakes on?"

She covered her face with her hands and stared at Hania through the gaps in her fingers, as if she could hide from the question he'd just asked. It was involuntary. It was childlike. What had the tired-looking Indian just said? Some*one*.

She recalled the truck that had crashed into the light pole in Glendale and the strange braking of her car, which she had assumed was the work of body consciousness—with a ninety percent probability, she thought ruefully—her animal self making a snap survival decision independent of the mind. But maybe it was something else. Something entirely different.

Hania had been examining her changing facial expressions with the concentrated focus of a tracker reading animal scents on the wind. Maya glanced over at the outcropping, noting the growls growing louder.

"Oh, you needn't worry about them," Hania said, watching her. "They are simple creatures. Their orders are clear. Do you want to know what those orders are?"

"Orders?" Maya said. "But they're animals."

"That's a limited view of things," Hania said. "Their instructions are to allow no one in the cave but you."

"Me?"

"Yes, and I think you owe it to your father—who saved your life—to go in. If only to thank him."

"*He* did that? How? How do you know all this?"

"I know many things, Maya. You had help. You are lucky. Not everyone has such good fortune. Now it's your turn to repay this kindness."

"You mean by getting mauled?"

"No. By passing by the line." Hania paused. "You can do it. He wants to see you."

"He does?"

"Yes. That's why you're here."

Maya said, "I believe you. I do."

"I'm glad of it."

"What should I do?"

"Sit," Hania said.

"Sit?"

"Be with it. Center yourself. Find the right state of mind. We are not going anywhere. Come only when you're ready."

She said, "How will I know that?"

"You will," Hania said. "Listen. Your father will die if he remains in that cave. He thinks one man can do everything. That's folly. I don't know where he gets such ideas. If I could pass by the wolves, I would."

She stared at Hania, said, "Just sit?"

"Yes. That's all that is required."

"OK," she said.

"Good. We're in agreement."

Hania pulled himself up, wished her well and walked back around the outcropping, leaving her alone.

Sit.

It was doable.

She saw an elevated mound of grass under a nearby tree, which looked like a good place to sit, whatever that meant. She would meditate. That seemed a reasonable approach. It couldn't hurt. And so, she crossed her legs, straightened her back and allowed her eyes to close. The resolve she'd made at Brandon's house came to mind. *Let it happen. Don't interfere.*

That would be her guide.

She sat.

She opened her eyes. The sun was far lower in the sky, just over the treetops. She was astonished. Significant time had passed. An hour, maybe. It was as if she'd just closed her eyes a minute ago. And she hadn't moved a muscle, a nearly impossible feat when she was anxious. *Interesting.*

She closed her eyes.

When she opened them, the sun was far into the trees, the day's light on the wane. She'd disappeared again. But there was more—a feeling in her body that was unfamiliar, like a stirring that seemed to come from ... her mind? She wasn't sure. It was mental *and* physical, or maybe it was both; a kind of shifting internally like an animal pushing at her insides. An animal awakened and stirred up.

She did her best to suppress the fear that came with that, for this sitting had to be accomplished, whatever might be happening. Maybe that odd feeling was nothing. Maybe it was the reason she was doing this. She glanced over at the outcropping, flashing briefly on the fact that was paramount above all else: *he* was close by. Maybe just a few feet away.

She stared into the woods. Night was coming on— nighttime in the wild. Maya Burke in the middle of nowhere with no idea of what was coming next. A swelling of pride asserted itself. Even with all the unknowns. Surely this was the farthest she'd ever ventured out of her comfort zone. What could possibly compare to this? She was glad she hadn't retreated. She'd forged ahead. She would continue with the sitting, heed Hania's words to come only when ready. What would be expected of her? A confrontation with the wolves? That would be crazy. She put that thought aside and closed her eyes again, deciding to place her trust in Hania and the Indians and in this process that was unfolding.

The sounds of the forest filled the air, the coos and caws of nocturnal creatures. There was frequent movement up in the trees, and she opened her eyes to see. A bright moon burned in a star-filled sky. It was full night. Again, time had sped by without her awareness of it.

She unfolded her aching legs and stretched out, squeezed her shoulders back and pressed out her chest, just to feel something other than that odd internal sensation that was growing more intense by the second. She had no reference for it, this force which had arrived out of nowhere and was overtaking her...

Let it happen.

Why not? Why else was she here? She would surrender to it. *Open up.* With that thought she felt more movement, a process unleashed, powerful and inexorable, which began with the most unexpected thing imaginable: a wail. A loud and primal grunt that came from deep within her. Unnerved, her eyes flew open. The darkness was ominous. She was breathing hard. Her heart was pounding. She guessed at what might be happening. It was naked fear coming up. The fear that had been simmering in her since she had started on the trail, which had grown monstrous and now had to be released.

Wide-eyed, expectant, she did not comprehend the details of what was happening, only that it had to happen. Perhaps it was an agony dissolving. *Open to it.* It was a sensation of both fullness and emptiness, and she shook violently, then grew still. Her mind, her thoughts ... something was happening. She'd forgotten why she was here.

Who am I? she thought. The question came out of nowhere. She'd lost herself. She was a young woman from Plainfield, Maryland, yes, but what did that mean? Was she what she'd done? What she believed? What she desired? The questions came, but no answers. The outlines of her life were washing away like watercolors in the rain, running off and out of sight.

The only certainty she could grasp with any confidence was the world within her reach: the grass beneath her, the rock outcropping a few feet away, the night and its invisible sounds. The owls, the wolves, the squirrels—they were real. Everything else was a dream.

She stood up, dusted herself off, pulled her sweater around her and lifted its hood up over her head, and rounded the outcropping. She knew what awaited her, what she had to do. The wolves saw her there, standing behind the arc of men.

She took a step forward, surging with newfound strength. Her mind—her own wolf—had receded, had given way to a deeper aspect of herself. The man-statues must have known she was there, yet none stirred except Hania, who rose and came over. He was holding a bulging leather pouch. He placed its strap over her shoulder. She didn't wonder, or care, what it held.

There was a strange feeling to the world now, as if every object was a symbol with multiple meanings and she was moving through a fabric made not of matter but of thoughts. The wolves were her power, the Indians her wisdom, and the mountain a blank canvas on which to create.

She walked up to face the line of wolves. They sprang to life, watching her. Tremors shot through her.

She stepped closer.

It doesn't matter. No thing does.

She had resolved to die, which meant to cherish the moment, whatever it held, beyond all else.

Forward, she commanded herself, even through the resistance of her body.

Suddenly she was consumed by a feeling of floating. Her physical form was gone, melted away like ice in a furnace blast. She was fully herself, and yet … she was another being entirely. Her life, this life, was changing in this moment which grew and stretched and reached beyond all boundaries and kept on going and didn't stop. She didn't know it but she was grinning. She felt … free. Of everything. She wanted to yell out—and maybe she did—*Thank you, thank you, Universe, thank you!*

An upwelling of gratitude surged in her, for everything and everyone, known and unknown. For the whole planet and all of its wondrous life forms. For the infinite and unknowable true reality. She was bathed in love and thankfulness for whomever she had touched or had touched her, even in the smallest way. *Mom, Josh, Brandon, Georgia, Fiske. Everyone—*

She peered through tear-soaked eyes at the wolf at her feet. The animal gave a quick glance up—a *wink?*—then lowered its head and padded away. The others followed. The pack had divided in half, creating an open path to the rocky platform. They watched Maya expectantly, their fiery eyes now still pools of calm.

She turned briefly to gaze upon the motionless men and noted their oddly blank looks. All except Tomas at the very end, whose face was lit in wonder. Hania implored her with his eyes. *Move!*

She stepped quickly past the stunned sentries to the rocky wall and scrambled up the footholds onto the stage-like platform. Below her, the wolves sprang to life, roused from their trance to resume their defiant barrier, just as the Indians lifted up their faces, and to Maya's astonishment, cheered!

"Flashlight!" Hania called out.

Maya opened the pouch and scanned its contents: bread, some dried meat, a water skin, candles, matches, batteries and a flashlight. She snatched up the flashlight, then turned and walked into the cave.

A cool, dark room. With air that seemed *hard*, as though it were rock itself. Each of her footfalls announced itself with an echo. There was a passageway at the back wall. She peered in, knowing what awaited her in that direction.

She glanced a final time at the moonlit trees outside, then lowered her head and stepped into the passageway. She had to stoop to advance through it.

As she advanced, the unearthly quiet was only broken by her breathing and the uncertain shuffling of her sneakers. The concentrated light beam shot around with her every movement, illuminating the long corridor ahead.

She came to a large chamber and saw that its ceiling was covered in black soot. Boulders were arranged in a circle on the floor. Along the walls, at waist level ringing the chamber, were drawings—hand-sized petroglyphs of horses and people, faded with age. Maya moved excitedly down the line, absorbing the images, wondering what they meant and who had drawn them. When she came to the last one, near the passageway from which she'd emerged, a chill passed through her.

She brought her face up close to the tiny webbed earth, the image that had followed her through the weeks. Or perhaps, she thought, *preceded* her.

She wondered which prehistoric peoples had drawn the petroglyphs, and why the last one had been added. But the ancients would not have envisioned a spherical Earth or its land masses, for they did not know it was a planet. Or did they?

She meandered over to the ring of boulders and sat on the largest one, pressing her palms against the cold surface, which was comforting. She liked being in the cave. She was *inside* a mountain, touching surfaces as old as anything on this world. She recalled someone once telling her, *Your head is up in the clouds, Maya. What you need is grounding.* Well, here she was, in the belly of a mountain. One couldn't get any more grounded than that.

Who had said that? She couldn't recall. Her personal history continued to be strangely inaccessible. But not all. Some vestiges remained, like the intense feelings that had brought her here, the nagging sense of emptiness grown to unmanageable size, and the suspicion that she was incomplete in a way she didn't fully understand or know how to remedy. And then her confused desire to do something about it all.

She heard a scraping sound nearby and jumped to her feet, alarmed, and spun around, shining the flashlight in every direction, its beam ricocheting off the walls. She heard a voice.

"Maya?"

In her alarm, the flashlight fell from her hand, hit the floor and rolled into a crevice, leaving its beam pointing up at the ceiling. Pale, indirect light shone in the direction of the voice. There, on the far wall, perched on a ledge in the gray dimness, sat her father, Ben Ambrose.

18

In the Belly of the Earth

His figure, shrouded in shadow, was up on a high ledge. In the dim light, Maya could see no details, just the vague outline of a body.

"It's you," he said simply, his words fluttering down as though on gently beating wings.

So, this is it, Maya thought. The moment. The moment she'd wanted for most of her life. It began with her father's voice. It sounded ... expectant. He obviously knew who was standing there below him.

A wave of anxiety overtook her excitement, and she hated that it was happening. She wanted to remain calm, to experience this fully, and yet she wasn't. She sensed stirrings within her, shadowy things awakened and seeking expression. Something was about to happen, and she didn't know what it was.

"Yep, it's me," was the best she could manage in response, which been uttered from a throat gone bone dry. She tried mentally counting breaths to center herself, but she couldn't keep track. *1, 2, 3, 4, 3, 2 ...* The moment, this opportunity so long awaited, which she'd envisioned in such detail and so intensely, was so burdened by expectation that she could barely manage it to remain in it.

She had placed tremendous import on what her first words to him would be, and had practiced a few lines back at Keith's house. But her ability to speak a single intelligible sentence had apparently deserted her. All she could access where her brain should have been was a jiggling blob of Jell-O. Unsteadily she lowered herself onto a boulder.

"I was the one holding you," her father said through the twilight.

What? I don't understand.

"The baby," Ben Ambrose explained. "The one you saw. The man holding her. That was me."

He was talking about a scene in the vortex vision in Dr. Porter's basement. How? But yes, she did recall that image. Had he read her mind?

"We kept a little stereo in your room, your mother and I," he said. "I would put on this song for you, *Country Girl.* You loved it. It always put you to sleep."

That image spooled up and played out in Maya's mind: the child in the arms of the dark-haired man, the music playing in the background. *Country Girl.*

Her hearing had become acute in the soundless chamber. She could discern his every movement, even his breathing from across the fifteen feet that separated them. It was labored, strained. There was a hitch after the inhale. Something was wrong.

"How do you know about that?" she said, finding her voice.

"What happens at one vortex can be observed from the others," he said. "I saw what you saw."

"Then you know where I was."

"Edgar Porter's house," he said softly.

She wondered if he knew what she was feeling at that moment. Did he know that the cold rock beneath her was bleeding through the fabric of her jeans, causing a near physical pain at the base of her spine?

And the anger that came, that took her by surprise. She expected it but not in the first moments. The all-consuming deluge came on too rapidly to repel. The waves built, and built, until they were towering, then they crested and crashed down, engulfing her. The next words that escaped her mouth weren't hers, but those of someone else—a child who had been abandoned, who was enraged. A beast who had seized the moment and would not release it. Maya jumped up to her feet.

"You left me," she called up to him.

No!

She recoiled. The rage! The rage. My god, she had just arrived. It was all wrong. But what could she do? It was already beyond her. She wanted to lash out, strike a blow, do *something*—anything but stand stock still in a claustrophobic netherworld of stony silence that could hide nothing. The intensity grew, even as she tried to think of ways to sidestep or derail it. Whatever mature power she had claimed outside the cave had deserted her. Her mind flashed for an instant on the world outside, now no longer real. War could have been raging, cities burning, populations dying, and she would have offered only a detached shrug. Nothing mattered. Nothing except this one interaction.

"I know there's nothing I can say," Ben said. "You must hate me."

"I don't *know* you."

"There were reasons for what I did," he said.

"Reasons?"

"There were dangers. To you and your mother."

"You're a fugitive. And Fiske." She paused, trying to get hold of herself. "I'm sorry. I don't mean to be this way. I don't know where this is coming from. It's like I can't help it."

Again the sound of his labored breathing jumped the distance between them. She waited.

He said, "I wanted to see you, Maya, of course I did. It killed me. It just wasn't possible. There were—consequences. I can't defend what happened. I believed what I did was the right thing. I still do."

"I didn't even know you were alive," Maya said, wiping away a tear as though it were a poisonous insect. She sighed.

"I'm sorry," he said.

A silence passed, an eternity.

"Maya?"

"Yes?" She was numb. She didn't know what she felt.

"Your mother."

"What about her?"

"How is she?"

"Fine."

Just that. *Fine.*

"What did she tell you about me?"

"She doesn't talk about you."

"Nothing at all?"

"No. Never."

Maya twirled a stray lock of hair, gazed over at the shadows on the walls, which looked like ghostly beings watching her. "She said you couldn't love. She said you loved ideas, not people."

More bile coming out. Why couldn't she control herself? How hard could that be? But maybe it was OK. Maybe he expected it.

"I found your journal," she said, changing the subject.

"You're here."

"Was that an accident? That I found it?"

He shifted on the ledge. "No," he said.

"What do you mean?"

"I sent you suggestions. Mental impressions. Hoping you'd hear, and you did."

"Why—if you wanted to remain a secret?"

A pause.

"Because I couldn't help it," he said.

Maya stood up and began to pace among the boulders. She peered up at his ledge. "I want to see you. Is that OK?"

"Of course."

"I'll come up," she said. She wanted to see his place, visit him where he lived.

"I'll come down," he said.

"No. I want to come up."

Another pause.

"All right," he said.

She grabbed the flashlight and shined it in his direction, which brought on a moan.

"What's wrong?" she said.

"The light," he said. "Please be careful."

She said, "I'll keep it low."

She looked inside the pouch and found a piece of cloth. She covered the lens with it.

A gentle slope of rocks led up to his ledge. Maya inched up on all fours, carefully keeping the lens covered, as the pouch swung from her side. When she reached the ledge, she placed the flashlight face down on it and pulled herself over to the wall beside him. Her head nearly grazed the ceiling. *Take a breath*. He was right beside her. Her heart was pounding, which she felt all through her body. She pressed her back against the wall and turned toward him.

She gasped.

She could barely make out his face. Long matted hair joined with a massive beard to almost completely obscure it. His cheeks—what she could see of them—were gaunt and pale, and his eyes, nearly invisible in the dim light, were submerged at the bottom of deep wells. His body was hidden beneath a thick fur coat. Emaciated hands and wrists poked out of the sides.

Father.

Maya recalled the photo that Fiske had shown her. But the being sitting beside her looked more like a caveman than the bright young man who had stood at the blackboard all those years ago.

"You look as if you've seen a ghost," he said.

Maya stared at him, feeling intense discomfort. Then he laughed.

The change in his expression had a profound effect on her. His beard shifted away from his mouth to reveal straight white teeth and she saw a brightness in his eyes, evident even in the low light.

"I must be a fright," he said. "That hadn't occurred to me until this moment."

"It's OK, really," Maya assured him. It hadn't occurred to her, either. But life had become just that—unpredictable.

She said, "How long have you been in here?"

"Three weeks," he said after a moment's thought.

God. He had no idea.

"Georgia said three months," Maya said.

"That's impossible."

Maya decided to let that go. What was the point of upsetting him? She said, "What do you eat? What do you live on?"

"Oh, I have food," he said, pointing to a small sack lodged against the wall beside him. Just to the side of it, Maya saw a hole leading into darkness. He said, "Don't be concerned, Maya, I assure you I'm fine."

He raised up his arms to demonstrate his vitality, making the opposite point instead. He was frail. Maya examined the half-starved figure of Ben Ambrose, her own flesh and blood, the lone man on earth whose genes she shared, the great leader of the Mandala underground. She made a decision at that moment. She knew what she had to do. It was the reason Georgia and Hania had brought her here. She would lead him out of this desolate hole, into the pure fresh air. Perhaps she even would play a role in his care, help this long-lost father of hers to become human again, for she did not know what he was at this moment.

"Come out of here with me," she said.

He said, "I'm not finished."

"You're weak. You're ill. I can see it."

"No, Maya. You're mistaken."

"Hania says you've been in here too long."

Ben Ambrose smiled on hearing the old Indian's name. But he remained steadfast. "I'll see you outside," he said.

An idea came to Maya.

"What do you do in here, exactly?" she said. "I'm curious."

"I work the vortex. I help bring about the change."

"I see," Maya said. "What I don't understand is how anyone will know that it's happening."

"A good question," Ben said approvingly. "It will start small, with barely perceptible changes in peoples' behaviors. If you analyzed the standard choice matrix for both the individual and the group, it would be abundantly clear that it's happening," he said, baffling Maya with the jargon.

"It's a good and noble goal," she said. "A lot of people believe in it. There's just one problem. You need to get out of here. You need to leave this place *now*. You're not well. Hania says—"

"Hania is wrong," Ben Ambrose said flatly.

Another idea came to Maya.

"Show me," she said.

"Show you what?"

"What you do. How you use the vortex. I've done it."

"What you did at Edgar Porter's house is child's play compared to what happens here," he said dismissively.

"I can do it, I know it," Maya said. "Don't you understand? I'm like you. I can *see*. I know things—"

"Wait a moment," he said. "Just a moment."

Maya watched his eyes close, and he fell silent, his awareness disappearing inward. After a minute, he turned to her.

"All right," he said.

"Really?" she said, surprised.

"Yes. But I control it. We just travel. No creating. And I stay with you the whole time."

"Just travel, no creating, you stay with me, got it," she said, having no idea what any of it meant.

"Come here," he said. "Come closer."

She scooted over until the sleeve of her sweater was touching his fur coat.

"I know you can meditate," he said. "I want you to do it for a few minutes. You'll need to still your mind, as I will do mine."

Still the mind. Right.

"Turn off the light."

She did so, and darkness engulfed them.

Her mantra drifted into her awareness and she used it, riding the familiar sound down through the layers of Georgia's onion to the mind's deeper strata. It was easy to do in the inky calm of the cave, free of the psychic noise that permeated the outside world. She could almost feel the absence of the electromagnetic radiation that passed through every inch of the planet's atmosphere.

She heard a buzzing sound, barely perceptible, like a mosquito at her ear.

"What's that?" she asked.

"You hear it?" he said, surprised.

"Yes."

"Good. Then keep listening," he said.

The numbness started at her outer extremities—her fingertips and toes and the tip of her nose—and moved inward toward her abdomen. It wasn't uncomfortable, just strange and different. Then she felt a jolt against her body, as if she'd been struck a blow.

Her eyes flew open. Though the cave was pitch black, she she could see. Only she wasn't *in* the cave. She was standing in a room beside … Uncle Buddy? Yes! The scene defied belief. It was impossible and yet it was happening. They were in a living room in a house with plush carpeting and high ceilings and a brick wall with tall bookshelves filled with books. Maya wanted to speak to him, ask him where they were and what was happening, but his form started to flicker. It became unfocused and blurry, losing its solidity. The whole room was undulating like a hot-weather mirage.

"Buddy!" Maya called out as she watched helplessly as he grew fainter and fainter, until … he was gone! And so was the room, and she was back in darkness. A limitless void peppered by a multitude of points of light. Stars! Impossibly, she was in space. How? There was no time to theorize. She heard the sound of breathing, which grew louder until it was a thunderous roar. She realized what she was hearing: her own breaths, expanding out to fill the waiting universe. She fought this observation, for a human being cannot float upon the arms of a spiral galaxy in the lifeless vacuum of space with the ease of a balloon sailing through a summer sky. And yet—

Trails of bluish-white stars crept in great curves around an unseen central point. Maya moved again—or *was* moved, she suspected—to a location directly above the galaxy's swirling center. Brilliant bright light was pulsing within it. The surrounding stars were falling into the funnel with the swiftness of paper boats disappearing down a waterfall.

Something pulled at her, at first mildly and then insistently. She heard her father's voice say, "Let go!"

Where are you? Where am I?

"…the inner medium…"

Help!

"Think future!" he said, and she was whisked into the light. A clamor erupted and then—

Quiet.

No—a droning. A chirping. Crickets.

Crickets? Maya gazed down at her body, praying that it was still there, finding her arms and legs. Yes, she was real, but *where?*

A world took shape around her: a bright sun overhead. Tall trees. Green growth everywhere. A lake with reeds bending in the breeze. Fish rippling the surface. A picnic table a few feet away.

She knew the place. Oh, did she know it, for she had been there many times. It was where she met her father, the dream she'd told to Buddy about it on the swing-set that day. Only it now it was happening and she was awake.

She would have been satisfied to sit quietly on the picnic table, exulting in the joyfulness she felt, for the spot had always been a welcome refuge. But there was the tap on her shoulder, and she turned.

Ben Ambrose was dressed in a white robe that reflected the sunlight so completely it appeared lit from within. He didn't speak, simply nodded for her to follow him her toward the nearby foothills. For the first time she passed beyond the borders of the dream.

They came to a valley where Maya saw many houses, including one that looked exactly like the old Burke farmhouse she'd grown up in, with its wraparound porch and white picket fence surrounding the lawn in a perfect rectangle. Children waved to her from perches in the trees. *Do you know me?* she thought, feeling drawn to them.

Her father led her to a house far different from the others, shaped like a pyramid and made of a smoky translucent material. Ben pushed open the front door.

The interior was unbroken by walls or rooms. It was a large airy space opened at the top to the sky and trees. Men and women in robes like her father's sat on pillows in a circle on the polished wood floor, their eyes open yet seeming to be looking at nothing.

A woman with a round face and almond eyes turned to Maya and smiled, then rose soundlessly and walked over and stood near the wall. Maya glanced at her father, who affirmed her thoughts with an almost-imperceptible movement of his head. In this place, wherever it was, you just *knew* things. Maya stepped over to the place the woman had vacated and lowered herself down onto the pillow.

The group—six men and five other women—glanced at Maya with eyes that slowly began to close. Maya's own eyelids became heavy, and she allowed them to drop. She felt a strange sensation, like a warmth flowing into her body from the direction of the man on her left, moving through her to the woman on her right.

Think future.

A sensation of motion came upon her and, to her shock, found herself floating outside, above the small opening in the ceiling. She peered down at her body on the floor below. *The top of my head*, she thought, incredulous at seeing herself from above for the first time in her life.

She felt more motion. Then the scenery shifted completely.

Skyscrapers rose up from an island city. Maya recognized it immediately. It was New York City.

But something was wrong. Something was different. The streets were empty—no marching crowds, no rushing taxis, no flashing neon. Just eerie quiet.

Maya saw a few people on the sidewalks now, walking hand in hand, in ways that gave her pause. The intensity in their faces struck her; it was as if something significant had just occurred.

An elderly man stumbled and fell down. A young couple rushed over to help him up. It was obvious by their body language they didn't know each other, yet they embraced in the manner of close friends. The couple held the old man tightly before releasing him and continuing on.

Maya felt more movement, and found herself hovering over the green expanse of Central Park. On the lawns, hundreds of people were basking in the sun, singing, playing guitars, pounding drums, stretched out or strolling in groups of ten or twenty. There were many such groups.

The tall buildings on the East Side stood like silent bookends at the park's perimeter, devoid of activity. Maya drifted over for a look. She approached a tavern, a restaurant, an apartment building. Doors were open but nobody seemed to be around.

She wondered about the rural areas of this world, this dream, this mystery she was taking in without question. And with that thought, she found herself far from the city, above a golden wheat field. On the roads here, too, groups were strolling and singing. Singing!

Nowhere did she see evidence of human struggle. Burden and discord were absent. Amid the strangeness, Maya felt at home.

The scene shifted.

An enormous hangar-like building took shape around Maya, a labyrinthine maze of offices, passageways and meeting rooms spread out under a ceiling so high that a layer of mist enshrouded it. Far below, along a great metal floor, work areas and cubicles stretched out as far as she could see, populated by workers in identical gray uniforms, staring at computer screens.

A man looked up, saw Maya, and after a moment's hesitation, began to jab a finger at her. "Look! Another one! Up there! Look!"

What? What did I do?

Panicked, Maya thought *outside*, and in a flash was on the sidewalk at the building's entrance. The grimness was here, too, permeating the city's concrete canyons. She looked up. Cars sped across the *sky*…

Someone approached. No—not a person but a synthetic, a robot, gliding above the pavement. Through its faceplate, it asked Maya where she was going. Unable to speak, Maya could only stare at it in horror.

The amber pupils of its mechanical eyes locked onto her. The pupils grew larger, then smaller, then larger again. Maya heard a hissing sound, as the machine drew closer. Maya desperately wanted to think *away*, but she could not form the word in her mind.

Several sharp cracks rang out nearby, bullets ricocheted off cars, and a frenzied crowd began to stampede down the sidewalks and street. The machine spun around and floated off, yelling, "Order! Order!"

Maya looked around helplessly.

Out! Please! I want out!

More movement.

Nighttime. Cool air. A star-filled sky. Maya saw the familiar outcropping a few feet away and the Indians in the clearing. Only now they were no longer sitting passively in a semi-circle but standing and talking. Some were eating. All were ignoring the wolves.

Maya watched as one of the wolves approached. She felt no fear. *I'm probably not even here*, she thought with satisfaction. She knelt down and extended out her hand. "Come here, girl. Come on, good girl," she said as if talking to an ordinary dog.

But the wolf didn't come. It began to shimmer and blur, just as Buddy had. Then, in a flash, it was gone, melted away into nothingness, and Maya felt her own form shifting.

The whirlpool of stars came into view, only this time above rather than below her. She knew what was coming and readied herself for the dizzying trip back.

The pressure of the ascent crushed her body. But did she have a body? She peeked at her arm, seeing only star-filled space.

She shot out of the vortex and halted in the air, in the dark. But not hovering, as before. Sitting. Sitting on a rocky ledge in the stillness of a pitch-black cave. She reached over and grabbed a handful of fur coat.

"Am I here?" she said breathlessly.

"I wouldn't have believed it if I hadn't seen it with my own eyes," Ben Ambrose said. "This is incredible."

19

Potential Future

Maya leaned against the cave wall and reveled in the heaviness—the solidity—of her body. She switched on the flashlight, careful to keep it low, and looked around. Everything was exactly as it had been before the vortex journey: the rocky ledge beneath her, the shadowy walls, the ring of boulders, the subterranean coolness, the passageway—and Ben Ambrose, staring right at her.

She said, "I have *no* idea what just happened."

"What just happened," he said with a smile, "is that you visited the probable future. More than one, actually."

"The dream!" Maya said. "The picnic table, the lake. I dreamed that place so many times." She turned away, embarrassed. "That's where we met."

"You brought all that with you," he said gently. "I simply used it as a gateway into the experience."

"The pyramid house," she said. "I never dreamed that."

"It ended before that, right?"

She nodded. "I never made it off the picnic table."

"I wanted you to be comfortable," Ben explained, "so you could go all the way in. And all the way in you went. That house is where the Mandala—or rather, projections of them—meet. That whole world is a mental construct. It doesn't exist, at least not in the way you think of existence. You see, Maya, the work isn't done on a physical level. It's *meta*physical. Meta means beyond, or transcending. You transcended the physical world."

"So where were those people?"

"At vortexes all over the world."

Maya shook her head, trying to take that in. "That felt like a dream," she said. "It still feels like a dream."

"Nonphysical work is always dreamlike," he said. "It's because you're not *here*. Technically, you're not 'of this place.' You're not even on Earth as you know it. Without the limitations of natural laws like gravity and time, you have more options at your fingertips. Experience moves fast—at the speed of thought. You don't *walk* anyplace. You just think it and you're there.

"This isn't anything new. People have been doing this for thousands of years. The ancients projected their consciousness just as you did. They didn't have external technologies because they didn't need them. Our world happened when people shifted to a different kind of experience, one that favors the rational thinking mind and a separation from nature."

He went on, "The physical world is just the outer crust of a multidimensional universe. It goes down *deep*. That's where the really interesting stuff happens."

"Hey," Maya said. "Those probable futures—that scary building and the happy people—is that what's coming?"

"You did see them," Ben said thoughtfully. "But this is more art than science. It's intuitive, subjective. Potentials are in flux and ever-changing, dependent on many variables. What you saw today might be more likely to manifest than the events trained remote viewers saw last week. Or less likely than what presents itself next week."

"What about my uncle?" Maya said, recalling the extraordinary sighting of Buddy. "Where was he?"

"My guess is that he's near a vortex."

Maya laughed. "That would be a pretty big coincidence, wouldn't it?"

"Not at all," Ben said. "Our world is punctured by thousands of minor vortexes. Energy constantly passes in and out of this plane at such places. If you calm yourself sufficiently, you can actually feel them."

Maya wrapped her arms around her knees and stared out into the dimness of the cave. "So, did I change the future?" she said, just kidding.

Ben's answer surprised her. "As a matter of fact, you did. But since you're not yet skilled in *consciously* directing the inner medium, you did it unconsciously. Look, there," he said.

She directed the flashlight beam at the floor below. A frightened wolf peered up at her from twenty feet away.

"Oh, my god!" Maya said. "How did it get in?"

"You invited her," Ben said.

"You said I was in the nonphysical world. That looks a whole lot like a real wolf to me."

"It's real, all right," he said. "Animals are more attuned to the subtle energies than we are. Our minds bind us more firmly to the physical. That wolf perceived you. Think about it, Maya. You changed the course of its life. Now, *that's* reality change. Simple life forms are easier to influence than complex ones, like us. Still, that was no small feat."

"Gosh, now I feel guilty," she said. "Can it get out?"

"Oh, I wouldn't worry about that. It's fulfilled the intention you set in motion. It's free to do whatever it wants."

As if on cue, the creature turned and disappeared into the passageway.

"Thoughts are tangible and real," Ben said. "They're not invisible nothings. 'You are what you think' isn't just a saying. Each thought is made up of energy packets, infinitely small. Smaller even than atoms. But like atoms, they behave according to laws—the laws of the inner medium. They're *used*. The inner medium draws them together into psychic structures which, in time, become physical events in the world.

"Vortexes simply act as amplifiers, speeding up the process. At powerful vortexes like this one, reality creation is jacked up to an unbelievably high degree. Harnessing all that power can be difficult, but I must say, you held your own. Now, developing the muscle for *large-scale* reality change is different. That can take a lifetime."

"Which is what you do."

"Try to, yes," he said, staring at the flashlight, still face down on the rock. He sighed. He seemed suddenly tired. He slumped. His last few words had been weak, Maya noticed, to the point where she had to lean in close just to hear him. Maybe the energy required for the vortex journey had worn him out.

"Are you all right?" she asked, moving in close.

"Fine," he said, lifting his hand to hide a grimace. "What else can I tell you?"

"What does the Mandala do?"

"We're in a certain business," he said. "The business of transforming intentions into events."

Maya considered that. She thought about all she'd learned over the past weeks. Everything, completely novel. Maybe what he was saying was true. Perhaps these theories did explain how physical events came to pass, or the way a certain potential future could be coaxed into being. Or maybe they were the first brushstrokes of truths that could not be fully known. Maybe none of it was true.

At that moment, she didn't care. Her interest lay not in the ideas but in the man, her concern for his well-being, for he seemed to be struggling mightily just to draw breath.

She wondered how much his utopian dream had cost him, and if he thought it had been worth it. She sensed the gaping hole in their personal histories, the empty space where a relationship should have been. She wondered if he felt it, too. Or maybe he was too immersed in his work to even take notice. Maybe he didn't care. She knew a little about people like him, men and women driven by grand ambition, who sought to change the world through the force of their extraordinary will. They were the people who made history, the leaders willing to pay the high price exacted by a single-mindedness of purpose, who steamrolled through life in a headlong rush to bring their dreams to fruition, often sacrificing people along the way, including the ones they loved.

In watching her father struggle to keep his body upright, to simply breathe, Maya was overcome by sadness. Maybe it was an assault of biology, a bending to the will of her DNA, for what was in her blood was in his, too.

It was more than that, she decided. It was about love. The love she'd been denied, the love she was owed.

"I don't think badly of you," she said.

He turned toward her, his movement slow and heavy.

She said, "I'm glad I'm here. I'm glad we met."

It was right to say that. She sat quietly. She rocked her body, back and forth, almost involuntarily, the way a child does, her feelings working themselves through her. When she ventured a glance at him, she saw that his eyes were fixed on her tennis shoes.

"Interesting," he said quietly.

"What's that?"

"The back of that shoe. Here, shine the light on it."

He leaned over and inspected her sneaker. "That's a yin-yang, and a creative interpretation at that," he said, staring at the sketch she'd made long ago in permanent marker.

"That it is," she affirmed. She smiled, choking back tears. *Imagine.* This stranger next to her, the man who had identified the yin-yang, was her own father.

"What's wrong, Maya?"

"Oh, nothing," she said. "I guess I'm happy."

She sat in contented silence, found herself wondering, *Is this the moment? Should I?*

She had been thinking about it since she first laid eyes on him—actually, for most of her life—but she was not sure she should try it. It could be awkward. But then, why not? There might not be another chance. She desperately wanted to hear the sound of it, to feel the word leave her lips. It was probably the wrong time, but she went ahead anyway.

"Dad," she said simply.

She waited. The word hung in the air between them. He didn't acknowledge it, just continued to stare down at her tennis shoe. Crushed, she shrank back, certain she'd made a grave mistake.

When she looked back over at him, she saw that his head was pitched forward, his arms limp at his sides. His eyes were closed. She moved in close.

"Are you OK?" she said.

She took his shoulder and gently shook him, watched in alarm as his head bobbed from side to side, the muscles of his neck gone flaccid. Frightened, she shook him sharply.

"Ben!" she said. "What's wrong?"

Slowly, with effort, his eyelids crept open.

When their eyes met, she *knew*. She knew why she was there, why Georgia had enlisted her on this mission, why Hania had urged her to push past her fears, and why she'd crossed the country on a journey that would almost certainly make her an alien to her former self, not to mention all the people in her life. It was as clear as the New Mexican sky.

"I'm getting you out of here *now*," she said.

Ben mumbled something and shook his head.

"You're sick!" Maya said. "Something horrible will happen if you stay in here. I'm sorry but I can't let that happen. We're leaving. We're most definitely leaving!"

"No—not finished—"

"You'll finish, I promise!"

She pulled him toward her, away from the wall, hoping to rouse him, to stir him, to get his mind working again, to jump-start him on a path out of the cold, desolate cave.

The creatures appeared without warning from the tunnel beside him. The bats poured into the chamber with the force of water shot from a fire hose, and angled for the open space in a mass that moved in a slow and ominous circle. Maya stared, her mouth agape. The beating of hundreds of wings created a terrific din, and she covered her ears against it.

She looked to her father for help. His eyes were closed. He was leaning forward. Instinctively Maya lay on her side and tucked herself into a fetal ball, wrapping her arms tightly around her head, pressing her knees into her chest.

The bats came at her, pounding her head, arms, abdomen and legs with the force of hurled baseballs. Her screams roused Ben from his stupor, and he jerked himself upright.

One of the bats was furiously nosing under Maya's hand. She could see the oversized ears close up, feel the pinpoint pressure on her skin. Another was probing at her shoulder, surprisingly hard given its small size. Each time she would shove it away, it returned as if pulled on a string. More bats alit on her. *I'm food*, she thought with horror.

Ben's voice pierced the din. It was weak and distant, and the words Maya heard she did not know. It was some other language. Immediately the bats stiffened, went limp and fell away. A few rolled over the ledge and smacked onto the floor below.

The cave returned to quiet. Maya remained still with her eyes shut until she had gathered the courage to peek out through her trembling fingers. Dozens of the stiff bodies littered the rock around her, and she kicked a few away, listening with satisfaction as they hit the floor below.

Beside her, Ben was speaking more in the strange tongue. The bats stirred. Maya's heart thumped, and again she wrapped herself into a ball. The bats took flight and re-formed, like fighter jets awaiting a signal to dive.

This time, though, they took aim at the lair from which they'd emerged. The long stream passed to within inches of Maya's face and disappeared into the small tunnel.

Again all was quiet. Maya loosened the vice grip around her head, felt her father's hand on her shoulder and unfolded slowly, like a newborn calf. She sat up and inspected her body, miraculously finding no cuts or bites, though the sleeves of her sweater were badly torn in places.

"I did that," Ben said miserably, avoiding her gaze.

"I know," Maya said.

"You have to go," he said, burying his face in his hands. "It's dangerous here."

"Ben, listen," Maya said intently. "I'm not trying to keep you from your work. You understand that?"

He nodded.

"Do you want to know why I'm here? The real reason?"

He stared at her.

"I *have* to know you," she said. "That can only happen if you're alive. If you don't want to see me, that's fine, I'll survive. But please just *exist*. Out there. Not in here, where you're going to—" Her words trailed off. She leaned in. "People are depending on you. Those men out there in the dirt. Georgia and Brandon. Help them. Help me."

Ben opened his mouth to speak but no words came. His body tilted toward her, like a tree toppling over. Maya held out her arms and he fell into them.

She smiled an odd smile—here was her dad, finally, literally, after all these years, in her arms.

She heard a voice down below.

"Hello!"

"Hania!" Maya called down. "Oh, thank God."

The old Indian peered up at father and daughter. "The wolves went home," he said. "And let me tell you, they were relieved. Ben, how are you?"

Ben couldn't answer. He was unconscious. Within seconds, Hania was there beside him, trying to rouse him, a look of concern on his face.

Standing in the clearing in front of the cave, Maya peered up at the bright moon and the jeweled multitude of stars sprinkled across the night sky. The heavens appeared unusually bright after the permanent midnight of the cave. A few feet away the Indians were emerging from the dark opening, carrying a sling on which the unmoving figure of Ben Ambrose lay. They handed him carefully down to their companions below.

Maya began toward them but Tomas held out his arm.

"Where are they taking him?" she asked, watching the men make their way toward the woods.

"They will care for him," Tomas said. "My father wants you to rest. He said you did a great thing. You should be proud."

"Where are they going?" Maya insisted.

"I don't know. Please do as he asks. It's for your own good."

Maya paused, checked in with herself. Tomas was right. She was exhausted, her body spent. Much had happened since she'd awakened in Keith's house in Taos that morning.

Tomas offered a bottle filled with a clear liquid. "Here, this will help," he said.

"What is it?"

"It's like a green drink. It's made from plants."

Maya held it up to her nose and sniffed at its pungent contents, then downed it all in a long swallow. "Good," she said.

"Come this way," Tomas said.

He led her to a trail, shining a flashlight so she could see the way ahead, staying close on the five-minute walk to a site where a campfire was burning. Georgia was sitting on a blanket near a tent, staring into the flames. She rushed over to embrace Maya.

"Georgia, is that you?" Maya said blearily.

"It is," Georgia said, guiding Maya into the tent and into a sleeping bag. Maya passed out before Georgia had even closed the tent flap.

She lay on her back staring up at the dark green of the tent fabric, faintly lit in the dawn light. Georgia was snoring in a sleeping bag beside her, oblivious to the cacophony of bird song raining down from the trees.

Maya quietly opened the flap and poked her head outside. The air was cool and refreshing. She saw her sneakers on the ground and she grabbed them and slid them on and quietly stepped out of the tent.

Standing in the dewy grass, she groaned. Her body was unusually stiff. She stretched out her arms and arched her back, hearing bones creak and crack in ways she'd never heard before.

She surveyed the forest, unsure of what to do. She sat on a fallen tree trunk and waited for Georgia to wake up.

The experience of the cave flowed into her mind, as did remnants of the dreams she'd had during the night, which had left her with the feeling of being anesthetized, as if some inner administrator had numbed her thinking facility while it sifted through all the new information—data which would have to be fathomed, organized and filed.

When Georgia stepped out of the tent, Maya plied her with questions, but the older woman would only focus on fixing breakfast: a hearty vegetable stew warmed in a large pot over the campfire, and a kettle of coffee. Maya ate and drank ravenously.

Tomas arrived at midmorning to take them to see Ben. Georgia doused the fire and hung the food from a branch, gathered her things and the three set off.

Rounding the familiar rock outcropping, Maya saw the Indians in the clearing, only not as figures sitting in the dirt or carrying a wounded man into the night. Now they were eating, laughing, smoking and regaling each other with jokes and stories. Maya saw Hania and waved to him.

Then she saw the reason for all the excitement: Ben Ambrose standing near the rocky platform, transformed.

Maya's mind reeled, unable to accept what her eyes were seeing. *This can't be*, she thought.

Ben's beard was gone and his hair was cleanly trimmed and combed back. His face, though still pale, had gained much in color, and his cheeks, which had been like sickly flaps, had somehow filled out. The red, swollen nose now appeared normal in size. In fact, much like Maya's own. He moved about easily. He was wearing blue jeans, a khaki shirt and wraparound sunglasses that looked glamorous—hardly the ravaged figure teetering on death's doorstep whom she'd encountered just hours earlier.

"I don't understand," Maya said.

"He's no finished product by any means," Georgia said. "But not bad, eh? They turned the vortex back on him. Used it for regeneration."

"What?"

"They channeled its healing power to help him."

"In one night?" Maya said.

"Well, no. Not exactly one."

Maya waited, holding her breath.

Georgia took Maya's hand. "Your nap took a little longer than that."

"How long?" Maya asked, bracing for the answer.

"Thirty-six hours," Georgia said.

"You mean I lost a whole day?"

"Stranger things have happened," Georgia said.

"Believe me, I know," Maya said. Her legs felt suddenly rubbery. Georgia erupted in laughter, just as Ben Ambrose started toward them.

20

Canis Lupus

Maya followed her father to a hillside a stone's throw away from the cave, where they sat knee to knee, facing the woods. It wasn't much of a private place, though, because Hania and the Indians came around every few minutes to check on Ben.

"He's *fine*," Maya wanted to say. "For God's sake, leave us be." But she did no such thing. This was their world, and she knew she was fortunate to be allowed into it.

Sitting beside him, Maya got to see the phenomenal change firsthand. It was astonishing. The flesh of his face and arms was still pale, his muscle tone loose, his body thin—but it was close. Miraculously close. The Pueblos had worked a miracle on him during Maya's long slumber.

"I don't usually wear these things," Ben said, touching the large sunglasses that hid much of his face.

"After that cave, I'm surprised you can see at all," Maya said.

He looked at her and smiled. They sat in silence. Maya was eager to launch into her questions, of which there were many, but she held back and decided to wait for a natural opening.

"It sure is gorgeous here," she said lightly. "Though I'm not sure where *here* is."

"To tell you the truth, neither am I," Ben said.

"Like I believe that," Maya said with a laugh.

He reached down and pinched a blade of grass from the ground and placed it in the corner of his mouth. Then, quickly, he flicked it away. "I imagine all this must be fantastic to you," he said.

"Actually, it's starting to feel normal," she said.

"Is it?"

"The things I've seen," she said, "no one I know would believe."

"There'll be more," he said.

"The change," she said. "That's what you mean. Maybe I shouldn't bother looking for a job. I mean if the world is going to turn upside down."

"Is that what you're doing—looking for work?"

It was an innocent question. Of course he knew nothing about her.

A loud cheer erupted over by the cave, out of sight.

"I wonder who's happier," Maya said, glancing toward the cave, "the Pueblos or the wolves. To tell you the truth, I'd be fine if there were no wolves in my life for a while."

"There won't be," Ben said, "except maybe at the zoo. I'm not a fan of those places. No animal should be caged."

Maya took that in. *Zoos, bad.*

Another long silence passed. He seemed content to just sit and make small talk, or no talk at all. Maya, on the other hand, wanted answers.

"So, what happens now?" she said when she could take it no longer. Then she quickly added, "I mean, about the Mandala and, you know, the change."

"You mean about us," he said.

"Yeah."

She shifted on the grass and waited, but he just sat there staring out at the trees, his last word buzzing at her ear. She swore herself to patience, tried to halt the nervous tapping of her fingers on her thigh.

"We live our lives," Ben said finally. "With a difference."

"A difference?"

"You said you needed to know that I exist, that I'm alive. Well, thanks to you, I am. You were right. Hania was right. I'm grateful to you both."

"Hey, you're into your work, I get that," Maya said, trying to put him at ease. "I mean, it's understandable—"

"Listen, Maya," Ben said. "I'm not sure how to make things right with you."

"History is … ever-changing," she said, quoting Buddy. "I understand that. You don't have to 'make things right'."

"No," he said. "I do."

"It can wait," she insisted.

She watched him out of the corner of her eye. *We're here, now.*

"In time," he said.

"OK."

That was fine. It was something. Or the hope of something. At that moment she wanted something more concrete, more *now:* to see him. The dark lenses over his eyes may as well have been steel doors.

"It's tough without the glasses, huh?" she said.

"Let's find out," he said, as he lifted them off. Squinting, in obvious discomfort, he said, "Not too bad."

He turned to her and she looked into her father's eyes for the first time.

"Blue," she said.

"Brown," he said, looking at hers.

No color match, she thought, feeling a pinch of discomfort. *No big deal.*

"Where were you before you came here?" she said.

"South America," he said.

"How often are you in the U.S.?"

He hesitated, then said, "It's best if we don't talk about details like that. I'm sure you understand."

"Sure," she said. "Are you married?"

He smiled. "You do get right to the point."

"God, I'm sorry. I don't know where that came from."

"It's fine," he said. "I'm not married. Are you?"

She laughed. "No."

Maya's mind went blank. "I had a hundred questions. Now I can't find a single one."

"You don't have to find anything," he said.

There was a faint sound in the distance, and Maya looked up into the sky. The sound grew louder, until it was obvious that it was an engine. Then it was two engines. Ben hurriedly put his sunglasses on and stood up, his expression intense as he searched the treetops.

"What is it?" Maya asked.

"It's the end of our conversation, for now," he said through gritted teeth. He scanned the eastern sky, his face frozen in concentration. Watching him, Maya imagined this look on him often, all the years he'd been on the run. The fugitive Ben Ambrose.

The roar of engines was now deafening, shattering the calm of the mountainside. Hovering over the treetops were two black helicopters, kicking up dust and sending leaves and branches swirling high into the air. Ropes were tossed down from bay doors and uniformed men reached for them. A loudspeaker bellowed, "This is the FBI! Stay where you are! Do not move!"

Ben took Maya's arm and they hurried toward the clearing, where they ran into three stout Pueblo men heading toward them.

The Pueblos led Maya, Ben and Georgia onto a trail and urged them to run. Ben, in his weakened state, struggled. The men on either side of him gripped his upper arms and whisked him along, his sandals hardly touching ground as the trail moved swiftly beneath him.

Maya, who could run a five-minute mile, kept pace easily. Trees and bushes whisked by, brushing against her arms and legs. At one point, she stumbled on a fallen branch and picked herself up, and hesitating a moment too long, was shoved hard by a strong hand at the center of her back. *Run!*

Dogs barked in the distance. Quickly the barking got louder and closer. Maya's spirits faltered. How could a near-emaciated man, a septuagenarian and a young woman from Plainfield, Maryland outpace K-9s, animals bred for the single purpose of running down humans? In seconds the escape attempt would meet its end in a way that Maya did not want to speculate about. After all these years, the authorities would have Ben Ambrose. And what of the Mandala? Could they go on without Ben?

The escaping group pushed on. The cave was far behind now, the loudspeaker's staccato commands fading from hearing. The dogs were about to arrive.

Something brushed against Maya's leg, moving rapidly in the opposite direction. Then, again. She looked down, seeing only blurred shapes.

And gray fur.

The wolves!

A bone-chilling clamor of growls and barks erupted out of sight, eclipsing the pounding of the runners' footfalls and the crackling of brush underfoot. The runners halted. Ben fell to his knees, staring at the ground.

In the nearby trees, an unseen war raged. Maya covered her ears against the wails, but no amount of pressure from her palms could hide what was happening. Then, as quickly as it had begun, it was over. A series of plaintive moans drifted over as the K9s wandered off, beaten. The wolves sped by and disappeared into the forest. All was still. Maya looked to Georgia for an explanation, but the older woman would only shake her head sadly.

Ben stood up wearily as the Pueblos assisted him with great care. The party gathered itself and trudged on, taking many different paths, stopping occasionally to rest. As darkness fell, a log cabin came into view up ahead.

Standing at its front door, Ben and Georgia bid farewell to the Pueblos, who disappeared back into the forest.

The cabin was a large single room overrun by dust, dirt and spider webs, furnished sparely with an old couch, a bed, a table and chairs, and a rocking chair. A lantern stood in one corner, which Georgia refused to light for fear of being seen outside. The only illumination was the moonlight streaming in through two windows.

The group was exhausted. Georgia fell heavily onto the couch and Maya settled into the rocker. Ben sat on the edge of the bed.

"What just happened?" Maya asked.

"They came close this time," Georgia said. "We should be fine now. We'll have no trouble here."

Ben said, "Maya, are you OK?"

"Hanging in there," Maya said, trying to maintain her cool. But it wasn't happening.

"Let's rest for a bit," Ben said. "Do you want the bed? I'm fine in the rocker."

"No, you go ahead," Maya said. "I've had plenty of sleep."

He said, "I'm going to shut my eyes."

"Me, too," said Georgia.

Ben lay back on the filthy white sheet. The bed bounced a few times on its squeaky springs before coming to rest. Maya looked over at Georgia spread out on the couch. Within minutes, both Ben and Georgia were asleep.

Which left Maya rocking in silence, and wondering how on earth they could relax so completely under the circumstances. They looked like slumbering lion cubs on either side of the cabin, without a care in the world.

Maya was OK with some time to herself. Her mind alit on little fantasies, and especially one: going out to breakfast with her father, talking with him and getting to know him. She wondered if that would ever happen.

He awoke around the same time as Georgia, looking fresh and rejuvenated, while Maya, still rocking, had barely taken her eyes off the door, waiting for the FBI to break through it.

"You needn't worry," Ben said, watching her.

"No, I do," Maya said, correcting the inaccuracy.

Georgia said, "We'll be out of here soon."

"They're looking for us," said Maya.

"They're being led away."

"How can you be so sure?"

"Listen," Georgia said, holding her hand to her ear. "Do you hear anything? I don't."

"That's not funny," Maya said.

"Seriously," Georgia said. "Do you see anything worrisome?"

"Well, not at the moment."

"So, right now there's no danger, right?"

"If they sprang for helicopters," Maya said, "I'm guessing they have cars."

Georgia said, "So what?"

Maya, rocking even harder, said, "I worry. I can't help it."

"Ah, but you can."

"I'm not so sure."

"But it *is* possible you're wrong?"

"Anything is possible," Maya said.

"Would you be willing to try something different?"

Maya watched Georgia, waited.

"Surrender," Georgia said.

Maya said, "That's what we're trying *not* to do."

"No,' Georgia said. "I'm talking about an internal process. I mean yield to the now. To what's happening in this moment. What's not happening is the police. What's happening is the three of us sitting here, talking."

Maya sighed. She knew what Georgia was getting at. It had never worked.

Georgia folded her hands in her lap. "Your mind is getting in the way," she said.

"Duh," Maya said. "But knowing it doesn't help."

"Disconnect from it."

"Difficult," Maya said.

Georgia said, "When you fight *what is*, you're pushing against life. Life doesn't like that. It's to your advantage to do the opposite of that."

"How?" Maya said.

"Simple," said Georgia. "Intend it. That's the starting point. Don't focus on the endpoint."

"What I really want to do," Maya said, "is intend a plan."

"We've already got one," Georgia said.

"Really? What?"

"Listen," Georgia said. "When action is called for, we'll act. You don't have to worry about that. Right now, we're sitting in this nice, quiet cabin where our only option is to wait. So why be miserable?"

"Because it's familiar?" Maya said, trying to make light of the situation, though the statement seemed depressingly true. She looked from Georgia to Ben. The expression on their faces was innocence—or control. It didn't matter what they were saying or that she couldn't do Georgia's exercise in Be Here Now, which she had tried and failed at too many times to count. Though the situation was desperate, she found herself reveling in the warmth and wisdom of her companions. They were like family. He *was* family.

Maya turned to him and said, "This global change of yours. This thing that's supposed to happen? When does it happen? Next week? Next year? Five years?"

"Unclear," he said. "There's an issue we have yet to resolve. We're well along, but there's one last piece of the puzzle. To get the change started, there's the issue of achieving critical mass. For that, we need—"

The curtains at the front window lit up. Outside, a car engine whirred, then fell silent. Footsteps sounded at the side of the cabin. Maya froze on the rocker as she watched the doorknob turn. A potential future flickered across the screen of her mind: her father and Georgia being whisked away in handcuffs, and she never seeing them again.

The door opened and Keith Seputa walked in.

"There's very little time," he said worriedly.

"Here's your *now*, now," Georgia said to Maya.

The group hurried outside and into the Wagoneer. Keith drove along the dirt road, as Georgia reached across the backseat to squeeze Maya's hand, a much-needed gesture of comfort.

When he came to a paved road, Keith shifted into a lower gear and began to descend the switchbacks, and in time they arrived at the outskirts of Taos. They sped along on the flatland on an empty highway for some time until they pulled into the parking lot of a roadside restaurant. A neon sign read BLUE DESERT DINER. The parking lot was empty but for one car.

"They're about to close," Keith said. "I have to go into town to deal with all this. You'll be fine here. I'll send someone out to get you."

"Thank you, Keith," Ben said. "For everything."

"You bet. It's great to see you, Ben. Good luck."

Standing on the gravel parking lot, Maya, Ben and Georgia watched him drive away. Maya scanned the moonlit desert landscape, bathed in a feeling of surrealness. The world looked pristine and new, as if it had just come into existence at that very moment: the immense star-filled sky. The dim outline of the mountains. The blazing full moon. And walking beside her, a man whose genetic makeup she shared, whose morphogenetic field informed hers in ways she could only hope to discover in time. He was a man who, until now, had been no more than a thought in her mind.

It would not be until many months later, as she sifted through the memories of all that had happened in an effort to make sense of it, that she would come to connect a portion of the journal to the incident about to take place.

If the events of our lives are meant to be learning experiences, it is up to us to understand and integrate their meaning. If you don't do this, you risk missing out on the meaning of your life. There exist clues, or synchronicities, that await your eyes, ears and mind, which can provide the needed insights. They beckon to be discovered.

The lone car in the parking lot belonged to Albert Fiske.

21

The Lure of Opposites

All those years ago, after Ben Ambrose had fled the familiar, comfortable world of Plainfield for the outlaw's life, never could he have predicted that the journey would lead to the nexus that presented itself now in the U.S. desert Southwest. But it was fate that had drawn him to this location. Opposing forces, by their nature, seek out their counterparts, and in their eventual joining are presented with an opportunity to crack the kernel of truth upon which the attraction rests. Perhaps that is why Albert Fiske, sitting on a stool at the long Formica lunch counter of the Blue Desert Diner, turned away from his unfinished sandwich at precisely the moment Ben walked through the door with his daughter and main lieutenant in tow.

Fiske eyed the travelers with astonishment. Maya glanced at Georgia and caught a worried look, which caused some distress, for Georgia had been unshakable until then, besting every challenge with a certainty that was far from the look on her face now.

For Ben, there was no escape. No helpful Indians to whisk him to safety, nor animal allies to defend him, nor Mandala agents to assist him past obstacles. All that existed in that moment was the old stucco building, the opposing forces within it, and a troubled history.

Two men sat on the stools on either side of Fiske, but otherwise the restaurant was deserted. A row of red-cushioned booths lined one wall, and many four-top tables were spread across a scuffed-up floor that had no doubt seen tens of thousands of footsteps.

Ben met Fiske's gaze. "Hello, Al," he said casually.

Maya looked on rapturously. *He expected this.*

Fiske stood up and gave a grand gesture of welcome. "Greetings to all," he said. Then he introduced the men beside him. "Agent Gaddis and Agent Andrelli," he said.

Agent Gaddis was an imposing figure, a thick-necked man with a barrel chest and arms the size of small tree trunks. Without saying a word, he strode over to the restaurant's front door, and after a quick peek outside, turned and planted himself in the doorway. Andrelli, a slender man with thinning hair and darting eyes, remained at Fiske's side.

Maya hardly recognized Fiske. When she had first met him in Washington, D.C., he came off as intense and blustery, but not such a terrible guy. Then there was the bar in Virginia, where he had squeezed her hands until she was writhing in pain. Now, he had the hungry look of an animal sizing up prey.

"We invested big bucks in surveillance, you know," he said, "and what happens? We eat at a hole in the wall in the middle of nowheresville and in walks our man. Talk about good fortune."

No, Maya thought. *Talk about synchronicity.*

Andrelli reached into his jacket, his hand moving toward a slight bulge beneath his left armpit. Fiske saw this and shook his head and said, "No. Not yet."

Maya looked worriedly at Ben, who, curiously, remained cool and composed. His gaze was directed at Fiske, his focus the same single pointed effort that Maya had seen in his eyes as he scanned the treetops as the helicopters arrived.

Maya saw a flicker of movement behind the counter, near the soft drink machine. A hand, maybe, or a shoulder moving out of sight. Someone was there. The Mandala? What could they do now?

The movement morphed into a man: a grizzled, pony-tailed fry cook with bulging, bloodshot eyes. He gave a pained smile, hesitated, then, without a word, dashed into the back room. Andrelli started toward him, but Fiske held up his hand. "Don't bother with it," he said.

Ben said, "How are you, Al?"

Fiske put his hand to his chin and made a show of thinking about it. "Honestly? It's been challenging of late, but I sense a *change* coming on, if you know what I mean. And I think you do." He laughed.

Ben strode up to Fiske in a catlike move, fluid and unexpected. Maya watched, thinking, *I don't know this man.* Georgia, who was near one of the booths, moved toward Ben, but stopped when she saw Gaddis coming at her. She backed off, and the agent returned to the doorway.

"You're still holding a grudge, Al," Ben said. "I feel it."

Fiske stared at Ben, said nothing.

"Your anger is unchanged," Ben went on, "even after all these years."

Looking on, Maya was mesmerized. The agents remained still and uncertain.

"Disappointing," Ben said. "Most men would have gotten on with their lives by now. They'd have done that long ago. But not you. A life spent in revenge isn't much of a life, Al. It's small. It's unworthy of a human being. Are you a human being?"

"What?" Fiske said, confused.

Maya was confused, too.

The next words Ben spoke carried an explosive charge, like grenades. "Twenty years!" he boomed out. "Twenty years, Al!"

Fiske fell back bodily as though he'd been hit, and reached for the counter to steady himself. His legs nearly came out from under him but he found support against a stool.

Maya stared dumbfounded at the scene unfolding before her. Ben's words were penetrating Fiske like blades. Ben seemed *larger*, though surely that could not be the case. Now he was practically on top of Fiske. The agents watched doe-eyed and spellbound.

"Look over here, Al, at me, that's right," Ben said. "Do you know what resentment does to a person over time? It's like cancer. It eats away at you. Do you feel it? Do you feel it right now, eating away at your insides?"

In a voice so weak as to be almost inaudible, Fiske said, "Don't make this about me, Ambrose. It's not. It's always been about you." Sweat traced down the side of his face.

"You're absolutely right," Ben said easily and with a smile. "It can't be about you because you're gone. You don't exist."

Fiske's forehead wrinkled in thought, as if he were seriously considering the validity of his being. His face was pale. He pushed off the counter and walked unsteadily toward the booth windows, gripping his stomach like he might vomit. Ben approached.

"You aren't standing here now," Ben said. "And you weren't sitting on that stool a moment ago."

Fiske mumbled, "What are you doing—"

"You're *gone*, Al. You've been gone a long time. And you don't even know it. You have no clue what's happened to you."

Fiske wiped a hand across his forehead. "Nothing's happened to me," he said.

"You were a man ... once," Ben said. "But you changed. You devolved, became a concept. Ambition. Naked, shameless ambition. Ambition without a conscience. A career. People paid for it, Al. I paid for it."

Fiske's swagger was a distant memory. He seemed empty, as though his life force had drained out of him.

He balled his hands into fists and stared toward the windows. "I can do this," he said to himself. "I know what's happening."

"No, you can't," Ben said.

Fiske's eyes raged as he spat, "You're viewing! You're viewing me!"

A hint of a smile crossed Ben's face.

Fiske looked up at the ceiling and let out a loud and startling wail. Maya recoiled, hearing the animal-like cry, which reminded her of her own primal scream in the forest. Fiske wheeled around toward Ben, his face blood-red.

And that was it. The moment everything shifted. It happened quickly and Maya saw it completely. When Fiske looked over at Ben, Fiske was himself again. His posture was erect and his voice strong.

"Oh, Ben," Fiske said.

Ben stared at him.

Fiske said, "Do you remember what you used to say?"

"What?" Ben said, as if roused from a dream.

"What you said about the work," Fiske said. "The work you loved so much. Oh, come on, you must remember."

Ben said nothing.

"You said we were a team," Fiske said. "You couldn't believe you were 'being paid' to do this. Remember? You loved it. Oh, you did. You were breaking new ground, doing things no one had ever before done. You wanted to make history. You did, Ben. All those trips. All those adventures. Come on, tell me you don't remember the things we did."

Ben was lost. Maya saw it and didn't know why it was happening. His look was far-away. Whatever had occurred to destroy his confidence and the devastating power he had claimed, was complete.

Maya wondered if he was even aware of it. He sagged. She wished him back into his strength, but he was thoroughly derailed, revisiting the past, lost in the old days; days spent rushing headlong into uncharted areas, of advancing the frontiers of a science that wasn't even on the map.

He was staring out the window. It was dark outside. He couldn't have been looking at anything.

"I remember," he said wistfully.

No, Maya thought.

"Ben!" Georgia called out.

He turned to her. Fiske moved to block the way. "Those days were something, weren't they, Ben?" he said.

"For a time, yes," Ben said.

"It changed, I know," Fiske said. "That was my fault, of course."

"The senator," said Ben.

Fiske said, "That was my mistake. I freely admit it."

Ben's chin was down toward his chest, his eyes locked on his shoes. Maya could hardly endure it. He said, "I never forgave myself for that."

"For what?" Maya interjected.

Both men turned to her, surprised at the interruption, surprised others were in the room.

"Go ahead, tell her," Fiske said.

A shadow crossed Ben's face.

"It was a Friday," Ben said. "Odd I recall that. We did the active remote viewing on a senator, Montgomery Ames. We got him to change his position on a bill that was up for a vote. It was just a test. The poor guy collapsed. He'd had a stroke."

"He recovered completely," Fiske said.

"You can really do that?" Maya said.

"Yes," Ben said.

Fiske said, "We learned from it. We stopped it. Nothing like it has been done since, until now, Ben. Until what you just did."

"It wasn't just one project," Ben said. "It was all of them. Your goal wasn't security, Al. It was control. That's what you've always wanted."

Maya sensed strength returning to her father. Ben moved toward Fiske.

"Whoa, stop right there," Fiske said, holding out a hand. "Take one more step and I'll have Agent Gaddis intervene in a way that will be very unpleasant for you. You can't handle all three of us."

Gaddis smiled at Ben, relishing his power. Ben backed away.

Fiske said, "This 'change' of yours—how is it any different from what we did? *You* want to manipulate people. So did we. The only difference is scale. Yours is huge. What if you're wrong?"

"We're not wrong," Georgia said. "We're giving people back their birthright, returning their God-given power. The power that was there before the veil came down."

"No," Fiske said hotly. "You're playing God. And besides"—he spoke to Ben—"you don't think *they're* going to let your little change happen, do you?"

Maya looked on, uncomprehending.

Georgia frowned.

"Doesn't matter," Ben said. "It won't change a thing."

"Won't it?" Fiske said.

"Won't what?" Maya said.

"Not a *what*, little girl," Fiske said. "A *who*."

"What are you talking about?" Maya said.

"The rulers of this globe," Fiske said. "The real ones. I don't mean governments. They don't control much of anything. You think you know what's going on out there, Maya? You think what you watch on the news is real? Those are shows, little girl. Productions crafted for your eager consumption. The *who* I'm talking about is the point-zero-zero-one percent of the population, the supremely powerful, the 'ambitious,' to use your father's term. World events don't just happen. They're designed, orchestrated. It's a grand symphony out there, a thing of beauty once you see it, created by virtuosos for a cold-blooded purpose. Do you want to know what that purpose is?"

"No," Maya said.

Fiske laughed. "Its purpose to keep the rich in power. You know—those nice people who finance wars, manipulate alliances, control markets, own the media and mold the careers of public figures who in turn do their bidding. You think you know history? Your degree is in storytelling, myth. Your father and I, we understand what's going on. We're minnows in a piranha tank, and unless he's changed, he's probably still denying it. I don't blame him. I'd want to forget it if I could. You're a slave, Maya, and you don't even know it. We all are."

Maya looked away. The air in the room suddenly felt thick and murky, like a doctor's waiting room packed with sick people. She glanced over at the windows—thin panes of glass shielding her from perhaps a radically different world than she thought existed. Maybe there was no point in "believing" anything. Things were changing by the hour, if not the minute.

"What do they want?" Maya asked.

To her surprise, her father answered.

"Control," Ben said.

"*You* believe this?"

Ben walked over. A look of compassion settled on his face. "It sounds crazy, I know," he said.

"It does," Maya said.

"History," Ben said, "in large part, is the story of these men. Why, you might ask? Why do they do it? Why does power corrupt? And why does absolute power corrupt so absolutely? Why are these men driven to dominate, and given the opportunity, eager to bring populations to their knees? I'll tell you why, Maya. It's about love."

"Love?"

"The absence of love. These men live in a far different world than we do. They develop differently. The tyrants, the despots, the controllers, the cabal masters—all those who grab and hold power at all costs—bring an innate lack with them, which is wholly destructive, for it cannot by its nature be sated, though they push ever harder to do just that.

"It's validation they seek, at a deep psychological level," he continued. "The domination, the bullying and control becomes pathological. The loop goes round and round. Theirs is a twisted attempt to be valued, a grasping for acceptance, a yearning for something they are unable to have because the capacity to recognize it is absent within them. This unquenchable desire, paired with indomitable will and access to great resources, creates an unholy alliance that drives them to madness, for they seek the impossible: to find in the outer world that which does not exist outside of the self."

Maya listened, trying to take that in. "Are they all like that?" she said.

"Being *like that* is the sole requirement for the club they're in," Ben said. "As in all clubs, those who do not share the prevailing view are cast out."

He pointed at Fiske. "He's right. Many global events are shaped. All sorts of machinations take place, out of sight, in back rooms, in the shadows. But the real insanity is that the elites believe their control is warranted, that it's for the good of all. To a man, they believe the end justifies the means, that ultimately their rule is just. That's the madness of it. And with advances in technology and communications, their minions can now reach into the minds of the multitudes, laid bare by the internet and TV." He stared, pleadingly, at Maya. "Do you see the insidiousness of it? All those people, all those innocents, unknowingly doing their bidding. But they can be freed! That's what we're doing. We'll wake them up. I promise, we'll—"

"Ben," Fiske interrupted. "Listen. I'm not disagreeing with you, mind you. But we do need to move on. I'm wondering if we—meaning you and I—might find a middle ground. A compromise."

"A what?" Ben said.

"Would you consider a proposition?"

Hearing that, Maya snapped to attention.

"Speak," Ben said.

"Come back," Fiske said. "Work for me. Let's try again. You were the best. You're even better now. Share it. Help us. Put the Mandala on hold, if only to make sure your plan is sound."

Maya held her breath, as her imagination took flight, rocketing off into the future—a future with a father in it, and a friend. The fulfillment of her most potent childhood dreams.

Ben walked the length of the floor, grazing his fingers along the Formica countertop. He glanced toward the windows and listened for a moment to the whoosh of a car speeding out on the highway. He peered over at Maya, saw the hope in her eyes and mouthed the words *I'm sorry*. Maya turned away, crushed.

Ben said to Fiske, "No. Never."

"Don't you even want to think about it? What about her?" Fiske said of Maya. "Surely you'll want to see her. Bonding could be difficult in federal prison."

"None of this will last," Ben said.

"Everything will change," Georgia added.

"We'll see," Fiske said. "I'm going to let you in on a little secret. So please, keep this between us. We're picking up your people right now, all over the world. It's over. In a few days there won't be enough Mandala left to change a lightbulb, much less planet Earth."

Fiske nodded to Agent Gaddis standing at the door, who stepped forward and grabbed Ben in a quick movement, pinning his arms behind him. Maya and Georgia ran to Ben, but Andrelli stepped in their way. Fiske moved toward Ben, but stopped suddenly.

Sounds were coming from the parking lot. Everyone turned toward the windows. Cars were arriving, scattering gravel beneath their tires.

22

Ruler of the Globe

Four black Land Rovers and a stretch limousine pulled into the parking lot of the Blue Desert Diner as regally as a presidential motorcade, rolling to a halt one after another spaced exactly the same distance apart. The engines fell silent all at once, returning the area to middle-of-nowhere quiet. The imposing cars remained still for some minutes, impervious to the outside world, shielding secrets behind darkly tinted windows.

The driver's side door of the limo swung open and a uniformed chauffeur stepped out. He reached for the back door handle.

Meanwhile, inside the diner, Albert Fiske was calling to his agents in rapid-fire commands, telling them to release Ben Ambrose. Maya and Georgia ran into Ben's arms.

The diner's front door swung open. Two tall men in dark suits stood in the doorway. Between them was a wheelchair, and in it was an old man. The men hoisted the chair up and set it down inside.

Edgar Porter nodded his thanks and pressed a lever in the chair's armrest, and the chair rolled across the linoleum floor, past the tables, past a speechless Fiske and his men, and past Maya, Ben and Georgia to the far side of the room. He stopped there and spun the chair around.

Agent Gaddis stared angrily at Fiske. "What the hell is this?" he said.

"We're U.S. Secret Service," said one of the tall men. He held up an ID badge. "This doesn't concern you, Agent. Just him." He pointed at Fiske.

"This is an operation in progress," Gaddis said.

"Listen up, Agent Gaddis," the Secret Service man said. "You're a good man. You'll be hitting retirement in three years. You've worked a few rogue jobs for our friend here, but, hey, no one's perfect. You want to keep that nice pension you've got coming? We're presidential commission. So, back off."

Gaddis insisted, "State your business."

"Our business is our own," Porter said.

Everyone turned toward Porter, whose eyes were fixed on the windows. There was a tapping on one of the panes, which spread to the next, and the next, until all the windows were rattling loudly. The outlines of several shadowy figures could be seen outside, each one holding a pistol aimed at Agent Gaddis.

Gaddis stared hard at Fiske, then at the Secret Service men. "All right," he relented. "All right. I get the point."

"Perhaps you and your partner would be kind enough to step outside," said Porter.

With that, they departed, glaring at Fiske as they left.

"Now, then," Porter said. "To the business at hand."

His gaze travelled from one person to the next, and settled on Maya, to whom he said, "My intrepid friend, congratulations. You found him. I'm impressed, and not for the first time."

Maya couldn't help but smile at him, even as she considered all she'd learned about him. Maybe he was dangerous, as Georgia warned, but Maya didn't share Georgia's point of reference. To her, Dr. Porter would always be an odd and fascinating character, the man who started her on her journey. If not for him, she may not have met her father. No doubt she'd still be in Plainfield, lost and confused.

But he had frightened her, too, that morning in his garden with his ominous words and unnerving laugh, which hinted at very different aspects of his nature.

He was staring at Georgia.

"Ms. Roussey," he said. "I haven't had the pleasure."

"Charmed, I'm sure," she said coolly.

"You know who I am?"

"Of course I do."

He bowed his head slightly, as much as he could, then turned his attention to Fiske. "Which leaves one little piggy."

"Edgar, why are you doing this?" Fiske said.

"Doing what?"

"Getting involved," Fiske said.

"Honestly," Porter laughed dismissively. "Getting involved? All I'm doing is stopping you from making yet another of your blunders. There were many and they were legion. For instance, there was no need to make a mess of poor Maya's home and upset her mother. You know we don't involve others."

"I knew it!" Maya said, glaring at Fiske. So he'd been behind the break-in. It was more reason to despise him.

Fiske pointed at Ben. "He's right here! You promised—"

"I promised nothing," Porter said icily. "Your work here is done. Now go outside and wait for me."

"No," Fiske said.

"You take a rather small view of things, sir," Porter said, wheeling toward Fiske. The Secret Service men stiffened, looking on. He said, "Please, do as I've asked. It's for your own sake."

"I won't," Fiske said.

"Suit yourself," Porter said and nodded to his men, who moved quickly toward Fiske. They took his arms, but he shook them off and stepped toward the door of his own accord. As he exited, he turned to Ben and said, "This isn't over."

Maya looked on, astonished. Was Fiske really gone?

"A most unpleasant business," Porter said, shaking his head. "I hope you can put him out of your mind. Now, sit, please, all of you. You must be exhausted after your travails."

He wheeled over to the table where Ben, Georgia and Maya sat. He looked Ben over closely.

"Tell me," he said. "How long has it been?"

"Twenty years, Edgar," Ben said. "Give or take."

"My my, how time flies," Porter said. "Look at you. You've hardly aged. What's your secret? Few of us can survive the onslaught of time unscathed. Least of all me, as you can plainly see." He paused. "Tell me, honestly, how are you?"

"Confused," Ben said, "if you want to know the truth."

Porter laughed. "You're wondering why I'm here."

Ben nodded.

"I'm here because want to share something with you," Porter said. "Something I generally keep under my hat."

"Which is?"

"I'm softening."

"Softening," Ben repeated.

"That's right."

"Meaning?"

"Just that, what I said."

"Edgar," Ben said. "You haven't said much of anything."

Porter laughed.

Ben leaned forward in the metal frame chair, put his elbows on the table. He said, "You once told me you'd rather die than lose your edge. Do you remember that?"

"I think so," Porter said.

"And yet, you're 'softening'?"

"Things change," the old man said, tensing his shoulders momentarily, waiting for a bodily distress to pass. "Honestly, I can't say when it happened. You would think one would feel more certainty in the winter of one's life. I feel—wistful. Yes, that's it. Nostalgic. Given to a longing for the past."

"*Which* past is that, Edgar?"

"Well, yours. Not to put too fine a point on it."

Maya watched the exchange, fascinated. The tone of their speech was like that of two men continuing a conversation started over dinner of the previous day, only they hadn't seen each other in years.

"I miss the old days," Porter said. "I know that must sound terribly maudlin. Forgive me. I've been thinking about our time at the university. That began as a lark, you know, a distraction. Simple research. But I came to love it. That's why I kept on for so long. You had no idea who I was. I love that about you, Ben.

Your obliviousness. It's a part of your charm. You can see the most exquisite of things, yet miss what's right in front of you. I still work my little vortex, but you already know that. I've even had a few minor successes, but I'm just a tinkerer next to you and your daughter here.

"When she showed up at my house," Porter continued, "I awakened as if from a deep sleep. I can't recall the last time I'd felt such ... enthusiasm. Growing old and infirm, despite the best medical science has to offer, has preoccupied me. So, I decided to get back into the game."

"The game," Ben said.

"*Your* game. Your 'change,' as you put it."

Ben's eyes grew intense.

"You see," Porter said, "I think I understand your mission."

Porter spoke directly to Maya: "Your father wants to elevate humanity out of its state of ignorance. In so doing, he hopes to create a new world of higher awareness and unbridled freedom. He believes that his compatriots, the Mandala, with their specialized knowledge, can direct such a change at a deep level within the world's collective psyche. As the great plan unfolds, 'the people' would be unaware of what's actually happening.

"Your father's partners"—he glanced at Georgia—"believe such a thing is possible. Others, like our overly zealous friend outside, think it would create a destabilizing chaos, a grave upset to the delicate balance that maintains our way of life.

"Further, your father believes that a cartel of men controls the fate of all human affairs through clandestine alliances and devious plots. He believes his work can unseat these unseen puppet masters." He turned to Georgia, looking self-satisfied, and said, "How am I doing? On the right track?"

"Let's hear the rest of it," she said evenly.

Porter turned back to Maya, said, "Your father thinks his underground of spiritual supermen can change the present situation using its special abilities to *nudge*, shall we say, humanity in a different direction. Perhaps they can. What do you think?"

"I don't know," Maya said honestly.

"The prudent, the cautious, point of view."

"Maya," Ben said, "you should know that Edgar here is talking about his own people. *He* is one of the elites, that group Fiske talked about. When Edgar sets his mind on something, it doesn't long escape his grasp. Ruthlessness, if the situation requires it, doesn't present a problem."

Porter smiled, amused. He said, "People like you think there is a master plan for world domination. You believe you're being manipulated. You think there's a Wizard of Oz pulling levers behind some mysterious curtain. Well, I'm sorry to be the one to tell you this, Ben, but that is pure hogwash. You must let go of such fantasies. I say that only to help you."

"Why are you here, Edgar?" Ben insisted.

Porter grinned approvingly. "You want to know the truth."

"If at all possible," Ben said.

Porter said, "I'm here to free you."

"What?"

"In fact, it's already done," he said. "The charges against you have been, well, disappeared. The details—of which there were many, for our friend outside had been diligent—have been managed. Effectively, where you are concerned, the deck is very much cleared. You're a free man, Ben. You can do whatever you please. How does that feel?"

Ben said, "Are you serious?"

"Quite. I have my connections. You've been out of the system for"—he glanced at his watch—"about two hours now."

Maya stared at him, astonished. "You can really do that?"

"It's one of the perks of being a ruler of this world," he said with a cold smile.

"I don't understand," Ben said.

"There's nothing to understand. You can return to civilian life," Porter said. "I know you've done nothing to earn the hardships you've had to endure. The way you've had to live saddens me. But I've always found that it's best not to dwell on the past."

"My God, Edgar," Ben said. "Thank you."

"But you already have."

"How?" Georgia said.

Ben said, "What about Maya?"

"What about her?"

"Is she safe?"

"Absolutely."

"And Georgia?"

Porter nodded. "She, too."

"What about Fiske?"

"Oh, you needn't worry about him," Porter said. "All he wanted was to grab you, cage you and break you. What he had in mind wouldn't have been pretty. You would have joined his team only to travel the same road once again. He'll be more closely watched, as will his project and its followers."

"He said the Mandala are being arrested," Maya said.

"A fiction," Porter said, "No such operation exists."

Again Georgia insisted, "What did you mean, we've 'already thanked you'?"

Porter laughed that same eerie laugh that had made Maya's skin crawl weeks ago. "You're eager to know the answer to that question, Ms. Roussey. Well, I'll give it to you. I want to see if your plan works. I may use it."

"Use it?" Ben said.

Porter said, "You, all of you, have made a trade with me. You've given me the technology of change—the deeper understanding of the vortexes, the inner medium, the Mandala, your grand plan, Maya's experiences, all of it—in exchange for Ben's freedom. I wanted all the pieces and now I have them to do with what I will."

"*How* we have we done all that?" Georgia asked.

"Unknowingly," Porter said, grinning. "I've been witness to all your communications, movements and plans, thanks to young Maya here."

"*Me?*" Maya said.

"How's that?" Ben said.

"Simple. I had a listening device placed on her. The discourse has been rather interesting," he said.

Maya looked down at her body, her sweater, her jeans, wondering—*where?* She recoiled in horror.

"What are you planning to do?" Georgia said.

"That's my business, Ms. Roussey. I will ponder that with great satisfaction in the comfort of my home."

He pressed a lever in the wheelchair's arm and began toward the door. He stopped and turned around.

"You were right about me, Ben," he said. "You were always perceptive. Goodbye and good luck, all of you."

The Secret Service men stepped inside and picked up Porter and his wheelchair and carried him outside.

Maya stood up and ran out after him. Standing in the parking lot, she said, "Where is it?"

"*Them*," Porter said. "Where are *they*."

"Yeah, whatever," she said. "Where?"

He stared at her with disdain, as if she were a panhandler who needed to be shooed away.

"Please," Maya said.

"One in your backpack, the other on your tennis shoe."

"Tennis shoe?"

She felt the impact of what she'd caused, with nauseating force. She had played the part of unwitting mole, single-handedly giving away the Mandala. She wanted to start walking down the highway and just keep going—anything to avoid having to face Ben and Georgia.

"Oh, don't fret," Porter said. "You wanted an adventure. You wanted out of your drab little suburbia. Well, you got it. The rest, as they say, goes with the territory. Now, goodbye."

He rolled toward the limo where his men were waiting for him. The chauffeur lifted him out of the chair and set him down on the backseat, then folded up the wheelchair and laid it carefully in the trunk.

The limousine and the Land Rovers started their engines. The headlights came on, and the vehicles crept forward, crunching gravel under their tires. They pulled out onto the highway. Maya watched the cars for some time, their red taillights growing smaller and more distant until they disappeared from view.

She kicked angrily at some rocks. There was nothing to do but go back inside the diner. When she stepped through the doorway, Georgia was standing at the counter pouring cups of coffee. She handed one to Ben.

"Java?" she said, holding out a mug for Maya.

"Sure, thanks. Just set it down."

Maya saw her backpack where she'd left it, on a booth table. She picked it up and examined the fabric carefully until she found a seam that had been re-stitched. She tore it open and plucked out a tiny rectangular device that was nestled inside. She dropped it on the floor and stomped on it until it was a brown smudge. The other device had been sewn into a fold at the back of the tennis shoe that did not have the yin-yang on it. At least there was that. Kudos to Dr. Porter for sensitivity. Or maybe he had a better chance of success that way. It didn't matter. She dug it out with a fingernail, dropped it on the floor and crushed it into a fine powder.

"I've ruined everything," she said miserably.

"No, you haven't," Georgia said.

"I'm never going to be able to live with myself," Maya said. "The rest of my life is toast."

"Didn't you hear me?"

"I heard you."

"We're not surprised, if that makes you feel any better."

Ben said, "Honestly."

Maya said, "No. It's a disaster."

"Listen to me," Georgia said. "Porter didn't *say* what he's going to do. What can he do?"

"What do you mean?" Maya said.

Ben said, "Remember I told you about the missing puzzle piece? The last issue we have to solve before we can initiate the change? Well, while Edgar was going on and on, the answer came to me. I know what we have to do."

"Really? What?" Maya said, feeling the weight of her burden start to fall away.

But Ben didn't explain. He just sipped at his coffee, gave a little quixotic smile and pointed at the door. "There's an enormous sky out there, with a few thousand stars that are begging to be admired," he said. "Let's check it out, eh?"

"I second that," said Georgia.

"Thirded," said Maya, as they headed outside.

The desert was vast and silent, the sky just as Ben had promised. Maya watched his gaze trace across the heavens. He was a free man now, no doubt seeing things from a very different perspective.

"I'm sorry about all this," he said to her.

"About what?" Maya said.

"Bringing you into this," he said.

"Are you kidding?" she said with a grin. "This is the best thing that's ever happened to me. I just hope the rest of my life isn't one huge downer after this."

They laughed.

"There's just one more thing," Ben said. "Something our Dr. Porter didn't count on."

Maya waited, desperate to know what that was, hoping he'd offer at least a hint, but he remained silent, with a look of satisfaction on his face.

23

Renewal

J eremy, I am so sorry," Maya said into the phone as she leaned back and swung her leg up onto the edge of her desk. "I can't see you tonight. I've got to work."

"Hey, no problem," Jeremy said. "Actually I'm in the same boat. I'm working late, too."

"Really?" Maya said, relieved. "Oh, that's awesome. Now I don't feel guilty."

"But New Year's Eve for sure," he said.

"For sure," Maya said. "I can't wait."

She eased back and looked around the office, which was quiet at this late hour. A few of the diehards who worked past eight were sprinkled around in the cubicles and the glass-walled offices of the Anderson Foundation, but otherwise the vast expanse of the fifth floor was still and empty.

Maya wasn't exactly sure why things were happening the way they were, but she'd decided to accept most everything without question and mostly was succeeding. The move to Washington, D.C., for one. The job at the Foundation. Her acceptance of every overtime assignment that had come up. She'd been fully immersed in her new life since she'd arrived, happy to pay whatever the price might be. She'd hardly even been back to Plainfield, just an hour's drive away, save for the occasional trip to see her mother or to pick up something she'd forgotten. Mostly her hometown was fading into in the rearview mirror of her life.

Jeremy Beven happened within two weeks of her arrival in D.C., as if by magic. She'd met him waiting in line at a carry-out near the office. He was a brainy 26-year-old lawyer from Philadelphia in his first job at the U.S. Securities and Exchange Commission. He was easy-going, well-traveled and possessed of a worldly, learned perspective that exceeded his years, a quality that lured Maya. He was shorter than her and wore thick glasses, and didn't have the star power of a Josh but she liked him, and wanted to see where this would go.

Maya, in fact, had found many surprises upon her return to the East Coast. She *liked* her first real job as an office assistant in the Foundation's development department, a wing of the medical research division run by Roger Anderson himself, the philanthropist friend of her father's and of the Mandala. Although most of Maya's job involved administrative details and tedious hours of research, which were not her strengths, she liked being a part of a large and important team.

"So, we're good?" Jeremy said, his voice drowned out by the scream of a police siren out on the street. A few seconds later Maya heard that same scream outside her own building, just a few blocks away.

"More than good," she said.

"I'll call you tomorrow," he said.

"You bet. Bye-bye, Jeremy."

"Bye."

Two hours later, Maya gathered her things, bundled herself up in her wool coat and set off for home, arriving just after ten o'clock. She threw off her coat, stepped out of her clothes, washed up and slid into bed, satisfied to snuggle beneath the thick down comforter she'd bought with a sizeable portion of her first paycheck. But before she turned off the lights, she reached under the bed for the treasure that she'd unearthed in her backyard all those months ago. Still she kept the journal close at hand, though she didn't read it much anymore. She would sometimes take a quick peek, or just hold it in her hands to feel the smooth leather cover. Whenever she did, invariably the memories would flood back in.

Her return from the Southwest had been difficult. At times the sadness and despair were overwhelming. The excitement of living all those days from moment to moment, taking in all those novel and extraordinary experiences, had instilled in her a desire for *more*. Each new day had been like leaping off a high cliff and soaring into the air—yet knowing she'd touch down safely. Not knowing *how* that would happen was the thrill. Anything could happen, and it often had. No day had been like any other. Even just that small taste of the outlaw life had created in her a yearning she knew would go unsatisfied in the workaday world she found herself in now.

She had lobbied feverishly in those final hours to remain with her father and Georgia, wherever they were headed. Passionately she had pleaded her case, though she could not articulate a single valid reason why they should take her along. She had certainly given it her all. In truth, she knew she'd be a burden, for their plans were complex and required speed. Despite her efforts, she was summarily told to return home and wait for contact.

And so, Maya's adventure in the West had given way to a far less exciting one in the East. Unpredictability had yielded to routine. She lived in a busy city and spent her time doing what most everyone else did: working, commuting, paying bills, planning meals, seeking likeminded souls, and, when possible, keeping up old friendships like the one she had with Josh, a last vestige of home. She endeavored to keep pace with life's plentiful, mundane details, even if at times she felt precious and unique, for whom else might she encounter who had traveled into an energy vortex to gaze upon Earth's inchoate future as it took shape in a shadowy pre-world that virtually no one knew existed?

In the morning, she put on a pot of coffee and nestled into the small loveseat at the center of the tiny studio apartment, and stared out the large window at the trees of Rock Creek Park. She drank the coffee and perused the internet news. As noon approached, she tidied up some, hung up yesterday's rumpled clothes, checked the unopened mail, washed the dishes and wiped down the kitchen counter. It was time to go meet her mother and Henry for lunch.

Standing in her building's front foyer, Maya zipped up her coat and peered through the glass door into yet another frigid late December day. Taking a last warm breath, she pushed the door open and made her way along the sidewalk of Connecticut Avenue to Zia's, a bistro down in Woodley Park, where she found a noisy, crowded dining room.

Muriel and Henry were waving to her from a high-backed booth. Maya walked over and slid in beside her mother. Soon, Henry had them raising their water glasses in a toast.

"To Maya's new life," he said. "May it be blessed with health, happiness and success."

"Hear, hear," Muriel said as they clinked glasses.

"Just look at her, Henry," Muriel said. "She's all grown up. When did that happen?"

"I'm right *here*, Mom," Maya said, shaking her head.

When *had* it happened? An image floated into Maya's mind of a young woman facing a pack of wolves in the high desert mountains, lit by the bright moonlight, feeling afraid and yet fearless. She had stood toe to toe with those creatures, secure in the acceptance of her own death. It was in that unlikely place that she had opened to the gift of surrender, slipped off the shackles that bound her. And who was the ally who assisted her, who propelled her beyond the threshold of fear into greater awareness, but the grey-coated *Canis lupus*?

Muriel was staring uncomprehendingly at her daughter's wondrous expression. Muriel—who had made a crossing of her own through a far different landscape than Maya's. When Maya first returned home, she assumed that the courage she was witnessing in her mother was some kind of psychological projection of her own growth. But she was flat-out wrong. Muriel's expansion was very much her own, with credit due to Henry and his approach to the drinking problem. Muriel had not only owned up to it, but she'd summoned the fortitude to examine herself with an unblinking eye—something she had never been disposed to do. And although her journey had its many lurches and derailings, it remained on track. None of it would have been possible without Henry and Alcoholics Anonymous, his own path to recovery. To Maya, it was a miracle plain and simple, which had made possible a steady reduction in tension between mother and daughter.

Henry was beaming, staring right at Maya, waiting for her to meet his gaze. When she did, he broke into a grin. He cleared his throat dramatically and said, "We have an announcement, Maya."

Muriel held out her left hand. A glittering three-stone, emerald-cut diamond ring sparkled on her finger.

Henry frowned. "Honey, you're doing it again."

Muriel said, "We've already had a toast."

"That was for Maya."

Muriel turned to him, understood what she'd done, and uttered something Maya had seemingly waited her whole life to hear.

"I'm sorry," Muriel said.

Maya laughed. She leaned over and gave her mother a hug.

December 31 was the coldest day of the year, dominated by an insistent, biting wind and a bright sun. On mornings like this, the two-block walk from Maya's apartment to the Cleveland Park Metro station was a grim-faced march during which she did not glance at anything except the sidewalk in front of her. She rode the long escalator down to the underground subway station and dashed into a train which had just pulled in.

Gripping a support pole, Maya observed the commuters wedged up against one another in the narrow seats—the bureaucrats, lawyers, teachers, clerks, students and all the rest—coming in from the outer city and suburbs. At each station stop a few would glance up from their books or magazines or phones, and stand up and head for the door, or after a quick scan of the station sign, resume their downward stare and continue on with their solitary activities.

Amid the bumps of the train tracks, as Maya swayed in the cabin, she considered her father's predications of societal change. The subject sometimes came to mind when she was in a crowd, though less and less often with the passing days. Would his great shift ever happen? She wasn't even sure she believed in it; doubt had been creeping in for some time. At times, the best she could muster was a slim acceptance of the possibility of it. At other times it seemed downright crazy, a fantastic fiction fabricated by a utopian dreamer. She hated to think that way, but she knew it might be true.

She considered the many impressive people she'd met, like Georgia and Keith, who believed in it wholeheartedly. What did they see that she didn't? Maya sensed no world-altering shift astir in the air. Events large and small occurred as they always had and always would. Strivers vied for power, wars raged on, peacemakers toiled, and everyday people struggled to keep pace with the demands of their lives, which often exceeded their reach.

Over the months, Ben's theories had receded from the sphere of interesting possibility to the realm of quixotic dream. The world was the world, its great motors chugging away the same today as they had yesterday and would tomorrow. Even someone who'd only been around a little more than two decades could see that.

The cycle of life turned inexorably. The march of days, of seasons, of the myriad beginnings and endings, advanced in accordance with the laws of nature, and perhaps, of God. If life was a miracle, then it was one that was largely predictable. In a few months, winter's frost would give way to spring's new green growth, pink blossoms would awaken on the cherry trees along the Tidal Basin, and creatures great and small would play their parts amid nature's ephemeral beauty. The lawns of the Capitol and the memorials would dance with life, as people arrived from many lands to learn about a bold idea some men had long ago for a new kind of society, whose story, like so many stories, would continue to unfold in dramatic and unexpected ways. The sleeping grass would awaken with new shoots, and children would wage their war on apathy and cynicism without even knowing of its existence.

Amid all this, Maya would enthusiastically pedal her bicycle along the forested path that ran the length of the city, listening to music on her headphones and doing her best not to crash into anyone going in the opposite direction.

But that time had not yet arrived. Today, the sky was a concrete gray, the temperature a frigid two degrees above zero. As Maya exited the Farragut North station, she speed-walked to her office.

Inside the lobby, she performed her usual cold-weather ritual: unzipping her coat as quickly as possible to revel in the burst of warm air that awaits anyone entering a well-heated building. A few feet away, a woman from another office seemed to be doing the same thing. Their eyes met and they smiled conspiratorially in recognition of a fact that exists at the heart of every cold winter: everyone is in it together.

Maya rode the elevator up to the fifth floor and made her way to the Anderson Foundation offices, settled in at her desk and draped her coat and scarf over the back of her chair. She was well into her morning routine, checking emails, when she heard a voice beside her.

"Hello, Maya."

She looked up from her computer screen. The man beside her was in his early seventies, tanned and in good shape. He smiled and extended his hand.

"Roger Anderson," the Foundation's chairman said.

Maya flushed, taking his hand. "Mr. Anderson," she said. "It's so nice to meet you. I've heard so much about you."

"It's Roger, please," he said. "I'm sorry it's taken me so long to come by. I want you to know how good it is to have you here, Maya. I've seen your father quite a bit lately. He asked me to say hello to you."

"Thank you," Maya said.

Roger Anderson leaned over and came in close. "It's about to happen," he whispered.

That was all, just those words. He walked off.

Maya knew instantly what he was talking about. The change. There was a kind of religious fervor about it among some of the people at the foundation. Maya was always mindful to be cautious about it, keeping her doubts to herself.

She set that issue aside and turned back to the computer screen. Among the unopened emails was one from her father. He would write to her now and again, sharing a few details about his travels, usually in a guarded way. She understood why. She clicked open the email.

> Maya, all on schedule. Pieces falling into place.
> Will jump-start the change through NY mass
> prayer. Get ready. xo Love, Dad

Maya stared at the paragraph, baffled. New York mass prayer? What was that?

Throughout the morning, between phone calls and emails, she tried to decipher the meaning of the message. But she was stumped. Then, just before lunch, she had an idea.

I know this.

She clicked open a folder in which she stored interesting articles she came across while web surfing. She was never quite sure why she kept them; she just had a feeling they'd come in handy one day. And often they did. Reading through the filenames, she found one entitled WORLD PEACE PRAYER. She smiled. She understood.

"NY" stood not for New York, but *New Year's.*

Tonight was New Year's Eve, when she would be going to a party with Jeremy. Yet much more could be happening.

Ben Ambrose was referring to the annual tradition of spiritual and religiously minded people to pray for world peace at midnight on December 31, Greenwich Mean Time. That way, their intentions would be synchronized, going out at exactly the same moment.

The theories of the Mandala had opened Maya's eyes to the power of coordinated intention and its role in creating events in the world. The aim of the Mandala and the people praying for world peace were essentially compatible, maybe even identical.

Worldwide, the Mandala, including Ben Ambrose, would attempt to use the power of the global peace prayer to build upon their own collective vortex meditation. The meditators, including those people Maya had seen in the pyramid house, would perform their collective intention for global change en masse, supported by tens of thousands unknowingly on every continent.

Poised at the Earth's power centers in the Middle East, the Himalayas, Central America, the American Southwest and all the other locations, the Mandala, energized by the inflowing energy of the vortexes, would make their demands, amplified far beyond what they could do on their own.

Maya considered all this, as more thoughts and feelings stirred in her, and images, too. In her mind's eye she saw her father, Georgia and Brandon, and many others including Buddy, all becoming still. Everyone connecting together as one.

If Ben Ambrose was right, critical mass would be reached and the change initiated. Humankind's collective consciousness would be elevated. The plan amounted to an enormous group meditation backed by the power of the Earth itself.

As Maya sat back in her chair, she wondered, would it work?

Epilogue

New Year's Day.

The morning hours travel through the globe's time zones.

In a coastal South American country, a prison guard hangs a new calendar on an office wall. On the upper page is a photo of a beautiful raven-haired woman. The guard admires it for a moment, then settles in at his desk and picks up the morning newspaper.

Unexpectedly, sadness engulfs him. *Why?* he wonders. Nothing is wrong. Life is good. He is in confidently in charge of his domain, the lord over these prisoners. He knows how to put each man in his place when necessary.

The guard tries to shrug off the discomfort but to no avail. It grows stronger. Struggling mightily, he tosses the newspaper aside, and without knowing why, walks to the prisoners' cell block.

Standing at one of the cells, he pulls out his key ring, and with shaking hands, finds the key and unlocks the door.

A battered, haggard man peers up at him through eyes that have seen too much. His crime: writing newspaper articles critical of the country's ruler. He has been tortured. His family, harassed. He has been forced to confess to crimes he did not commit. He is an innocent man awaiting execution.

The guard swings open the door. "You are free to go," he says. "I can't bear it. Please, go."

The prisoner hobbles down the hall and away, as the guard falls to his knees and begins to weep.

At precisely that moment, many thousands of miles away, in a small town in the American Midwest, a twelve-year-old boy is being harshly chastised for being inattentive in class and acting aggressively toward his classmates.

"I can't help it," the boy pleads, honestly, for indeed it is true.

"He can't concentrate on *anything*," says his exasperated mother, sitting beside him in the principal's office.

"Math," the boy says suddenly. "I can do math."

His words surprise him as much as they do her.

In an instant, the boy is overcome by a sudden expansion of comprehension for subjects that are far beyond him: geometry, calculus, probability theory. The epiphany shakes him to his core. His aggression disappears, never to return again.

Halfway around the globe, huddled with his men in a military tent in the mountains of a battle-torn country in the Near East, a warlord who has committed countless atrocities, who has ordered the deaths of thousands of innocents, leans over a territorial map and falls into a momentary hallucination. He imagines the enemy general as his own brother. With trembling hands, he takes out a cigar and lights it. He continues his plotting, but it will not go on much longer.

Further to the east, a young Chinese woman stands unsteadily in a rice paddy on a misty afternoon, crushed with grief at the loss of her sister, killed in a robbery. Inexplicably, she feels hopeful. She *knows* that things will improve, that the agony will pass, that she'll know peace again. She ventures a smile, a gesture she has not allowed herself in many months.

The tide gains momentum. All populations feel it. It comes from within each man and woman. Beneath the level of their conscious awareness, biochemical processes shift, neuronal pathways change and entrenched psychological blocks clear. Pure energy surges up from the deepest depths of the collective psyche. In a timeless moment never to be forgotten, all the world's peoples know fully and beyond doubt the power of their humanity, the limitlessness of their potential and the promise of their heritage.

In New York City, an old man falls down on a sidewalk. A young couple rush over to help him. They embrace in the manner of close friends, though they have never met.

And walking along the sidewalk near her home, Maya Burke stops suddenly, overwhelmed by excitement. It is the same feeling stirring in her father, as he stands on a mountaintop in Peru and takes in the glorious view. She knows, just as he does, exactly what is happening.

About the Author

Warren Goldie was born in Brooklyn, New York. He holds a degree in biology and has been a full-time writer for more than twenty-five years. Drawn to existential and metaphysical inquiry from a young age, Goldie pursued these interests through creative writing and daily meditation. He has worked as a writer and editor for Steven Spielberg, as a screenplay analyst, and as a writer for numerous publications and websites. He was a featured playwright in Playwrights Showcase of the Western States and the Baltimore Playwrights Festival.

Made in the USA
Middletown, DE
23 April 2017